"Let me kiss you, April."

Rex smiled, his smile alone overloading her senses. "I promise to be a gentleman and stop when you tell me to."

Stop? The man had her surrounded. He blocked out the whole world with his body, sparked all those achy places he'd awakened with his magic hands while massaging her.

"Just one kiss to see if you like it." And then he lowered his face toward her with exquisite slowness, allowing her a chance to retreat.

Decision by indecision.

The instant their lips met, April knew this would be like no kiss she'd ever experienced before. He seemed to explode with emotion. His muscles gathered against hers. He tucked her into all the sculpted places of his body, enfolded her in a layer of hard, aroused male.

Her every sense was heightened, focused on him intently. The steady beating of his heart. The feel of him draped over her. Her every breath became his as his mouth prowled hers hungrily, coaxing her lips wide, thrusting his tongue inside, devouring, demanding a reply.

She replied with the only answer that made any sense. She kissed him back

Dear Reader,

Once upon a time I worked for a Fortune 500 company and lived the whirlwind life of a career woman on the road. I discovered firsthand how easy it is to get caught up in the challenge of the job to the exclusion of all else.

Rex Holt is a man who loves his life on the road—or so he thinks. Once April Stevens arrives to help him research the market for the Sensuous Collection, he realizes there is a whole lot of life he's missing out on. It doesn't take much more than some steamy nights between the sexy sheets to convince April that Rex is the man she wants to enjoy her life with, but there's one not-so-little problem....

Blaze is the place to explore red-hot romance, and I'm excited to write for a series that excels in steamy happily-ever-afters. I hope April and Rex's story brings you to happily-ever-after, too. Let me know. Drop me a line in care of Harlequin Books, 225 Duncan Mill Road, Don Mills, Ontario M3B 3K9, Canada. Or visit my Web site at www.jeanielondon.com. And don't forget to check out www.tryblaze.com.

Very truly yours,

Jeanie London

Books by Jeanie London

HARLEQUIN BLAZE

28—SECRET GAMES
42—ONE-NIGHT MAN
53—ABOUT THAT NIGHT...
80—HOW TO HOST A SEDUCTION

BETWEEN THE SHEETS

Jeanie London

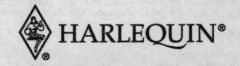

HARLEQUIN®

TORONTO • NEW YORK • LONDON
AMSTERDAM • PARIS • SYDNEY • HAMBURG
STOCKHOLM • ATHENS • TOKYO • MILAN • MADRID
PRAGUE • WARSAW • BUDAPEST • AUCKLAND

For Ann Josephson, Kimberly Llewellyn and Tara Randel, the brilliant brainstorming buddies who helped me fan a tiny spark into a flaming love story. And special thanks to Francine Bauer for introducing me to the fascinating world of nibbies!

ISBN 0-373-79094-5

BETWEEN THE SHEETS

Visit us at www.eHarlequin.com

Printed in U.S.A.

1

To: Wilhemina Knox (mailto:president@luxuriousbedding.com)
Date: 3 Mar 2003 07:59:54-0500
Subject: Effective Stress Management

Install glory holes in the employees' bathroom stalls for a low-cost method of stress management!

Studies prove that the regular release of sexual tension contributes to the effective management of work-related stress, improving overall mental and physical performance. Condom dispensers located beside tissue holders will adequately meet all OSHA standards and state health requirements.

"Glory holes, hmm?" April Stevens frowned down at the hard copy of an e-mail post. She'd never heard of a glory hole, much less seen one, but she had no trouble grasping the concept. Or imagining the protruding body parts and variety of sex acts that might be performed through one.

As an investigative researcher for J.P. Mooney Investigators, Ltd., the premier agency in the Dallas area, April had witnessed a variety of oddball human behaviors during her eight-year tenure. The recommendation of glory holes in bathroom walls as a way to relieve work-related stress was a definite first.

Scanning the e-mail header, she noted the address and glanced back at her boss. He sat behind his desk, primed and ready for her reaction, as though he'd sensed sex was the very last thing in the world she wanted to think about right now.

But her boss wasn't a mind reader, so she cocked a hip against the edge of his desk and gave nonchalance a stab. "Did someone send this post to Wilhemina as some sort of joke? I can't imagine she found it funny. It's...well, *raunchy*."

John Patrick Mooney steepled his fingers before him and grinned a grin that April imagined had stopped quite a few hearts some thirty-odd years earlier. An undeniably attractive man in his sixties with knife-creased features, steely gray hair and piercing black eyes, he had this whole I've-seen-it-all-and-lived-to-tell attitude that people often found intimidating. The grin softened his appearance considerably.

Not that he needed softening for April. Not at all. Years ago John and Paula, his wife, had opened their home to April. And she'd worked for John in some capacity since her junior year in high school—the year her search for her birth parents had introduced her to the world of private investigation. A world that had fascinated her enough to go into the field herself.

She'd convinced him she'd be an asset to his team despite her youth. He'd been insightful enough to give her a chance to prove herself. During her years with the company, she'd worked her way up from an administrative assistant to her current position as investigative researcher. While John Patrick Mooney might intimidate some people with his hard stare and deadpan expression, he didn't intimidate April. She'd seen up close what a fair and even kindhearted man he could be.

"It is raunchy," he said. "And you're right. My sister-in-law didn't find it remotely funny."

April could well imagine. Professionalism was the end-all and be-all of Wilhemina's world. She was a woman who'd forged a corporate career for herself during a time when executive management positions were filled by men through the good-old-boys' network.

Wilhemina had chosen career over marriage and made no apologies, which meant that at holidays she showed up at John's house to commune with family. This also meant that she and April were kindred spirits because April had attached herself to the Mooney family, too.

"Why did Wilhemina send this?" she asked. "What's up?"

"This post isn't the only one to come across the Luxurious Bedding Company's computer network." Reaching across his desk for the copy of the e-mail post, John held it up between them. "It's one of over *six dozen.*"

"Oh my." An image of the proposed glory hole sprang to mind and April shook her head to clear it. "All to Wilhemina?"

"No, she's only one of the recipients. Someone is stalking employees at corporate headquarters with similar posts on a variety of, er, *diverse* topics. They're showing up in the different departments—executive management, operations, sales, human resources, even the warehouse."

"Suggestive e-mails popping up during business hours." She gave a short laugh. "I'll bet that makes for an interesting day on the job."

"No joke. Wilhemina said the place has been bedlam. And the timing couldn't be worse. She's preparing to launch the Sensuous Collection. It's a high-profile launch and a risky time for the company. These posts are distracting the employees from their work. 'Sex on the brain' is the way she described it."

April would just bet. Whether a person was offended or titillated by the idea of what two employees might do with a stall wall and a cleverly positioned hole between them, one thing was clear—that person would be thinking about sex.

And thinking about sex was exactly what April didn't want to do. She couldn't afford a case of sex on the brain right now. No way. No how.

"The *Sensuous* Collection?" She urged John to get on with his point so she could figure out why he was telling all this to her. "Didn't Wilhemina tell me at Christmas that the reason she accepted this presidency was to get the company back on its feet after they crashed with the Cuddly, Cozy Winter Collection?"

Let your nights be about more than sleep, she'd recited the jingle to April over eggnog. *Get cuddly and cozy with our Cuddly, Cozy Winter Collection.*

A seemingly clever marketing campaign for a collection of sheet sets that should have translated into public recognition, huge sales and a solid bottom line. However this particular marketing campaign had proven so cuddly and cozy that consumers complained the advertisements had gone too far to promote the sensuality of their product. Morality groups had protested and the backlash against the Luxurious Bedding Company had resulted in the company's reorganization. Not to mention earning a defining nickname for the mattresses, bedding and sheet sets.

The Lus*turious Bedding Company.*

April remembered John telling Wilhemina she was crazy to take on a company in the throes of consumer condemnation. The board had thrown out the former president for getting them into such a mess. But Wilhemina had waxed poetic about the challenges and argued that she had a blowout strategy to turn the disapproval rating around by capitalizing on their new image.

"Is the Sensuous Collection Wilhemina's blowout strategy?"

John nodded. "It's a line of luxury bedding that will compete with the European manufacturers, who apparently dominate the market. She's hooked up with a high-ticket marketing consultant to help capitalize on their *lust*urious image."

"Is someone unhappy with the plan? Is that why they're stalking the employees with these sorts of posts?"

"The posts are being generated in-house at corporate headquarters."

"Oh." A disgruntled employee then. "Where do you fit in? Can't security track down the stalker with the network administrator's help? Shouldn't be that difficult."

"Apparently that's not the case." He set the e-mail post back on the desk and lifted his black gaze. "The posts are originating from computers all over headquarters, forwarding files to everyone in the address book."

She whistled. "That must generate a ton of traffic. I don't imagine it's feasible for the administrator to monitor all the posts."

"It's not. Wilhemina tried curtailing network activity in various departments to give the administrator a chance to track the problem posts, but every time activity slows down, the stalker stops sending the raunchy posts completely."

"So our suspect is operating on the same premise as a computer worm or a virus. Very clever, really." Good, bad or otherwise, April appreciated resourcefulness when she saw it. "What files get forwarded?"

"Mainly information dealing with the Sensuous Collection, which has raised the issue about whether these posts are meant to obstruct the collection's launch."

"You're talking about corporate espionage?"

"It's a concern. Selling details about the Sensuous Collection could translate into big bucks if a rival manufacturer introduces a competing product line before the Luxurious Bedding Company launches. Wilhemina has turned the problem over to in-house security to conduct an internal investigation.''

"Has she asked you for advice on the investigation?''

John tapped his fingers on the desktop and met her gaze thoughtfully before answering. "The investigation is pretty clear-cut. The only thing they can do is eliminate their employees one by one. This isn't a mom-and-pop organization. While it's not Fortune 500, the Luxurious Bedding Company is large with the opportunity for spectacular growth if this collection takes off like the projections indicate.''

Which still wasn't explaining why John was holding on to that post. April must have looked confused because he said, "Wilhemina's got a rogue element—a high-ticket independent marketing consultant. Rex Holt's his name.''

"Never heard of him.'' And she'd prefer to keep it that way. She didn't need to be thinking about any man on a list of suspects who had the potential to get his jollies from stalking an entire company with the kind of posts she'd just read.

Not at this particular time in her life, at any rate. "If he's independent can't she just replace him? She'd eliminate one suspect from the equation.''

"He's not a suspect.''

"No?''

"Wilhemina has worked with him a number of times before when she was running Duval Foods International. She doesn't think he has anything to do with the posts or corporate espionage. She's so sure that she's betting her career on it.''

That was saying something. "Yow.''

"Yow is right,'' John agreed. "She's got a mess on her

hands. The board of directors is understandably edgy after being burned with the Cuddly, Cozy Winter Collection and they're pushing to opt out of their big bucks contract with this guy. Wilhemina says it's way too close to the launch to bring in another independent consultant and she needs Rex Holt to pull off this launch. Apparently he's big potatoes.''

''If she's so convinced her big spud isn't guilty, what's worrying the board?''

''Aside from the fact that Holt is the only one besides Wilhemina who has free run of the company at every level from operational to executive management, he also has means and opportunity. He consulted for a competitor a few years back. Wilhemina believes his past experience in the industry is working to their benefit but the board thinks it means loyalty to a rival manufacturer. Given the fact that he's out-of-house, I see their point. The guy's positioned to do a lot of damage.''

''Do you think Wilhemina's made a mistake?''

''I've been married to her sister for thirty-five years. Trust me, that one doesn't miss a trick.'' He shook his head decidedly. ''But even so, I've been looking into this guy's history the past few days and Holt's MO doesn't jive by a long shot. He's got references up the wazoo and he's considered one of the top marketing consultants nationwide. Big-name corporations are lined up for his services.''

''Then she wants you to find out who's sending these posts?''

''No.''

''No?''

''Wilhemina has decided to buck the board on this but she's up against a time limit. Holt will be moving his base of operations out of corporate headquarters to conduct marketing studies around the country. She needs to cover her ass—and his, too—while he's out on the road. This is where we come in.''

We. That one word and the way John leveled a steely gaze her way shot April's internal alarm system into the red zone. ''But you just said her in-house security is investigating and they've exhausted the computer angle.''

''I'm pulling you off the computer.''

April knew what was coming next and launched into evasive maneuvers to avoid yet another lecture about how twenty-five-year-old women should be out living life, rather than viewing it through a flat-screen computer monitor.

''I'm an investigative researcher, remember? I'm supposed to work behind a computer.''

''You're an *investigator.* You call yourself a researcher, but I don't have researchers on my payroll. Only *investigators.*''

''But that's what I do. I *investigate* through the computer. Some agencies would call me an information specialist.''

''You work for *my* agency, April. I employ investigators who can work behind a computer *and* in the field.''

Could she help it that she was more comfortable with binary and circuitry than she was with English and humans?

John heaved a sigh that drove the alarm indicator in her head right off the gauge. The man was gearing up for an argument. She recognized the raised brows, the stiff neck and the squared shoulders as surely as if the word *A-R-G-U-M-E-N-T* had been tattooed across his forehead.

She took a judicious step back. Unfortunately, her sweater caught the edge of his in-box as she did. John came halfway out of his chair in a vain attempt to catch it, but the whole tray toppled off the desk with a clatter.

''No, no, don't get up,'' she said, sinking to her knees to collect the scattered papers. ''I've got them.''

She could feel his gaze on her as she gathered the various

documents and envelopes and quickly restacked them. By the time she returned the tray to his desk, her cheeks were hot and John was watching her with an expression of resignation that only made her blush burn hotter.

Backing away to minimum safe distance, she took a calming breath and another crack at appearing nonchalant. But John still looked resigned, which meant he wasn't buying her act.

"Do you know what a *nibbie* is, April?"

A *nibbie?* Definitely not the question she'd expected. A change of tactic, then, so he could try to make his case for getting her off the computer. "Yes."

"Would you mind explaining the term to me?"

"Nibbies are teeny-tiny tufts of fabric that ball up on sheets. It's a casual term. You might have heard them called piles or pills."

He shook his head. "These…*nibbies* are a big deal?"

"To some people, I guess."

"Well, I suppose that fits. Wilhemina made a point of saying that whoever I sent needed to know what a *nibbie* was. She called me obtuse when I told her I didn't know what she was talking about."

Under any other circumstances April would have smiled at John's indignation. Most people wouldn't consider calling the man anything but *sir.* Then again, most people weren't his wife's sister, a formidable woman who was more than up to the task of handling her sister's equally formidable husband. But April couldn't even rally a grin. She'd walked right into this one.

"Sort of like the *Princess and the Pea,*" he said, grinning at his own cleverness, which in April's mind only supported the accusation of obtuseness.

She only shrugged, afraid to open her mouth and step in any further. Personally, she couldn't see what the big deal was. She'd never noticed whether she slept on sheets with *nibbies* or not. The only time she was horizontal in a bed was when she was fast asleep, unconscious of *nibbies,* piles or pills. Unconscious enough to be unaware of anything else that might take place in a bed, either.

He leveled that steely gaze on her. "Sounds to me like you've got a good bead on the subject. You're the right person for this case."

"And what exactly is this case?"

"Inside surveillance."

A moment passed before she managed to speak past the alarm shrieking in her head. "Inside surveillance? You want *me* to go…*undercover?*"

"As Rex Holt's in-house marketing assistant."

Undercover? A laugh sprang unbidden to her lips, along with a denial that she managed—*barely*—to squelch before it actually popped out of her mouth. Good thing, too, because butting heads with John would only make him dig in his heels.

She started to pace. She didn't sit still well on the best of days, but with John springing fieldwork, no, *undercover* fieldwork on her…

Glancing at the most recent Mooney family portrait that included a stoic John, a smiling Paula, their daughters, sons-in-law and seven grandchildren, she clasped her hands behind her back and forced herself not to pace, although the urge to move was physical.

She was manic at the best of times but when she got nervous…April Stevens aka *April Accidentally* had learned to curtail her actions rather than risk knocking anything else off John's desk, or heaven forbid, the étagère, which housed all sorts of sentimental items.

John knew more about her than anyone on this planet. Surely he could be reasoned with. "Wow, real undercover work," she forced herself to say lightly. "Why don't you take the case? You live to go out in the field and it's been a good year since you've gotten out of this office."

"Aside from the fact that I don't know a damned thing about *nibbies,* I promised my wife that I'd get you out from behind the computer. She said you've been holing up since you and Jeff broke up. She thinks you're pining."

"I'm not pining."

Man, she should have known she'd wind up back here despite diversionary tactics. The planets must be aligned, because short of quitting her job and moving to Canada, April couldn't seem to avoid John and Paula's attempts to force her to get social.

"I appreciate the concern, John, but what is it you don't understand about hard work? I *like* working hard. I'm good at my job. Where's the problem?"

"You're good at the computer end of your job. You don't have enough experience in the field. And like Paula pointed out, you need to make time for a life."

"I have a life. A good one. You know how active I am in the adoption society—"

"More time spent behind the computer."

"If memory serves, I just took off a morning last week to attend the preschool graduation of one of your little rug rats."

"A *real* life. You barely come out from behind the computer for holidays. When was the last time you were out with friends? Or on a date?"

April could hear Paula's arguments as though she were actually broadcasting them through her husband's mouth. "I was just out with the girls a few weeks ago for Marietta's bachelorette party. I'm sure every female in this place will corroborate my story."

"What about a date?"

"I haven't met a guy I'm interested in."

She wouldn't mention that if she happened to meet one she'd run in the opposite direction.

"Cut me a break, April." John spread his hands in entreaty. "What am I supposed to do? This is Wilhemina we're talking about here. Paula's on the warpath. She wants me to help her sister and she wants you out from behind the computer. This is a straightforward job. You pretend you're this guy's assistant and keep your eyes on him. You can handle this. Getting out of the office will be a challenge."

Challenge? Oh, John was right about that. She inhaled deeply and tried to appeal to reason. "Send Sherry. She's much better at this sort of thing."

"Sherry's married. We don't have any idea how long it'll take in-house security to complete their investigation. It makes more sense to send *single* you."

"Just because I don't have a husband doesn't mean I don't have important things going on in my life, you know. I happen to be in the middle of an adoption search."

A bald lie, since she'd just reunited Dawn Conover with her birth sister and hadn't been assigned another search yet.

"Bring your laptop. You can work your search into your cover. An occasional break will keep you fresh."

"Sherry will blend in much better."

His dark gaze settled on her thoughtfully. "You'll blend in just fine. Don't borrow trouble."

John didn't have to define borrowing trouble, and while April appreciated his confidence in her abilities, the simple truth was that jumping into new situations was not one of her strengths, at work or in her personal life.

Unfortunately, she hadn't been nicknamed April Accidentally for no reason. She was high-strung by nature and whenever she got nervous, accidents were the likely result, which didn't make her prime undercover material.

Of all the crosses she might have to bear in life, April considered this one tame, if rather unfortunate. She accepted her flaws right along with her strengths and coped with them.

"John, this isn't a good idea."

He arched a grizzled brow at her. "Is the sex part making you uncomfortable? I was sure you could handle it."

Before her breakup with Jeff, April might have been able to handle glory holes and bedding companies. But now...

"The sex does bother me a little, to be honest." Unwilling to elaborate on the reason why, she quickly added, "I'll have to be close to spy on this guy and you said everyone in the company has sex on the brain...shouldn't you send a man?"

"I told you, I checked him out. He's okay. This is a babysitting job, April, plain and simple. All you have to do is make sure Rex Holt doesn't make contact with any rival manufacturers. This is not difficult stuff."

"A baby-sitting job?" She tried not to sound panicked or resentful and didn't think she succeeded on either count. "Since when have you had baby-sitters on your payroll?"

John steepled his hands before him and looked at her over his fingertips. "This is the perfect job for you. Wilhemina needs a professional in place and she trusts you. She asked me to send you specifically, if that makes you feel any better. If anything unusual catches your attention, you report it. Should any questions be raised about this guy's integrity, you'll be able to testify that he conducted good business on the road."

Both Wilhemina and John had lost their minds, April decided. It wasn't that she wasn't well trained or competent, but just the thought of heading into the field made her adrenaline pump so hard she could barely hear past the rush of blood in her ears.

"I know you've said Wilhemina's people exhausted the computer angle, but give me a crack at it. They're not as good as I am. I can track those posts. I'm sure of it."

"We're not being hired to investigate. We're being hired to baby-sit. Wilhemina wants you. Besides, who else in this firm will be able to hold his own with *nibbies,* piles and pills?"

"*Nibbies,* piles and pills, oh my!" She pushed off her perch on the chair arm and started pacing again. Babbling was not a good sign, it usually indicated another step toward panic. If John had been paying attention, he'd have noticed.

He wasn't. Or perhaps he was just ignoring the symptoms.

April could have appealed to him to send someone else. If she was pathetic enough, she might just wear him down and she wouldn't have to make excuses to Wilhemina until Easter. But that would mean standing up for herself and she wasn't so hot at standing up for what she wanted on the best of days. And especially not with John.

So she scowled instead.

He scowled right back.

Whoever lasted the longest would win.

Unfortunately, John had the edge. If he was determined to send her to the Luxurious Bedding Company how could she possibly refuse him? Besides being her boss, John Patrick Mooney was also the closest thing she had to a father. He'd come into her life at a time when she'd desperately needed a friend, after her adoptive parents had died tragically in a ski-lift accident during a long-anticipated second honeymoon.

Learning of her situation through their church, John and Paula, whose own daughters had been either married or attending college at the time, had opened their home to April so she could avoid toughing out four years of foster care until reaching eighteen and adulthood.

A very decent thing to do, considering the circumstances of their first meeting.

She certainly hadn't meant to trip John as he welcomed her into his home, but she'd nearly sent him sprawling right through the decorative glass door. The poor man had still been sporting the goose egg a week later when she'd moved in.

Fortunately, he hadn't held the accident against her. He'd taken her under wing through the ups and down of her high school years, including her decision to pursue her birth parents.

Though she'd been unable to locate her birth parents, April had found a family with the Mooneys. They'd become her family-by-love, as she liked to call them. She'd become a friend to John's daughters and Auntie April to the grand-kiddies. Aside from occasional bouts of *too* much concern for her well-being, they were perfect. She honestly didn't know what she would do without them.

No, she wasn't going to practice her standing-up-for-herself skills with John. And he knew it.

Leaning back in his chair, he stared at her with dark eyes that saw right through her.

"Why are you so worked up about this job? What's the real problem? I can't help unless you tell me."

Busted. April clasped her hands behind her back and stared hard at the Mooney family portrait. The last thing she needed was a case that would put her in direct contact with sheets—which would invariably lead to thoughts about what couples did between them.

But she couldn't tell John that now, could she? Telling the truth would mean admitting she'd sworn off relation-

ships that involved sex for the rest of her life because she
was a disaster in bed. Bonafide hopeless. Evidenced by the
fact that Jeff had nearly aspirated during their last sexual
encounter, in the very whirlpool tub he'd sworn would help
her relax.

In all fairness, April couldn't have known he was going
to lick her *there*. He'd been underwater, after all, and if
she'd known he'd been perched so precariously on the
bench, she would never had jumped, no matter how ticklish
she might be.

But she hadn't known, so she had jumped and Jeff had
lost his balance, cracked his head and almost drowned.

Bum luck? Not exactly.

She'd had three lovers in the space of six years and
enough near-misses to come to the conclusion that April
Accidentally was simply too high-strung to have sex. She
could barely stay in one place long enough to run a background check on a suspect.

She worked in front of a computer all day, true, but she
didn't sit, she *stood,* with the keyboard taped to a treadmill
no less. The only time she ever got horizontal was while
sleeping.

She simply couldn't handle another romantic encounter
that wound up with some form of CPR, or worse yet, a
body. Jeff had claimed she was being ridiculous, accidents
happened—especially to her, she'd silently agreed—and had
refused to let her break up with him.

But that was a refusal more easily made than kept. April
had broken off with him and sworn off men—for their protection and her peace of mind. After serious soul-searching,
she'd made the decision to give up the one thing that she'd
wanted all her life—her very own family. She'd never have
a husband or children. She'd never even have an orgasm,
for goodness' sake.

But this was all need-to-know information that John didn't need to know. Not only didn't he need to know, she was fairly certain he wouldn't *want* to know. The idea of his own daughters having sex had him waxing poetic about storks flying around with pink and blue bundles. She had no intention of admitting any of this. Not even to get out of this case.

April had handled losing her beloved adoptive parents to tragedy. She'd handled the defeat of sealed state records after an exhaustive search for her birth parents. She'd handled accepting that her future didn't include her own family or happily-ever-after or mind-blowing orgasms.

She could handle going undercover to spy on Rex Holt. Even surrounded by sexy bedding and a slew of raunchy e-mail posts.

All things considered, life could be a lot worse.

She met John's searching gaze and forced a smile. "I don't have a problem with the sex. No problem at all. I'll go undercover as the in-house marketing assistant."

And try not to get nervous, cause accidents or think about the family she'd never have and all the sex she was missing.

2

To: Rex Holt (mailto:consultant@luxuriousbedding.com)
Date: 7 Mar 2003 08:55:41-0000
Subject: Interoffice Relations

Weekly group sex sessions will promote teamwork between departments!

Studies prove that sex promotes closeness and cooperation; group sex will offer a budget-friendly method of improving interoffice relations. The confidentiality clause of the P & P manual will protect all parties from personal repercussions.

Rex Holt frowned at his computer screen, right-clicked his mouse button and forwarded this and the accompanying 162 e-mail posts to the Luxurious Bedding Company's president, Wilhemina Knox. Contemplating group sex as a viable support skill wasn't exactly how he'd planned to start off his Monday morning. While he could live with the thought of two women pleasuring a male co-worker, the flip scenario made him cringe.

He found the effects of the sexy Sensuous Collection and these suggestive posts far too distracting for his taste. Trying to concentrate on work when his blood was maintaining a constant temperature somewhere between simmer and boil was proving damned difficult.

Reaching for his coffee mug, Rex took a healthy swig.

Maybe caffeine would help. Then again, maybe not. At least not with a dozen promotional photos of the Kama Sutra Sports Set littering his desk. Bedding the company classified as "gaming sheets," the 720-thread-count Egyptian cotton set was imprinted with adventurous sexual positions and included a game piece for consumers to spin and add variety to their erotic lives.

A variation of Twister, he supposed.

Averting his gaze from the zoomed images of couples with twining legs and thrusting parts, Rex gulped more coffee. At this rate he'd show up for his ten o'clock marketing strategy session with a hard-on.

Again, not exactly how he'd planned to start off his week. But then, this job at the Luxurious Bedding Company wasn't turning out to be what he'd expected either.

The titillating sheet sets in the Sensuous Collection were the topic of every marketing strategy session, budget meeting and operational planning review. But Rex hadn't felt any threat to his professionalism until some clown had started sending these suggestive posts through the company network, lending the whole project a decidedly raunchy edge.

Fetishes, fantasy role-playing, bondage, glory holes…the posts ran the gamut. Sex had become the topic of conversation among employees in corporate headquarters—over the water coolers, in the copy room and even on the lunch line in the cafeteria.

Sex on the brain, Wilhemina had called the phenomenon, which begged the question: who needed group sex in the conference rooms to improve interoffice relations?

No one, as far as Rex could tell. Everyone appeared to be relating fine. The warehouse supervisor had caught two employees testing out the stock in a shipping truck, and a petition urging executive management to implement the glory hole proposal had circulated through the departments. While no one had actually been bold enough to sign it, the petition had left more buzz in its wake that had spurred the sexy talk even hotter.

Unfortunately, Rex was no better than the rest of this bunch. Though he'd had no lapses in professionalism to his credit, he'd been thoroughly preoccupied with all the sexy distractions. Had he known that sex would start occupying a top slot in his thoughts when he'd contracted this project, he might have reconsidered accepting the job, even though it had meant a chance to work with Wilhemina again.

His gaze slid back to the Kama Sutra Sports Set. Most companies wouldn't have taken so much risk, which is exactly what had made this project appealing. Rex understood and agreed with Wilhemina's position—capitalize on their image and turn a negative into a positive. It was a bold move, one the company needed at this stage of the game. And Wilhemina Knox was just the woman to make it. Rex planned to make sure she had all the statistical ammunition she needed to make her new company gain big.

Gathering up the photos of the Kama Sutra Sports Set, Rex made the trip between his office and the conference rooms, wishing San Francisco rather than Atlanta was the number one stop on his itinerary. At least in the Golden Gate City a lovely flight attendant named Susan would be ready to help him satisfy his overactive libido.

It was the *only* city with such a distinction.

The migratory nature of his life precluded long-term relationships. He stayed in a place only long enough to get a new project underway. Then he headed out on the road to conduct marketing studies that provided him with the demographics he needed to offer the cutting-edge marketing strategies that had earned him a name in the industry.

Mobility suited him. He scheduled holidays in his Chi-

cago hometown to visit his family—includi
sisters and their broods—and managed some
life despite his global geographic workplace.
skiing buddies in Aspen, fishing chums in Mia
ing pals in Albany. His social circles even incl
casional female acquaintance.

But his rather single-minded focus on work had been interfering with his social life recently, not leaving him much time to cultivate any new relationships with the fairer sex. He didn't have one potential date in his black book for Atlanta and not much time to meet anyone while in town.

Rex had been so distracted by spending every waking moment surrounded by sexy sheet sets and suggestive e-mail posts that he'd even considered breaking his rule and mixing business with pleasure. Unfortunately not one woman at the Luxurious Bedding Company had even piqued his interest. Maybe his sisters were right—he was so wrapped up in his work that he forgot to live.

With these sobering thoughts in mind, Rex arrived in the conference area in time to meet Wilhemina before she made her entrance.

Wilhemina Knox was the reigning corporate queen of the Luxurious Bedding Company. A formidable-looking woman somewhere in her late fifties, she favored designer suits that sat well on her statuesque shoulders and exuded a no-nonsense competence that had earned her staff's respect.

Flagging him in the hallway outside the conference room, she motioned him to hang back while the vice president of sales and the marketing director continued inside.

"I'm glad I caught you before you went in." She met his gaze, an action that barely required she tip her head back, though he stood well over six feet.

"You got the posts I forwarded?"

"I put Jacqui to work on them."

nodded. "I know the drill."

"Unfortunately," Wilhemina said with a frown, "I'm discouraged that between her and security they haven't been able to find anything, but trust me, Rex, we'll get this sorted out."

"I have no doubt."

And he didn't. Wilhemina ran a tight ship. Even with a rat running loose on board.

Inclining her head in acknowledgment of his compliment, she said, "I imagine you're looking forward to a break from this madhouse."

"I'm always glad to get out on the road. Traveling is one of the job perks."

"Very diplomatic. But you'll be missed, I promise. You've been a smooth fit again. I'm impressed."

"Thanks. Smooth transitions facilitate my work and as always your staff has been top-notch." The sex on the brain issue aside, of course.

"Good. And speaking of, I'm providing you with a support person for the marketing studies."

That got Rex's attention. "We agreed that given the nature of the Sensuous Collection and the current climate around here I should work alone."

"After reviewing the launch schedule, I reevaluated. We're running close here. Decisions need to be made and I don't want to risk running behind. Everything depends on the success of this launch. You know that."

He nodded. Contractually Wilhemina had the right to insist on in-house representation for the upcoming marketing studies, which didn't give him much room for an argument. But the last thing he wanted to tackle right now was the vast amount of work in front of him with an assistant who had sex on the brain.

The logistics of the marketing studies and focus groups

he'd be conducting shortly not only meant traveling to various cities to interview respondents but also recording their reactions to the Sensuous Collection products.

By the time he'd concluded this project, he would know whether men and women had more orgasms on red satin sheets or fewer, more powerful orgasms on gray jersey. He'd know what percentage of single women between the ages of 21 and 35 slept naked. He'd be able to estimate how many children were conceived every twenty-three seconds on a Luxurious Bedding mattress.

This abundance of information would have to be compiled after each study, which translated into hotel suites with two bedrooms, a shared office and lots of conversations about sex.

"I understand your position, Wilhemina, and your caution," he said. "But I thought you understood my concerns about distractions. I appreciate that we are on a close schedule and I don't want the chaos happening around here to follow me out on the road."

"You're absolutely right. So I brought in someone from our West Coast operation. Someone familiar with the Sensuous Collection but unaffected by our current network dilemma. That should solve the problem, don't you think?"

"You're providing me with an assistant focused on work rather than sex, right?" He smiled to segue them through the moment. "Are you willing to put that in writing?"

"Only after I run it through the legal department."

"You're not inspiring my confidence."

"I promise she's very competent." Wilhemina motioned to the conference room. "Go meet her. She's already inside. I need a word with Leah first."

Wilhemina glanced in the direction of the approaching human resources manager, but Rex didn't move because her statement had just registered.

She?

Tossing a glance back over her shoulder, Wilhemina asked, "Is there a problem?"

Maybe. Maybe not. The answer to that question all depended on his new assistant.

Turned out today was his lucky day.

He knew both men sitting at the conference table, flanking a wisp of a woman with light brown hair, translucent skin and wide eyes so deep a shade of blue they seemed almost violet.

Growing up with four younger sisters had given Rex a unique perspective on the fairer sex—of their temperaments, their quirks and their differences. As the odd men out, he and his father had developed a sense of humor to cope and their standing joke had been that all women were flowers. His sisters ranged from the high-maintenance hothouse variety to a sturdy weed that thrived in the toughest conditions.

Given that take, his new assistant was a wildflower, or maybe a wild violet with her unusual eyes. He could only see her from the waist up, but in a glance, he took in the slender body and slightly too-erect posture, pegged her in her mid-twenties, right about the same age as his youngest sister.

"Hey, Rex," Dalton Tucker, the VP of sales, said, before turning his attention back to the woman beside him.

Rex inclined his head in greeting, his curiosity piqued by his new assistant. He'd made a career out of evaluating people and translating observations into marketing strategies. Everything about this fresh-faced woman told him she was a fish out of water.

"The man of the hour. Wilhemina brought this lovely lady into corporate to assist you," the marketing director, Charles Blackstone, said, smiling down at the lovely lady in question. "April Stevens, this is Rex Holt, our independent consultant."

Charles reached for April's hand and damned if he didn't bring it to his lips in a move reminiscent of some silver-screen movie star.

Not to be outdone, Dalton reached over the table to pour a glass of water, which he offered to her. "Here you go, April. You'll need this. Trust me. These marketing strategy sessions tend to get steamy ever since we started gearing up for the Sensuous Collection launch."

Squaring off in one corner was Charles, the heavyweight champion trying to hang on to his belt. In the other corner was Dalton the challenger, the hotshot VP of sales—ten years younger, better-looking and a well-liked guy who was a serious threat to the title without any effort.

But Dalton typically went above and beyond the call of duty, which upped the level of competition between these men to include every interaction Rex had ever witnessed. Who was the most competent at his job? Who made the brightest light shine on the company? Who had the most impressive conquest of the previous evening? These two were a regular half-time show.

They'd made every effort to include him in their testosterone war, but Rex had declined the invitation. He did wonder what April thought of all the attention, though. Her smile was in place but she looked breathless.

"Hello," Rex said, pouring a cup of coffee from the sidebar. More caffeine was definitely in order. "A pleasure."

She gave him a high-beam smile and he was surprised at just how much that smile did to relieve the tension radiating from her. She was a very beautiful woman. And one who should have had eyes in the back of her head because she slid her chair out just as he circled the table and walked behind her.

He'd meant to put his cup down and then shake her hand, but he wound up scuttling backward instead to avoid a collision, barely avoiding the hot coffee that spilled over the rim.

She shot to her feet in a fluid motion that made him do a double take at all the long slim curves her blue silk suit didn't hide. She wasn't so much wispy, as willowy…and embarrassed, he decided, as his gaze settled back on her face.

She obviously realized that she'd almost taken him down, because a blush stole into her cheeks. "Oh, I'm sorry."

He shook his head and extended his hand, aware that all eyes were on them. "Welcome to the team."

That high-beam smile returned, despite the blush that didn't look as if it would be fading anytime soon. "I'm looking forward to working together. Wilhemina told me about you."

Their hands met and sparks flew *literally*. Static electricity snapped. April turned to pull away.

Rex didn't let her go.

She was one jumpy lady but the shock of the moment quickly passed as he guided her slim fingers into his and squeezed reassuringly. "Good things, I hope. I wouldn't want you to regret becoming my assistant." He certainly wasn't.

"Oh, no. I'm counting on learning a lot."

"We both will, I'm sure."

He'd already learned a lot today, starting with just how much he'd been ignoring his sex life lately. One look at April Stevens and his mood improved big-time.

Strands of fine hair had escaped from the clip at her nape and she blew them from her eyes before tucking them behind her ear. Rex dragged his gaze from that manicured pink fingertip as it threaded through her hair.

Now if his luck just held, April would be single.

Forcing himself into motion, he set his cup on the table and took his seat just as Jacqui Scott appeared in the doorway. "Good morning, everyone."

She moved into the office with confident strides that encouraged the notice of every man in the room. An attractive woman with an abundance of curly hair she wore loose around her shoulders, she wasn't too far behind him in age, probably around thirty.

"What are you doing here, Jacqui?" Charles asked.

"Kaye asked me to sit in for her. She's on a conference call with the L.A. office. Some crisis with an order."

Rex had dealt chiefly with executive management during his time in-house at the Luxurious Bedding Company, but Jacqui Scott had been the exception. As the network administrator, she'd crossed his path every time he'd been the unlucky recipient of a suggestive post. And the one he'd received this morning would guarantee him yet another visit.

Her gaze rested briefly on April, but she dismissed his new assistant with the barest smile of greeting before sliding into the seat beside Charles. Her gaze skimmed across the product display boards at the front of the room that depicted the lovemaking couples of the Kama Sutra Sports Set.

"Wilhemina told me you received another post, Rex," she said. "I'll need to check out your system after the meeting."

"Drop by my office." Drinking his coffee, he affected a slightly bored mien. As usual, the Sensuous Collection and the suggestive posts placed sex front and center.

"So you're the poor Joe of the day," Dalton said. "What was it this time? I hope not another suggestion to supply male employees with panty hose so we can develop our sensitivity."

"You can ditch that idea completely," Charles said. "Not going to happen in this lifetime."

"I think you'd look good in a pair of thigh-highs with garters, Charles," Jacqui said silkily, glancing at the men from beneath her lashes and saving Rex the trouble of managing a diplomatic reply. "But you'll like today's suggestion much better. Group sex to improve interoffice relations. Isn't that right, Rex?"

He nodded.

"As in you and a friend paying me a visit in my office?" Dalton asked Jacqui hopefully.

Jacqui's gaze shot to Charles before she said, "Or you and a friend visiting me."

Charles laughed and Dalton cast a sidelong glance at the water glass in front of April, a warning about the oncoming conversation. She only smiled.

"I hadn't noticed interoffice relations suffering, which makes this recommendation moot." Rex tried to move them past this topic and give his wide-eyed new assistant a break.

Unfortunately, Jacqui dismissed his attempt with one wave of a manicured hand. "It's my experience that interoffice relations can always use improvement."

"Given your managerial experience, we'll have to take you at your word." Dalton hoisted his mug in salute. "Rex is a corporation of one."

"The lone ranger." Charles laughed.

"We happened to have designed the Rodeo Line for lone rangers," Jacqui said. "'Rope 'Em and Ride 'Em with Supple Leather Sheets Made from Doeskin, Calfskin and Suede,'" she recited the slogan, an obvious attempt to inspire images of what roping and riding in bed might entail.

Both Charles and Dalton watched her with glazed expressions. April didn't say a word, but he sensed she paid close attention to every word of the exchange.

Rex took another shot at interjecting sanity into the conversation. "You seem very well-informed about the line's marketing and you're the network administrator. I don't see much room for interoffice improvement."

Jacqui frowned. "Spoilsport. I thought you were the man who came up with the slogan 'Experience the Bed, 1001 Things to Do Between the Sheets.'"

"For the Sensuous Collection," he pointed out.

"Between our sheet sets and the suggestive posts, everyone is in the mood around here," Charles said. "Except you, Rex. What's up with that?"

"I'm here to work."

"Admirable." Jacqui shrugged in a way that conveyed she didn't believe him. "Most men would be enthusiastic about the idea of a few women pleasuring him."

"The opposite scenario undermines my enthusiasm."

Now she laughed, obviously letting go of her irritation. He noticed April couldn't contain a smile, either.

"You should enjoy yourself while you're here," Dalton said.

"He's right." Jacqui smiled. "Everyone else is."

Rex was spared from further comment when Wilhemina and Leah entered the room and forced the conversation back to business.

"Good morning, everyone." Wilhemina greeted her staff and took her place at the head of the long table. "Have you all had enough coffee to tackle the Kama Sutra Sports Set?" Then she glanced his way and said, "Rex, I trust you've met April."

"We've been introduced."

"Then let's get to business. Are you ready to brief us on your objectives for our gaming and adventure lines?"

"My focus for these lines will be to assess how far we can push the public with our advertising." Reaching for his folder, he went to stand beside the computer where his presentation was set up and ready to roll.

"You're planning the usual run of studies?" April asked in that pleasant, breathy voice that fit right in with the overall excitable impression he'd gotten of her. "Accompanied shopping observations, focus groups, blind testing against our competitors' products."

Rex nodded, before casting his gaze around the table as a distraction from her big violet eyes. Flipping on the display, he pressed a series of commands to bring up his first slide.

"Everyone here will monitor several online discussions and consumer panels. Given my preliminary studies and hindsight from the response to the Cuddly, Cozy Winter Collection campaign, it's clear the key to success will be in proper market placement and how well we reach the target audiences. We can't know where to hit hardest until we have an idea of how consumers will react to the overt sexuality of these lines."

"Which is exactly why Rex is here to advise us." Wilhemina said. "Let's face it, folks, we're dealing with tricky products to place in a mainstream market."

"No joke." Dalton shook his head. "I don't have a clue how I'm going to instruct my sales force to sell sheets that come with a dual-temperature vibrator and a cock ring."

"You will after I turn in my executive summary." Rex motioned to a product display board beside the viewing screen that depicted the "Kama Couple," as the couple demonstrating the Kama Sutra Sports Set's sexual positions had been unofficially named. While not a cartoon, the Kama Couple was animated with very lifelike flexing muscles and twined limbs. "Don't discount the impact of the new terminology, either."

Missionary Mania, as this particular position was called,

depicted the Kama Man on top of the Kama Woman, whose legs were hooked around his waist.

Rex glanced around the table to find April looking at the display. Her wide eyes grew even wider, just about the same time Rex's pulse kicked up a notch.

"That's right, Dalton," Wilhemina said. "Rex's suggestion to have product development rename the positions on the Kama Sutra Sports Set will make the line much easier to present."

Leah nodded. "Missionary Mania isn't nearly so clinical as the missionary position. The term invites fun."

"You're right about that." Charles laughed. "Posterior Passion sounds more inviting than doggie style."

Rex resisted the urge to massage the growing ache in his head. He assumed Wilhemina's executive staff had been a normal group of people before corporate headquarters had been inundated by sex. But that was a big assumption. He hadn't seen much proof and he'd been in-house for several weeks already.

He launched into a translation of his slide show before any more conversation could start up. Part of his job as a marketing consultant was to effectively present complex statistics to businesspeople who weren't statistically oriented. Only two of the six people seated around the conference table had a clue what he was talking about.

At least he assumed his new assistant did.

She never took her eyes off him while he presented the numbers. To Rex's amazement, he found her gaze made his blood pump hard. He was aware of this woman and the way her every breath made her chest rise and fall invitingly.

And the way she shifted around in her chair, giving him prime glimpses of her curves, as though sitting still was testing her patience. And the way she nibbled on her lower lip as he directed everyone's attention to the Kama Couple and discussed potential target markets for the gaming sheets.

He obviously hadn't been making enough time for women lately because he was reacting to April Stevens with an intensity he hadn't experienced before. Keeping to the point of his presentation proved damned near impossible when his thoughts kept snagging on her every reaction to the sexy Kama positions.

Did the way her eyes widened when he presented Her Tip-Top Thrill mean she liked to make love on top? Or did the way she gnawed on that full lower lip when he presented Bound Boy Bliss mean she liked to take charge and bind her lovers?

Had she ever had any lovers?

Something about her fresh-faced looks and that tentative demeanor made him wonder. And her sexual status wasn't the only thing he was wondering about. Why was he tripping over his words as he addressed the Jackhammer, a sexy position that had the Kama Man pleasuring his Kama Lady standing up? Did her blush extend below her collar, down to the swell of her breasts?

April definitely wasn't the only one demonstrating a propensity for hot blushes at the moment. Rex was feeling his fair share of heat, only it wasn't rushing north into his face but south, proving beyond a doubt that he hadn't been making nearly enough time to date lately.

Something about the way his new assistant was checking him out undermined his usually solid control in a way she shouldn't have. April hadn't spoken a dozen sentences yet he found her reactions to his presentation a lot more stimulating than the presentation itself.

Luckily he'd be wrapping up things in corporate headquarters today and leaving for Atlanta first thing in the morning, which meant he would have April Stevens all to

himself in less than twenty-four hours. Sharing a hotel suite
with this lovely lady suddenly seemed to be the perfect way
to kick off his week. He could investigate consumers' reactions to the sexy sheet sets and perhaps explore this unexpected, yet undeniable chemistry he felt for her.

To: J.P. Mooney (mailto:john@mooneyinvestigators.com)
Date: 7 Mar 2003 05:02:12-0800
Subject: First Contact

Hello my favorite brother-in-law,
I promised to keep you posted about the investigation and
I'm happy to report that it's underway. My security chief
has his people working hard running background checks
on my employees and he was agreeable to your suggestion that we start looking very closely at the network administrator. In the three months I've been here, I've found
Jacqui competent at her job as long as I keep a tight rein
on her. But the same could be said of all my staff. Unfortunately with the launch, everyone is behaving very out of
character and as my experience with them is limited, I'm
at a disadvantage.

Sex on the brain. You laughed at me, John, but I wasn't
kidding. If you could have been a fly on the wall at our
marketing session this morning—half the time I marvel that
I'm able to keep a straight face, which leads me to…April.

Paula mentioned how worried you were about forcing
her out from behind that computer so I thought I'd let you
know how she made out. Fine, so stop worrying. I know
she's a daughter to you and you're understandably concerned for her welfare. I also know you'd rather keep her
hidden away at work with you, where she'll be comfortable and you can keep away all the bad guys. But, John,

April will never be comfortable unless she gets out to meet new people without *you* hovering over her shoulder.

Paula is right about giving her a little nudge. There, I've said it. In thirty-five years, I've done my level best never to take sides but April is a smart, beautiful girl who should have a life. If I wasn't convinced before, I was the minute I saw her with Rex today. I got them together during that meeting I mentioned above and stood outside the door to watch. You should have seen her! She almost swallowed her tongue when he walked in the room. I know she found him attractive because she almost torched him with a cup of hot coffee. Rex took it in stride and behaved very gallantly. I told you he's *perfect* for her. I've never met a man so gifted with handling people. He'll have her eating out of his hand in no time.

Which would make me very happy. He's a wonderful man who works too much and she's a normal healthy young woman who should have a wonderful man in her life, i.e. *sex*. There, I've said that, too. You've got to toss her out of the nest and give her a chance to fly. She'll soar. And she knows her Auntie Wil is just a phone call away if she needs me. Trust me, John, she's not going to want *anyone* but that to-die-for man she's working for.

I know she technically works for *you*, but I don't mean *you*. Although you know if you weren't my dear sister's husband…

Wil

John stared at the computer screen and decided sex on the brain sounded about right. He'd warned Wilhemina she'd have to be crazy to consider taking this job. Turned out he was right. She was damned certifiable.

3

SOMEHOW APRIL had gotten it into her head that a man who commanded as much respect in his field as Rex Holt had to be middle-aged with a serious type A personality.

Wrong-o.

The Rex Holt she'd been sent to baby-sit was about the last man on earth to need a baby-sitter. He was laid-back, very charming and positively drop-dead gorgeous, which meant that every time he turned that dark chocolate gaze on her, she went straight to pieces. Every time he spoke with that rich silk voice, her insides fluttered and her memory echoed with the sound of his voice as he'd calmly discussed sexual positions from the Kama Sutra Sports Set.

Ladies' Luxury Laptop and the Sexy Slam-Dunk.

She was in so much trouble here.

To add insult to injury, Rex Holt had to be a gentleman, too. He hadn't said a word when she'd arrived at the airport late this morning, even though he'd been specific about the time to meet. He hadn't asked for an explanation either, which was good because April hadn't wanted to explain how she'd accidentally packed her purse in the frenzy to get out the door, which had meant searching through all her suitcases while the taxi waited....

As they moved through the line toward the ticketing counter in the airport, he kept eyeing her rolling luggage.

"Can I help you with all those bags?" he asked.

"I've got them, thanks," she said *again*. Granted, he'd

packed light by comparison. But he was a man. A garment bag, suitcase and laptop case might outfit him for their Atlanta stint but she wasn't so lucky. Glancing up, she met his gaze. Mistake. One glimpse into those eyes made her breath catch.

"You'll check them?"

"Except the ones I need on the flight," she said around that trapped breath. "I want to use the downtime to review the product line."

Learn the product line was a more like it, but April couldn't tell Rex Holt that. She'd spent the entire weekend immersed in Market Analysis 101 to learn what acronyms like ESOMAR, ANOVA and CAPI meant so she could play a convincing marketing research assistant.

There'd been so much to learn that she hadn't had a chance to even glance at the Sensuous Collection, an oversight that was bound to blow her cover if she didn't get a grip on the product line PDQ.

The product line wasn't the only thing she had to get a grip on. She chanced another glance at Rex, who was still frowning down at her luggage, an expression that didn't minimize his good looks one tiny bit.

And he looked *so* good with his deep russet hair and olive skin. Too good. Even though she wasn't conducting an investigation, this man was technically a suspect until cleared of complicity by in-house security. She cautioned herself that suspects were suspects no matter what they looked like, but Rex's mouth kept doing her in. He grinned wickedly. He frowned intensely. He made a woman who'd sworn off relationships that involved disastrous sex think about what she might be missing.

That mouth could make her imagine the soul-deep sort of ache that would build and build toward a mind-blowing climax, an explosion of the senses that could eradicate reason and make a woman swoon—or so April had heard. She'd never actually experienced the phenomenon firsthand, had never been able to relax long enough to reach the finishing line.

Oh, she wasn't incapable or anything like that. She had absolutely no problem satisfying herself when she was alone. Being alone *with a man* was the problem. She got so nerved out that the experience always ended up in disaster long before she or her partner ever reached fulfillment.

Exactly what had happened with poor Jeff.

Then there'd been Vic. He'd wound up with a dislocated shoulder and a sprained ankle when a foray into light bondage had ended with a broken bed frame, a mattress on the floor and a trip to the emergency room still locked in the handcuffs that had done him in.

He'd been convinced she could relax if she was in control.

Wrong.

Kenny had wound up in surgery to repair torn ligaments after an unexpected make-out session in the front seat of his classic Firebird. He'd totally wiped out his knee wrenching it between the gearshift and the steering wheel.

He'd been convinced spontaneous had been the way to go.

Wrong again.

The memories only reaffirmed that she'd made a logical decision to give up sex, which also reestablished that she was in way over her head on this case. *That* fact had been obvious the instant Rex Holt had stepped foot in the conference room at Luxurious Bedding Company's corporate headquarters yesterday.

It wasn't bad enough that the man was too good-looking to be allowed. No, he had to be charming, too. And so tall that she felt like a china doll standing beside him, those broad, broad shoulders taking up more than his fair share of space.

Inhaling deeply, April reined in her thoughts, only to find Rex still eyeing her bags, as if it was killing him to let her carry them unassisted. Which was just so gentlemanly, darn it.

Finally, the line shuffled ahead and they reached the ticketing agent, where all her plans to work on the flight were almost waylaid before they got off the ground. She had to fight to keep her carry-on bags and only won the battle after the ticketing agent made a big show of measuring the large one to ensure it would fit in the overhead compartment.

By the time she fell into step beside Rex for the walk to the gate, April wished she'd just checked the bags in the interest of time.

When airport security personnel swarmed the monitoring station while their carry-ons were undergoing inspection, April *knew* she should have checked the bags.

Whatever the problem was, it had to do with her luggage.

"What do you have in there?" Rex asked her.

"Just some work." She didn't volunteer any more information. She didn't need to because two security workers were currently opening the bags to begin a search. Rex was about to find out exactly what she'd packed, along with everyone else within ten feet of the monitoring station.

A man standing in the line behind them complained loudly enough for them to overhear. "Now what's wrong?"

Rex shot the man a frown, then glanced at her, brow raised in question. "The Fetish Collection?"

She only nodded, unable to do anything more than stare as the security people pulled out items from her bags, painstakingly examining each one before laying it on the immobile conveyor belt in full view of the crowd.

The black sheet set with pockets built into the sides to hold sexy goodies like...

The dual-temperature vibrator with a clear plastic casing that could be filled with ice water for a sensual experience guaranteed to earn a shiver...

The pair of Pleasure Pearls Ben-Wa balls that clicked together noisily in their clear plastic box....

"An impromptu consumer study. I wouldn't have thought of it," Rex said conversationally. "Got a notebook? You can start documenting peoples' reactions."

April didn't bother answering what she assumed had been a rhetorical question. She didn't bother looking at Rex either. She didn't need to see his face to recognize his amusement.

But she couldn't figure out what he found funny about the looks the security personnel kept shooting their way. Or their suggestive sniggers. Or the nearby passengers' barely muffled comments about where they were planning to use those sheets.

"We'll have to confiscate the handcuffs, sir," a security worker said.

"Think we'll be able to manage without them?" Rex asked.

Another rhetorical question she didn't bother answering, not when his question was drowned out by the amused voices all around them and the sound of blood pounding hard in her ears. She just glared up at Rex, scowling her displeasure that he had all these people thinking the Fetish Collection belonged to them *for personal use.*

"We're marketing consultants working on the launch of a new product line," April explained.

Maybe it was her squeaky-voiced delivery. Or maybe it was the blush. But her explanation only drew more attention. The crowd inched closer to the monitoring station, every pair of eyes within ten feet darting down to assess the neatly packaged leather restraints, stainless steel nipple clamps and the—what on earth was *that?* Oh, that must be a cock ring.

The expressions ranged from shock to amusement and strongly suggested no one was buying her explanation. Rex only snorted when the impatient man behind them didn't bother lowering his voice to make a crack about perverts sleeping with women young enough to be their daughters. A *gross* exaggeration as Rex was only thirty-two.

To Rex's credit he didn't seem bothered by the stares and lewd comments, although he would have been well within his rights to blame her for this whole embarrassing delay. He remained good-natured in the face of adversity, which showed a great deal of restraint under the circumstances.

She, on the other hand, demonstrated no such restraint. The security personnel took their sweet time cramming all the items back inside her bag and the attached case. By the time they'd made room for the Naughty Nipple Cream and the Kegel Balls and snapped the latch on the case shut, April was barely containing the urge to run back in the direction of the terminal.

What on earth had John been thinking? What had Wilhemina been thinking? They both knew better than anyone that she simply wasn't cut out for fieldwork. Not even inside surveillance. And especially not to surveil a man who was so darned handsome that her tongue tangled in a knot every time he looked her way.

She was screwing up already and she wasn't even out of Dallas. Not good. But she didn't get a chance to dwell on how she'd just cost them another ten minutes before Rex touched her. One brush of his warm fingers on her hand, and she felt a jolt that zapped every thought out of her head.

"It's okay, April," he said. "There's no law against sex toys in Texas. We won't wind up in prison."

And now he was on to her. She couldn't decide if she was annoyed that he'd noticed her anxiety or touched that he'd made an effort to reassure her. Not that she could be reassured with everyone in a ten-foot radius thinking they liked kinky sex.

"I had no idea those gizmos would cause a problem," she said as soon as she'd caught her breath and they were on their way again.

Several flights appeared to have arrived, slowing their progress by forcing them to pick their way through the crowds. "I even remembered to take my pepper spray off my key ring."

He only shrugged. "It's the tightened security measures. Slows down the travel process."

"Well, we're almost at the gate, hopefully with no more—"

April cut off abruptly when the luggage handle was ripped forcibly from her grasp. Spinning around, she realized that someone's garment bag had snagged the wheel of her roll-on, sending it thumping along the floor and nearly tripping an inattentive passenger, who hop-skipped over it at the last possible second.

But not before he kicked the smaller case—which security obviously hadn't reattached properly—and knocked it away. The latch burst open as soon as it hit the floor. There was a loud crack and the items spilled out.

Here we go again. April winced as the plastic casing on the vibrator shattered. The box holding the Pleasure Pearls exploded in a burst of clear plastic shards. The balls shot away in different directions.

"Another impromptu consumer study?" Rex asked.

April didn't dignify that question with an answer, but

leaped into motion, deciding damage control was the better part of valor. Diving for the case, she missed the ball she'd been reaching for when an errant foot kicked it away.

Suddenly Rex appeared at her side, shielding her from the crowd with his big body.

"Hey, lady, you lost your dildo." Some jokester handed her the vibrator with the cracked casing.

April issued a weak, "Thanks."

Rex plucked the vibrator from her hand and said, "Grab the rest of these things. I'll get your bags back together."

He sounded positively jolly and she glanced around to find him reattaching the case to her roll-on with a wicked grin.

April didn't need to be asked twice. Lunging forward, she grabbed the leather restraints, which were still bundled inconspicuously in their packaging, handed the bundle to Rex and took off for a Pleasure Pearl Ben Wa ball that had landed under a newspaper dispenser.

It was while on her knees reaching for the ball that she noticed the sneakers. A pair of spiffy clean child's sneakers attached to two sturdy legs. Lifting her gaze, April took in the fists jammed into the shorts pockets, the bright print Hawaiian shirt covering the solid body of a towheaded boy who couldn't have been more than four years old.

People were whizzing past them at rush hour speed but he didn't appear to have a parent nearby. Sure enough, one look at those round blue eyes revealed the little guy was positively terror-stricken.

Wedged in the shadows between two newspaper dispensers, he looked as though he'd been overwhelmed by the crowd and had sought the nearest hiding place. At the moment, April could completely relate with the need to hide.

"Hello."

No reply. The child was clearly too scared to even cry

and the sight of him toughing it out in the shadows tugged at her heartstrings. She could relate to losing parents. She'd lost two sets in her lifetime, though never at this little guy's age.

Sitting back on her haunches, she met his gaze at eye level. "Did you lose your mom and dad?"

Still no reply, but she caught the flicker in those big blue eyes and knew she'd hit the bull's-eye.

"I lost my mom and dad once, too. We were at Disney World. I wasn't holding my mom's hand because I was eating an ice-cream cone. All of a sudden I was alone."

She smiled reassuringly. "I was really scared, but I knew my mom would come to get me. So I tried to remember exactly what she'd told me to do if I ever got lost. She'd said to find a policeman or someone with a name tag that worked close by. And she told me not to talk to strangers. Did your mom tell you something like that, too?"

He blinked, which April interpreted as a yes.

"Great. Well, since I'm a stranger, you don't have to talk to me, but how about if I ask one of the airport people with the name tags to call your mom and tell her where you are so she can come get you. I'll bet she's looking for you right now."

He managed a small nod.

April kept smiling and stood, hoping to flag down a passing airport employee. She had no intention of leaving this little guy alone and wouldn't traumatize him any further by forcing him to leave his hiding place to go in search of help. She turned to find Rex right behind her.

"Oh, Rex. I'm glad you're here. Would you mind—"

"I'll take care of it," he said, indicating that he'd overheard the exchange. He parked her roll-on beside her and headed back into the crowd.

"That's Mr. Rex," she explained to her new charge.

"He's a friend of mine so he'll go get someone who can find your mom."

The little guy kept his hands jammed tightly in his pockets but April noticed the *Star Wars* light saber attached to his belt. John's grandson had one like it, so she struck up a one-sided conversation about how she and little Joel liked to play Jedi knights.

She hadn't yet heard a page over the intercom system before a woman burst through the crowd. "Jake!"

One glimpse at the petite blonde and the little guy dissolved into tears. So did the panic-stricken mom.

Rex appeared a second later with an airport security officer and a man who was obviously the dad, judging by the two other towheaded children hanging on to him.

It turned out that Jake's family was on their way to a vacation in Hawaii—a fact corroborated by their matching Hawaiian shirts. While Jake was still too traumatized to smile, his mom and dad offered profuse thanks.

"Glad we could help," April said, grabbing her roll-on bag, afraid to look at her watch because the chances of making their flight after this delay were slim. "You all have a nice time on your trip."

She wasn't quite sure what she could say to Rex that might make up for causing so many delays, so she just held up the Pleasure Pearl and said lamely, "Got it."

Turned out no explanation was necessary. Rex led her to the gate, explained the situation to the agent, grinned that killer grin and managed to make arrangements for the standby list on the next flight to Atlanta.

"We've got an hour to burn," he said. "Let's get coffee."

He didn't come out and say he needed a cup, but April got the distinct impression he did, especially when he stood at the counter and ordered five additional shots of espresso.

She had the most amazing effect on people. It was a gift.

After receiving her own decaf cappuccino—heaven knew *she* didn't need any caffeine—she sat across from him at a table, used a stirrer to swirl the foam and contemplated what she wanted to say. This morning had not gone according to plan. She'd needed to slip smoothly into this man's life, not convince him he'd been saddled with a total idiot for an assistant.

April knew she'd be okay if she could just get a grip on her nerves. Unfortunately, Rex Holt was exactly the kind of self-assured man who made her a nervous wreck. He was just too personable, too charming…. She should have stood up for herself and insisted that John send Sherry on this case.

"You handled that boy very well," Rex said.

"Oh, thank you." She glanced up into dark chocolate eyes that studied her curiously. "The poor little guy was terrified."

Rex nodded and reached for his coffee. He had long, tanned fingers with neatly trimmed nails, and she followed them as he tipped the cup to his lips.

"Sorry we missed the flight," she added.

"We have some breathing room."

"Thankfully."

She must have sounded too relieved because he arched a dark brow. "You don't go out on assignment often, do you, April?"

Definitely the last question she wanted from him. "Actually there's another assistant who does most of the out-of-house work, but she's…on maternity leave," April lied, seeing a pregnant woman walk by and spouting the first thing that came to mind. "Why do you ask?"

He sat back in his chair. The grin was twitching around

his mouth and she was struck again by what a handsome man he was.

She *really* didn't need to be testing out her field skills in front of this man.

"You seem nervous," he said. "I'm trying to figure out if it's you, me or the situation that's making you feel that way."

He was much too gallant to come right out and say that it would be a long few weeks of working together if she couldn't relax. He didn't have to. April had known that from the instant she'd laid eyes on him.

"I assume all the responsibility," she said with forced lightness. "I'm pretty high-strung on the best of days."

"So you're okay with the logistics of us working together? I can get you a separate hotel room. We'll manage."

She was so tempted to accept. The absolute last thing she needed was to be sharing a suite with this utterly attractive man. She'd never maintain her composure having conversations about the kinds of items that had been rolling all around the airport today.

But accepting Rex's offer wasn't even an option. She needed to be close to see what he was up to. She couldn't get much closer than sharing a suite.

Unless she was sharing his bed.

That thought appeared totally out of the blue and April squelched it as images of the broken vibrator and the leather restraints popped into her head. She had enough against her without letting her imagination run wild. "The logistics are fine, Rex, but thanks for the offer."

He nodded and his hair caught the light overhead, drawing her attention to the glimmers of rich russet in brown hair not quite as dark as his eyes. Such an unusual color. Such an attractive color.

"You're okay with our topic of study?" he asked.

"Of course. What's not to like about dual-temperature vibrators and nipple clamps?"

He chuckled. "I'm going to take the Fifth. Given the responses we've gotten today, I'm hoping this isn't indicative of the consumers' reactions to all the lines. Amusement and shock don't translate into high-gross sales and I don't want to be called a dirty old man again."

"Which part bothered you—the *dirty* part or the *old* part?"

Her question earned a full-fledged laugh and April felt the sound straight down to her toes, another example of the way this man was affecting her. And shouldn't be.

"Both."

"Forget it. That guy had to have been blind. We look like businesspeople, certainly not a couple having a May–December romance. You're not old enough for one thing. And I'm not young enough." She frowned before adding, "That's a dismal thought."

He cocked that brow again, as though not quite willing to debate the point, and set his cup on the table. Leaning forward, he closed the distance between them. "I found your impromptu consumer study very interesting. We got some varied reactions."

She only nodded, thinking him very gallant to find something positive in that debacle.

"We've got our work cut out for us trying to figure out how to market this product. If what I saw today was any indication, establishing a baseline about who'll be receptive to the sexier sheet sets isn't going to be easy. There was a middle-aged woman nearby who couldn't stop laughing. I'd have pegged her as the one to call me a pervert."

"The guy who did the honors couldn't have been much older than you are. His younger girlfriend probably just left him."

"I hope he didn't offend you."

"At least he didn't call me old, but I don't think I've ever been so embarrassed." That was saying something. April Accidentally was *very* familiar with embarrassment.

"I'm surprised you brought along the whole collection. The literature wasn't enough?"

"I suppose it would have been if I'd have thought about it. But I didn't want to forget anything so I just stuffed everything in my bags."

"You'll do just fine on this job, April. Try to relax."

She'd heard *that* before—from John just a few days ago, in fact. She forced a smile, but there was something about Rex, a perfect stranger—a *suspect,* for heaven's sake—making the effort to reassure her that touched April someplace deep inside.

As deep inside as Rex seemed to see with his melting dark eyes. He'd seen right through her to recognize she was completely nerved out about doing her job, even if he didn't know exactly what that job was.

It wasn't enough that this man was so gorgeous she couldn't forget she was a woman who would never have a normal relationship or a mind-blowing orgasm or a happily-ever-after. No. Rex Holt also had to be so nice that he made it difficult for her to remember that he was a suspect.

So she sipped her cappuccino as the million-dollar question roared through her head: just how was she supposed to conduct inside surveillance when observing the suspect made her think about what they could be doing between the sheets?

4

REX PLUGGED the last surge protector into the wall outlet and stood back to survey his handiwork. He'd transformed the suite's formal dining area into a work center to rival his high-tech office in Chicago with an array of computers, peripherals and telephone/copy equipment.

He made it his practice to ship his office equipment ahead so it awaited his arrival in each scheduled city—a trick he made a mental note to share with his inexperienced new assistant before they moved on to Tampa. Given that she'd brought what must have been half her house to the airport today, she clearly didn't appreciate the terms *drop* and *ship*.

Glancing at the closed bedroom door April had disappeared behind an hour before, he smiled. The suite at Atlanta's exclusive Bancroft Hotel seemed uncharacteristically homey today with its plush sitting room, spacious dining area and small kitchen where he could cook, a hobby he enjoyed whenever time permitted. No doubt the prospect of seducing a very lovely lady accounted for the change.

There would be a seduction—*if* he could figure out what was making her so nervous. She was wound way too tight and it was a problem he intended to make every effort to handle because he found April an interesting woman and a study in contrasts.

He liked her ability to laugh at herself. She'd blushed furiously while people had commented about her suitcase of sex toys, yet she'd exhibited a calm, take-charge compassion that had managed to reassure a frightened child.

He'd wanted to know more about her and got her talking on the plane. She wasn't currently involved with anyone—a good thing—but given her hesitation to discuss her love life, he questioned whether her experience included casual affairs, which was all he could offer.

His mobile lifestyle made the logistics of conducting long-term relationships ugly at best, so he avoided them at all costs and contented himself with casual affairs when mood and time permitted, which definitely wasn't often enough. But he intended to go for it with April if she was interested.

The opening bedroom door dragged his attention to the lovely lady herself who appeared with a laptop case slung over a shoulder. She still wore her traveling clothes, jeans and a sweater, which alone was nothing more than a comfortable outfit. Yet on April, casual clothing clung to her every slim curve as though it had been poured on. The woolly pink sweater molded her full breasts in staggering detail.

"Wow! You've been busy." She gave a low whistle, her gaze skimming over the equipment. "Got any room for me in here?"

She patted her laptop case absently, but there was nothing absent about the way Rex found himself taking in her appearance from the top of her soft brown hair to the tips of her manicured fingertips. His powers of observation were on in full force.

"Of course," he said. "What have you got?"

Slipping the case from her shoulder, April deposited it on the table. "Just my laptop. You've got everything here. I won't need to use the business center downstairs for much."

"I'll network you to my system so you can access all the equipment."

"Great." She moved around the table through the small pathway between the table and the desk, her gaze darting from scanner to laser printer to fax machine.

He watched her feet skim inattentively across the cable connecting his late-model system to the power supply and made another mental note to tape down the cable before his system wound up a pile of electrical circuitry on the floor.

Too late.

She snagged the cable. Rex saw the exact moment reflected in her face, in her mouth that formed a perfectly round *O*. She stumbled and reached for the table edge.

Grabbing the monitor before it went over, he had the wild thought that it might be safer on the floor beside the mini-tower, protected from the hotel sprinkler system and his whirlwind assistant. If he could just work lying down…

The keyboard went over in a clatter and April lunged for it, catching the cord in a spectacular save just before it hit the floor.

"Got it." She heaved a relieved sigh when their gazes met across the table.

Her eyes reflected her emotions like a window and he recognized relief and embarrassment, not only in her face, but in the way she held herself frozen in midwince. A blush stole into her cheeks, a color that made her violet eyes seem even richer in hue, her skin even more translucent.

Something about her reaction suggested this wasn't the first time she'd dealt with such accidents and her look of inevitability brought Rex to his senses. Relinquishing his hold on the monitor, he plucked the keyboard from her grasp and returned it to the table.

"Nice catch." He smiled.

His smile had an incredible effect. April exhaled a pent-

up breath, relaxed her primed-and-ready-for-disaster stance
and he realized then that she'd been awaiting his reaction
hadn't expected him to make light of the incident.

Rex couldn't say what it was about her relief that affected
him, but it did.

Then with a light laugh, she breezed away and the moment passed. But not without leaving Rex with a few new
insights. The first was that April was vulnerable behind that
breezy laugh and her blushes, no matter how quickly she
rebounded.

The second was that she had the most curious effect on
him. Technically he shouldn't be feeling anything but relief
that he wouldn't have to rush to an office supply store to
replace his monitor. But segueing her through that uncomfortable moment made him feel ridiculously pleased with
himself.

"Let's look at your laptop and get you set up," he said.
"This is top-of-the-line equipment. The Luxurious Bedding
Company issued you this?"

She lifted those big violet eyes to him again and damned
if his pulse didn't step up its beat.

"No. It's mine. I need an up-to-date system to conduct
adoption searches."

More unexpected information. "Your own?"

"Afraid not. I abandoned my search years ago. I was born
in a sealed record state. The woman I'm helping out now
has a real good chance of tracking down a birth sister. She's
been waiting a long time and I'd rather not let the trail get
cold. But my search won't interfere with my work. I promise."

She seemed so earnest that Rex had no doubt she meant
what she said. Leaning back against the table, he folded his
arms across his chest and pursued the topic, curious. "You

couldn't locate your family, but you help other people find theirs?''

She nodded, her gaze flicking up to high beam. ''I learned so much with my own search it seemed a shame not to put the knowledge to use. I've been active in my local adoption society ever since college.''

''Really?''

Really, he soon discovered when she launched into a breathless tale of winding, often frustrating searches into the adoption system and how some states facilitated search efforts while others used legalities to thwart them entirely. She explained how luck could play a huge role in a search and how the outcomes weren't always happily-ever-afters, although even unhappy answers were often better than unanswered questions.

Clearly these searches were her passion and he found her passion fascinating. As fascinating as he found watching her, her excitable movements drove home the fact that he had a long way to go before he could even contemplate seduction. Her nerves were making her downright dangerous, he decided while watching her sweep a hand around to illustrate a point, only to miss wiping out a table lamp by a bare inch.

''You're knowledgeable,'' he said hoping to keep April in her comfort zone, now that she'd finally stopped talking long enough to draw air. ''I imagine the people with the adoption society consider themselves lucky to have you around.''

She shrugged, looked slightly embarrassed. ''I'm sure that's more than you ever wanted to know about adoption searches.''

''Not at all. Turns out that I'm very interested in things that interest you.''

''Oh.''

"Did you bring your cords?" he asked, deciding his best bet was to keep her off balance and reacting so she didn't have time to analyze what was happening between them. "If not, I should have something that'll work."

She circled the table to unzip her laptop case and whipped out a tangle of electrical cords. "Here you go."

The instant their fingers met sparks flew. April gasped and said, "Oops, sorry," before spilling the cords into his hand, careful to avoid touching him again.

She bolted toward the sitting room and leaned against the sofa, her nerves clearly back in force. Rex watched her retreat, glancing at her sneakers with rubber soles that should have grounded her from creating static electricity on the carpet.

He had the vague thought that this woman conducted more voltage than a lightning bolt and made a mental note to call the front desk to have the hotel provide a mat for the floor of their work area. An extra precaution since April would be networked to his system and might inadvertently share her electromagnetic gifts.

"Great, you've got everything you need here. Give me a minute and we'll be all set." He connected her system to the switch box. "I've got cable access to the Internet. Do you need anything else?"

"Oh no. That's perfect. But what about virus protection, Rex? I'll be searching all sorts of databases. Are you protected? I'd feel horrible if I gave you anything."

"I'm a responsible adult. I make sure I have protection."

There was a beat of silence before April laughed, a ripple of sound that made him smile. "Good, then we won't be in for any unexpected surprises."

"Oh, I don't know. Not all surprises are unwelcome. You've been full of them since we met and each one is proving more interesting than the last."

"Me? You mean because of my adoption searches?"

No, he hadn't meant her adoption searches but he wouldn't elaborate. Not that he would have minded knowing how she felt about abandoning the search for her birth parents. As a man with four sisters, working-class parents and a genealogy dating back several generations, Rex had no frame of reference for how she might feel about not knowing her heritage.

But he wouldn't ask. Not when he had more important mysteries to solve.

"Your adoption searches are interesting," he said, switching seats at the table and booting his system. "But I was referring to what a pleasant travel companion you are. My assistants are always a roll of the dice since I don't get to choose them."

"I'll bet."

Forcing his attention to the screen, he enabled the settings that would allow April access to his system then asked, "Want to see the agenda for tomorrow?"

"Yes, please."

He clicked open his time management program. "I'll download the schedule to your desktop."

In one energetic move, she covered the distance between them and stood hovering above his right shoulder to view the screen. Though she held her hair back so it didn't brush his cheek, Rex could still smell the faint floral fragrance that had embedded itself deep in his psyche during the flight to Atlanta.

"Direct observations and depth interviews?"

He nodded, inhaling deeply and enjoying the way her scent filtered through his senses. "The marketing researchers will have respondents scheduled for shopping experiments. I'll conduct one-on-one interviews after each one."

"What will you want me to do?"

"You'll start cleaning the data, check the sequencing of the questions and the consistency of the answers. I'll examine the results at night. The key here will be to keep up. We've got a busy few weeks ahead."

April nodded. "Tell me about the marketing research company we'll be dealing with."

"My first choice is always Yodzis and Associates. They have offices in most of the major cities, but I work with a few others when need dictates."

"Why do you like this company?"

"They streamline my work process by being professional and organized. They also have a large participant base, which lets them pull together studies on a dime if something comes up that I need to investigate quickly."

Standing up, April made a move to back away, so Rex pulled a chair out and said, "Sit. Let's go over the game plan as long as we're here."

She slipped into the seat, propped her elbows on the table and rested her chin on her clasped hands. "Are these the same researchers you dealt with when you conducted the research for America Sleeps?"

Her question distracted him from the way the purple lights in her eyes flickered beneath thick black lashes. "You know about my work with America Sleeps?"

"My boss mentioned it. I think he was trying to convince me of the merits of going on the road with you."

"Needed convincing, did you?"

"Some," she admitted. "Nothing personal. I just haven't ventured away from home base that much."

"Some people enjoy working on the road."

"You're one of them?"

He nodded and she gifted him with a smile that said she'd guessed as much. That smile did amazing things to her face, and his pulse rate. Full pink lips parted just enough for him to see the straight white teeth below. That smile also sparkled in the depths of her eyes and dispelled some of the nervous energy that seemed to be so much a part of her.

One glimpse of a relaxed April so completely undermined his focus that Rex forgot what he'd been about to say. Which didn't really matter, as she seemed happy to lead the conversation.

"So what's the attraction of the open road?"

He'd been asked variations of this question many times— especially from his sisters, all of whom believed he should find a bride and settle down in Chicago to raise little Holts to entertain his nieces and nephews. He kept a stock answer handy.

"Keeps me fresh. The work is always changing and providing new challenges."

"Being challenged is important to you?"

"Some wise person once said, 'Variety is the spice of life.' And as we only get one go-around, I figure I might as well make the most of it."

"True enough, but it's interesting how your focus is work."

There was something so wistful about her expression that the question popped out of his mouth despite his intention to keep the conversation on business. "Are you making the most of your life, April?"

"That's purely a matter of opinion."

"So what's your position? Do you or don't you?"

"I do," she said quickly.

Too quickly.

Leaning back, Rex smiled as another piece of the puzzle fell into place. There was something so vulnerable about her right now he was reminded of his youngest sister Betsy—

the only one of the Holt clan besides himself still unmarried, which had created a bond between them in recent years.

Rex got the sense that April didn't often open up and share her feelings. Perhaps she didn't have many people to talk with. Or maybe she simply wasn't comfortable sharing her thoughts. Whatever the reason, April reminded him of Betsy whenever she had something weighing on her mind.

"So who doesn't think you're making the most of your life?"

"My boss," she said, shaking her head. "He's on this quest to force me out of the office."

"So your boss is more than a boss. He's someone who cares about you. A friend?"

"He's sort of like a father. He worries too much."

"*Sort of* like a father?" Rex asked. "I assume that means he isn't your adoptive father."

"John and his family took me in after my adoptive parents died when I was fourteen. Sort of like a stray."

"*Sort of* like a father. *Sort of* like a stray." He couldn't help but chuckle. With her chin tilted proudly and her shoulders held back, April seemed about as straylike as a thoroughbred. "You don't deal much in absolutes, do you?"

Her eyes widened and he got the sense that he'd surprised her with his question. But her smile made another appearance, curving her mouth upward, and Rex liked that she had the ability to look at herself with amusement.

"No, I guess not. Not the best of qualities for your marketing assistant, I'm afraid."

"Not necessarily. The work isn't all about statistics. It's about the ability to read people and interpret their reactions. *Not* an absolute science."

"I don't know. From what I hear, you're very gifted at interpreting people's reactions and translating them into statistics businesses can bank on."

He inclined his head in acknowledgment of her compliment, not missing the way she attempted to turn the conversation around to him again. "Accuracy does count for a lot in my work."

"And you aim to please?"

"I do. My reputation, and consequently my success, depends on how well I advise my clients." Folding his arms across his chest, he directed the conversation back to her, much more interested in watching her relax and open up. "I assume your job operates in a similar fashion, otherwise you wouldn't be so concerned about making sure you get it right."

"That's the second time you mentioned my job performance, Rex. Have I given you the impression I'm worried?"

"You said you haven't had much experience in the field."

"True enough. But I'm still competent at what I do."

He bit back a smile. She put on a good show, but she was up against a man who made his living by observing people. Her bravado didn't fool him for an instant. Given her comments about her boss, he suspected she wasn't quite as confident as she presented herself. "You must be competent or Wilhemina wouldn't have sent you. She's topnotch and we both know how important this launch is to her company."

"Also true. I'm a hard worker. If I'm not sure of something, I'll ask, and I trust you'll make it clear what you want me to do."

"I will."

"There we are. We'll get along fine. I'll learn lots from you and you'll report good things about me to my superiors."

"Which will reassure that boss who worries too much."

"Here's hoping." She exhaled heavily, sending wisps of silky hair flying off her forehead. "He needs to find something else to worry about because he's making me—" She stopped in midsentence and eyed him accusingly. "How do you do that?"

"What?"

"Keep steering the conversation back to me."

"I thought you were doing the same thing to me."

Something about this seemed to disturb her, judging by the tiny frown that wedged itself between her brows. "Naturally, I'm interested in you. You've got quite the reputation."

Now it was his turn to eye her dubiously, because he recognized evasive maneuvers when he saw them. This lovely lady didn't want to talk about herself. Being the curious person he was, Rex couldn't help but wonder why.

"A reputation I won't enjoy for long if I don't get to work." He shoved his chair away from the table, deciding a little distance was in order right now. Not only to get April off her guard, but to give him a break from inhaling her delicate fragrance that was throwing his senses into high gear. "I'll get our model together. We'll hit the ground running tomorrow with the Fetish Collection."

"You just jump right in with the tough stuff, don't you?"

"The gaming and adventure sheets present the biggest challenges. I scheduled them first so I'll have time to study whatever comes up."

"Makes sense," she said. "Do you mind if I set up my equipment."

Since he'd already networked her system, he wasn't exactly sure what she had to set up, but he told her to have at it. Maybe she wanted to check out the software he worked with or view their schedule for the remainder of the week, either way, he took advantage of the opportunity to catch his breath.

After sorting through the stack of boxes he'd had Luxurious Bedding ship to the hotel, he'd located the box containing the sheet sets and unfolded the queen-size sleeper sofa that would serve as his display.

As he'd explained to April, the Fetish Collection would be his toughest placement in the launch. Sexual fetishes had the ability to arouse or offend a consumer, as he'd experienced firsthand back at corporate headquarters in the employees' reactions to the suggestive posts.

Finding a balance between these extremes would be tricky and to tell the truth, he was glad he'd scheduled this sheet set to kick off the analysis after witnessing the responses of the people in the airport earlier. Looked like he'd need all the time he could get to pull together an accurate assessment.

Digging through the box, Rex pulled the sheets from the bottom, stripped away the plastic packaging and arranged the fitted sheet over the mattress. Made of a blend of fibers that the Luxurious Bedding Company held the patent on, the Fetish Collection sheets were more supple than vinyl, but just as water-repellent.

The sheets came in various colors with sexy names like Blushing Pink, Tempting Tan and Red-Hot Red. He hadn't requested any specific color for his inventory and noticed that operations had shipped him Brazen Black, the same color April had in her luggage today.

Of all the Fetish shades, Brazen Black was the gaudiest, a shiny color that brought to mind whips and chains. Considering this would be the focal point of their suite, he'd have preferred something a little more tasteful. But he wasn't surprised that delivery and shipping had dispatched this color. Brazen Black suited the mood of the corporate office employees of late.

He set the dual-temperature vibrator aside—he'd seen enough of it in the airport today—and turned his attention instead to the other items in the collection, which upon closer examination could have been packaged under the heading of 101 Things To Do With Leather….

Fit to be Tied Restraints—Indulge in consensual, playful bondage with these comfortable, faux fur-lined bonds. Buckle closures fasten securely yet allow for easy release and long tethers accommodate restraint in many locales.

He wished the airport security guards hadn't spared them the joy of unwrapping these restraints earlier. The reactions of the crowd would have been telling to say the least.

The long leather tethers conjured an image of a lovely bare body spread over the shiny black sheets. Funny, but that body looked like it might belong to a lady who'd been divested of a woolly pink sweater and a pair of bun-hugging jeans….

Who's There? Blindfold—Add mystery and suspense to any sexy encounter or simply enhance the other four senses by wearing this comfortable leather blindfold lined with faux fur.

Boy, wouldn't that lady be surprised to know what was on his mind right now?

Power Play Paddle—Whether on the giving or receiving end of this palm-size leather slapper, the Power Play Paddle delivers a variety of sexy sensations from a tickle to a sting.

The idea of marring her creamy skin with a paddle didn't do much for him, but the tickle part raised possibilities. The sound of her laughter, her long, pale legs scrambling to get away…of course he wouldn't let her. On second thought, the stinging part might not be so bad if a few gentle strokes warmed up her bottom, made her ache for *him*….

Take Control Cock Ring—Add pleasure and pressure with this adjustable cock ring that ensures a snug and secure fit and provides a snap for instant release.

Rex damn sure wouldn't mind one of these if his thoughts kept traveling along this path, or if April proved as lovely divested of that woolly pink sweater and those bun-hugging jeans as he imagined.

"Ouch!"

Startled from his sexy musings, he glanced around to find the woman currently fueling his imagination on her knees beneath the table, massaging the top of her head.

"You okay?" he asked.

She glanced his way scowling, her gaze dropping to the Take Control Cock Ring he still held, then lower to the bed with its array of sexy apparatus. She quickly busied herself with rerouting the wiring from his system to hers.

"What are you doing?" he asked.

"Trying to get the cords to reach so I can set my laptop on the bar."

Rex set the cock ring beside the Pleasure Pearls, which promised to drive any woman to orgasm, and headed toward her. "I don't mind sharing the table. There's enough room for us both."

"Thanks, but the table's too low."

He watched her thread the cable around a chair before standing, a fast, fluid motion that drew his gaze back to the woolly pink sweater. "Too low for what?"

"For me to work."

He eyed the bar skeptically, clearly missing some integral piece of her logic. "Those chairs don't look very comfortable."

"I won't be using one."

He wasn't sure what to make of this revelation, but as he watched her lay the cord across the only walkway to the kitchen, he made a mental note to tape down that cord, too, before her system wound up in pieces on the floor. "You stand?"

"Yes."

"Back trouble?"

"No, I just don't sit very well. As I'll be spending a good bit of time on the computer, I want to be comfortable."

April clearly had this all worked out so Rex kept his mouth shut. What interested him even more at the moment was why she was working so hard not to look into the sitting room, where the Fetish Collection sat front and center in all its suggestive glory. Was the array of sex toys making her uncomfortable?

"The sofa pulls out into a queen sleeper," he said. "I figured we'd keep it open as our model since we'll be dealing with it tomorrow."

"Great."

One deadpan word that told Rex everything he needed to know. Earlier she'd claimed the subject matter of their research didn't bother her. Not only had she declined his offer of separate rooms, but she'd joked about the sex toys. So what was making her uncomfortable now?

And April was uncomfortable. She hovered somewhere in the high digits on a fidgety scale of one to ten.

"What do you think of the color?" He contemplated the sheets, watching her reaction in his peripheral view. "I wish they'd sent something a little less—"

"Shower curtain?" she said dryly, keeping her gaze fixed on her laptop.

"Dungeon," he replied just as dryly. "Though now that you mention it, I suppose that shiny water-resistant look does resemble a shower curtain."

She didn't reply, just started tinkering on her laptop, connecting the mouse, arranging the pad, *not* looking at him.

Something was definitely up.

"Will you give me a hand getting all these doo-dads into the pockets?" he asked. "I want to see the Fetish Collection in its entirety so I can take a look at my script for tomorrow and make sure the two line up."

"Uh, sure." She turned around, avoiding his gaze, suddenly all business.

Rex bit back a smile, certain he'd found the answer he needed.

The sex toys weren't making April nervous. *He* was.

5

APRIL HADN'T BEEN in the Atlanta offices of Yodzis and Associates for twenty minutes before understanding exactly why Rex chose this firm as his preferred research company. They'd arrived at the crack of dawn to prepare for the first run of concept testing. The staff greeted them in the reception area with smiles and proceeded to treat the man as if he was the ruler of a small kingdom.

"We've taken care of it, Mr. Holt."

"We'll make the arrangements right away, Mr. Holt."

"Just let us know if you need anything else, Mr. Holt."

Mr. Holt handled the attention as though it was his by birthright, commandeering the offices and establishing himself as if the place was his castle and the staff his royal subjects.

The man was so damned charming that every staff member from the supervisor on down, hopped to do his bidding as if it were a privilege.

"It's been three months since we've seen you, Mr. Holt."

"We've stocked plenty of your favorite espresso, Mr. Holt. Would you like a cup?"

The staff of Yodzis and Associates ran the place on par with the motherboard of her high-power computer system, managing not only to accomplish every single task on Rex's hefty to-do list, but to accomplish it to his satisfaction.

April had firsthand knowledge that this was no small feat. She'd spent her first night in Atlanta sharing a suite with the man and familiarizing herself with his project outline and upcoming schedule.

A perfectionist from the word *go,* Rex Holt crossed every *t,* dotted every *i,* and left virtually nothing to chance. He clearly took the research process very seriously, which she guessed was to be expected, given these studies provided him with the data necessary to consult his clients.

The man didn't miss a trick, either, a fact made evident when they were ushered into an observation area off the main conference room where he would begin the first run of testing. The room boasted a wall of nonreflective glass where she could observe him and provide the support he needed while conducting his interviews.

The room in itself was nothing special. Filled with various data-collection tools—an audio recording device, video recorder and a mobile computer system with a docking port. What made this room unusual was that sometime between late yesterday afternoon and this morning, Rex had arranged to have the computer system set on a podium so she could stand.

He surveyed the makeshift computer setup with a satisfied gaze. "What do you think, April? Will this work for you?"

"Beautifully. Thank you."

"My pleasure," he said in that deep silky voice that sent a shiver down her spine. A *shiver,* for goodness' sake.

He swept that dark gaze over her. Not a glance, but a caress. The chemistry between them was so potent that April could barely breathe. She tingled beneath his gaze, a ridiculous reaction to a man she'd only met a few days ago.

The absolute last thing she needed from him right now was an assault by his thoughtfulness when she was already so incredibly aware of him. Such a simple gesture, a small kindness, but one that told her he'd been paying close attention to the little things about her. April backed away to put some breathing room between them since the man seemed to be sucking up more air than was his due.

She saw the inevitable crash reflected in Rex's face the instant she collided with the opening door. He reached for her as the door nailed her shoulder and sent her sprawling forward. He caught her soundly in his arms, pulling her hard up against his chest to steady her.

For one startling moment she registered the feel of her breasts molded against hard muscle, registered the fact that Rex didn't seem to be nearly as startled as she was by the perfect fit of their bodies before an anxious voice said, "Jeez, I'm so sorry. Are you all right?"

April sprang away from her tall protector, almost colliding with the man who'd entered the room. He sidestepped her neatly.

"Fine. I'm fine." She knew she couldn't have sounded less fine.

Retreating to minimum safe distance, she clasped her hands behind her back to curtail any more livewire movements, willed her heart to slow its pace. She couldn't do a thing about the blush. It blossomed full-force, prickly and uncomfortable, no doubt turning her face as red as a strawberry.

Rex watched her too closely to help matters, and the new arrival, a man with neat hair and wire-frame glasses, looked so mortified that she had the ridiculous urge to comfort *him*.

"Excuse me, ma'am. I'm very sorry."

"My fault." April forced a smile that lacked credibility because of her blush. "I stepped in front of the door."

"What's up, Matthew?" Rex asked, taking control of the exchange and segueing them back to work, much to April's relief. "This is April Stevens. April, you lucked out today. Matthew will help you run the equipment and he's the best Yodzis and Associates has to offer."

The moment passed. The heat in her cheeks waned. A little at least. Rex checked the position of the video camera while Matthew extended a hand in greeting. "Which is exactly why Mr. Holt requests me. Do you have everything you need?"

"Looks good," she said.

He eyed the equipment as though he wanted to ask about the unusual setup. Perhaps because of their mishap, he refrained.

"Everything looks great, Matthew. But let's keep the coming and going to a minimum," Rex said to them both. "Every time the door opens in here, light shines through the observation glass and distracts the respondents."

April nodded.

"Of course, Mr. Holt." Matthew exuded an efficiency that suggested Rex would get whatever he wanted no questions asked. "Here's the copy of today's schedule you asked for."

Rex accepted the clipboard and stood there, tall, muscular and oh, so handsome in dress slacks and a light gray Egyptian cotton shirt that seemed striking against his tanned skin. Flipping pages, he scanned the material with a no-nonsense gaze. "The respondents meet the eligibility criteria. Backups?"

"Several per session. Should be sufficient."

"Good. I've got these groups scheduled back to back all day. I don't want any downtime."

Matthew nodded. "As usual, Mr. Holt."

"How about you, April?" Rex turned that lethal gaze her way. "Do you need anything before I head into the conference room? Matthew will get the equipment rolling."

"I'm all set."

She wouldn't have dreamed of prolonging Rex's departure. More than she needed information, she needed a wall of observation glass between them so she could catch her breath. Her reaction to this man was nothing short of overwhelming and she was convinced he was some sort of test— give up men and the sexiest man on the planet pops up as the final temptation.

Making her way to the computer, she smiled a polite farewell and got down to business. She had to establish her cover as a competent marketing assistant while assessing her suspect. She didn't have a spare second to lust.

April's function would involve monitoring the interviews that Rex conducted in the form of focus groups. Product had been shipped from the Luxurious Bedding Company and a display bed covered in the Fetish Collection occupied the focal point of the main conference room. Unlike the display in their suite, this Fetish Collection wasn't nearly so—what had Rex called it?—*dungeon.*

This sheet set was a tasteful shade of seashell pink. She couldn't recall exactly what name, but knew she'd read a list of available colors in the literature. Pink was far less menacing than shiny black leather.

Rex set a cup of coffee at the head of the conference table and after perusing the stacks of product shelved behind the chair, he said, "How are we doing on the audio, Matthew? Can you hear me?"

His voice transmitted over the microphone that dangled from the ceiling above the conference table.

"Loud and clear," Matthew shot back.

"Good." Rex took a seat at the table, sipped his coffee and reviewed a folder of papers. "How about you, April? All set?"

She clicked the system mouse to move through the data-collection program, checking the various screens to ensure she was using the same software she'd familiarized herself with last night. "All set."

He nodded, never lifting his gaze from the paperwork. Shortly afterward another staff member popped her head into the room to signal Rex the first run of respondents was assembled.

Rex stood, glancing at his watch. "Right on time. Please send them in."

A half-dozen women from a variety of life stages and occupations filed into the room, all carrying name cards and an assortment of beverages. From the moment Rex smiled that killer smile, introduced himself and instructed the respondents to place their name cards on the table facing him, April realized she'd only glimpsed a infinitesimal percentage of this man's charm.

"He's something, isn't he?" Matthew said from behind the video camera, which hung from a ceiling apparatus and was positioned through the observation glass. "We work with consultants from all over the world and there's no one even close to Rex's caliber. The guy's a legend around here."

"He's something, all right," she agreed.

A very skilled, highly impressive something. April might be most comfortable behind a computer, but she was a well-trained investigator, skilled in assessing people, even if she preferred not to deal with them face-to-face. She recognized star quality when she saw it and Rex had star quality, plain and simple.

Watching him in action was nothing short of amazing. He smiled his blinding smiles, laughed easily and maneuvered the discussion with a deft skill that never seemed prying or forced.

He questioned the respondents about their lifestyles, their shopping habits, their bedding preferences and his easy manner encouraged the women to answer freely. He made notations on a notebook, backed up the questioning if someone said something that interested him and explored the minds of average consumers with such skill that they weren't an hour into the day before April understood why John had referred to Rex as *big potatoes.*

The man had a true gift for dealing with people. He read each of the respondents accurately, handled each in a way to make her comfortable enough to talk honestly about an intimate subject. And he did this all so fast he made April's head spin.

There was no question about why she'd had such a difficult time keeping the conversation focused on him last night. She may be an information specialist, skilled at manipulating data and extracting information from the Information Superhighway, but this man made his living by manipulating conversations and extracting information from *people* face-to-face.

She was in so over her head here that she couldn't help but wonder if Wilhemina had lost her mind. John may not have known what she'd be up against with Rex, but Wilhemina surely had when she'd asked for "someone she could trust."

Which brought to mind this past Christmas Eve when they'd been chatting over fruitcake while waiting to leave for midnight mass.

Just because I've chosen my career over my own family doesn't mean I've neglected my personal life, April, Wilhemina had told her.

They'd been discussing the similarities in their devotion to work and April remembered thinking that John and Paula must have recruited another family member to help eject her from behind the computer. As if it wasn't enough that she was only one against the entire Mooney family already.

Maybe asking for April was Wilhemina's attempt to support the family cause. She wouldn't put something like that past Paula and Wilhemina when they put their heads together, but John? He knew those two were double trouble—he'd commented on it often enough—and would never have gone along.

Or would he? Had they finally worn him down?

Pulling up her e-mail program, April jotted off a post to Wilhemina right then and there, asking point-blank if she was trying to play matchmaker. Sexy sheets and Rex Holt. Such a potent combination April was convinced she'd been set up. Once she hit Send, she felt nominally more in control and went back to watching Rex work, marveling at his skill and telling herself she could handle this man who maneuvered people and conversations as deftly as her computer multitasked.

Couldn't she?

Yes.

Fortunately, Matthew reminded her that she was here to assist Rex, in addition to spying on him, when he produced the first stack of respondent surveys. So while April busied herself inputting data, she kept one ear on Rex's discussions and picked Matthew's brain about the marketing consultant he so revered.

Turned out the young man possessed a wealth of knowledge about Rex he wasn't shy about sharing. "I don't know too many people in the industry who haven't heard of him. He teaches me something every time he walks through the door."

April peered through the observation window to where Rex sat at the conference table charming his respondents into a rather animated conversation about what they looked for in their sheets. "He expects a lot from you all."

"He's reasonable. You'd be surprised how temperamental these marketing consultants can get. Yodzis and Associates provides a service and…well, since we're dealing with people, sometimes things don't always work out as expected. Rex trusts us to do our jobs and always plays fair."

April recognized the sincerity behind the words and couldn't help thinking that men who were renowned and respected for their sense of fair play usually didn't involve themselves in corporate espionage. One more character trait that would serve Rex well if suspicion was ever cast his way in court.

Not that any judge and jury couldn't just look at the man and see his integrity. She watched him through the window, the fluorescent lights sparking off his russet hair, the way he moved from the table to the display bed with long-legged strides and a grace that should have been at odds with his size.

"Go on, Bonnie-Jean," he was saying as he leaned over the bed to reach for a pillow. "Please follow that thought. You're telling me your interest in this sheet set depends on what position you're sleeping in?"

An attractive woman in her early fifties with bright blue eyes, Bonnie-Jean gave Rex a smile. "It would definitely factor into my decision whether or not to buy them."

April stepped back in front of her computer, recognizing a cue in the sound of Rex's voice. There was a note of interest that told her he was on to something. She typed S-L-E-E-P-I-N-G P-O-S-I-T-I-O-N into the appropriate cell in the spreadsheet, her attention focused back on the conversation in the main conference room.

"So you're saying that you sleep differently on different nights?" Rex asked.

"It's not the nights really, but my husband and I definitely go through phases. If we're in our *intimate* phase…" The woman smiled. "This sheet arrangement would work out fine. But if we're in our butting-heads phase, my husband would wind up hanging off the edge of the bed to get away from me. All that stuff on the side of the sheets would annoy him. You know, the apparatus.''

April chuckled. With the click of her mouse, she pulled up the file with the respondents' profiles.

Bonnie-Jean Hickman, 50, business owner—floral shop.

While April had never been involved in a relationship long enough to warrant *phases,* she knew Bonnie-Jean's claim was valid when several women around the table nodded their agreement.

''So couples have styles of sleeping,'' Rex said. ''Ladies, you're nodding. You all know what Bonnie-Jean's talking about?''

More nods.

''Let's explore this. Tell me about how you sleep, Marina.''

Marina Torres, 38, elementary school teacher.

''My husband and I spoon in the middle of the bed so the pockets on the sides of the sheets won't bother us.''

''Would you think about sleeping like spoons when you were considering whether or not to purchase these sheets?''

Marina shrugged. ''Not when I was buying the sheets, but it would make a big difference whether I left them on my bed all night.''

''So you may put the sheets on and remove them before you sleep. Treat them as a specialty item rather than conventional bedding. How would your sleeping position factor into this decision?''

''It wouldn't.''

''What would influence your decision then?''

Marina smiled. ''How well your sheets worked and whether or not I was too tired to get up and strip the bed.''

Several women around the table laughed. Rex only nodded, but even through the window April could see the spark of amusement in his dark eyes.

"How about you, Carolyn?" he asked. "How do you sleep and would your position affect your decision to buy these sheets?"

Carolyn Rogers, 42, legal receptionist.

"My boyfriend and I start off the night facing each other like we're hugging."

Rex reached for his notebook, made a notation before he looked up and asked, "So far we've got hanging off the bed, spoons and hugging. Any others?"

When one woman tried to describe how she and her significant other slept, Rex looked stumped. He finally asked her to illustrate the position on paper.

While April may not be very comfortable around people, one area she excelled in was research. With just a few keystrokes, she'd pulled up close to a thousand hits on Web sites featuring information about sleeping styles. A few more strokes and she narrowed her search specifically to couples' sleeping styles.

She visited the Web site of a psychologist who'd based his twenty-five year career on the study of how couples' sleeping language indicated the emotional well-being of the relationship. Scanning the pages, April scrolled through the photographs that demonstrated each sleeping position in full color.

"April," Matthew said, dragging her attention from the computer screen. "You're on."

She glanced up to find him pointing at the window and Rex and the respondents in the room beyond. "What?"

"Mr. Holt wants—"

"April," Rex's voice resounded over the speaker. "Please join me."

"Oh, thanks," she said to Matthew then slipped from the

observation room, trying not to allow too much light in through the opening door.

She popped her head inside the conference room a moment later and Rex motioned her in. Smoothing her hands over her skirt, April entered and greeted the respondents with a smile.

"Ladies, this is my assistant, April. She comes directly from the client who is sponsoring our focus group today. She'll help us clarify the positions you're talking about." He turned to her and she saw a smile in his dark eyes. "April, you've been following our discussion?"

"Yes."

"Good." Circling the table, he motioned to the bed. "Come on over here. Ladies, gather around. I want you to talk us through these positions."

It took a moment for April to realize what Rex intended, another to comprehend that he expected her to lie down on that bed with him. Direct contact. Exactly what she didn't need with Rex Holt in front of an audience....

"Take off your shoes, April." He toed off his own butter-soft leather slip-ons.

Then he climbed into bed.

The sight shouldn't have been erotic, given the logistics— an audience, an observation window, a video camera—but there was no way watching this man climb into a bed *couldn't* be erotic. That he was fully clothed didn't minimize the effect of his long, sculpted body unfolding as he spread out over the sheets, a fact apparently evident to every woman in the room if the way they all watched was any indication.

His dark hair and tanned face looked striking against the pale pink pillows, his button-up shirt and knife-creased trousers a silent invitation to be removed piece by piece.

"Come on, April, join me." He extended a hand and she had no choice but to accept it.

Smoothing her skirt, she slipped into bed and stretched out, careful not to brush against him. Her heart began to race. A voice in her head warned over the alarm bells that had started peeling wildly...*calm down, calm down, calm down.*

She breathed deeply, surprised that lying beside him left her with a curious feeling of déjà vu, which made no sense at all given that she had never even seen the man lying down.

Unless she'd been fantasizing about him.

As she'd slept so restlessly last night, she couldn't discount the possibility. Just knowing Rex was in the room on the other side of the wall, in bed, perhaps naked...

"All right, Bonnie-Jean," Rex said. "Let's start with the butting-heads phase."

Rolling to his side, he draped his knee over the mattress. "Like this?"

"Hang your arm down," she directed.

"And where are you sleeping when your husband is hanging off the side of the bed like this?"

"On my right side with my hands tucked beneath the pillow."

April mimed the position and Bonnie-Jean nodded.

"I sleep the same way all the time. My husband's the one who changes. But see how the pockets with all that stuff in them are in the way."

"I'm catching one with my arm and the other with my knee." Rex shifted around to illustrate his point.

"It's a wonder your husband doesn't fall out of bed," Marina commented. "I couldn't sleep like that."

"Actually, he has." Bonnie-Jean laughed.

"So you sleep like spoons during your…" Rex hesitated. "Intimate phase, isn't that what you called it?"

Bonnie-Jean nodded.

"With your husband on the inside or outside?"

"Outside."

Rex rolled over and suddenly he was pulling April against him, much too close, much too *male* for her peace of mind. She actually tingled when his warm strength cocooned her, molded every solid inch of him around her.

His chest pressed full-length against her back. His crotch pressed against her bottom so she could feel the slight bulge nestled between her cheeks. His thighs slipped beneath hers, knee-to-knee, and if that wasn't enough, he hooked an ankle over hers to pin her beneath him.

She wanted to ask if it was really necessary for him to take the closeness so seriously. They were only supposed to be *demonstrating* sleeping positions, after all. But she couldn't come up with a way to phrase the question that wouldn't make her sound stupid in front of their audience.

"Does this sum up your sleeping arrangement, Marina?" His breath came in a warm burst against her ear and to April's utter mortification she actually shivered, a head-to-toe vibration that she sincerely hoped Rex hadn't felt.

Marina approached the side of the bed to orchestrate their arrangement. "My husband's leg crosses mine over the thigh. Like this." She patted Rex's knee to motion him to slide his leg upward.

April felt every inch of that warm weight dragging a trail up her calf, her silk hose and his trousers sliding sleekly against each other.

"Like this?"

Marina clapped her hands. "You got it. Nothing fancy, just really close."

Really, really close. April's temperature rose by slow degrees, a dizzying combination of nerves and awareness.

"All right, Carolyn. Your turn." Rex clearly was as comfortable conducting business on these pale pink sheets as he was sitting at the head of the conference table. "Show us what you were talking about."

Carolyn Rogers was an attractive divorcée in her early forties, a receptionist who'd recently gotten involved with a partner from her law firm.

"We face each other," she said. "My boyfriend lies on his left side and I lie on my right."

Rex turned over, and encouraged April to slide into his arms with a dashing smile. Meeting his gaze squarely, a bravado that was absolutely, positively all show, April rolled against him.

"Now thread your legs together with yours on top, Rex."

He wedged a knee between hers and slid the other on top as directed. Wrapping an arm around her waist, he held her close.

"Well, this is cozy." He laughed, a rumble she felt deep inside his chest, or more accurately, *her breasts* felt deep in his chest, because they happened to be the closest body part.

"Ah, to have such passion again." Marina heaved a great sigh. "You and your boyfriend want to fuse together, eh?"

Carolyn grinned and the women nodded appreciatively, gathering around the bed as though proximity might pass along some of the magic.

April, however, felt far from magical. She was barely staving off the effects of Rex's hard body and her own case of nerves. The need to fidget was becoming torture.

"The Honeymoon Hug," she squeaked out, needing to hear her own voice as a distraction.

His chest kept brushing her nipples so lightly she feared

she'd wind up with nipple erections for all these women to see.

And Matthew. And the videotape...

"The what?" Rex asked.

"This sleeping position. It's called the Honeymoon Hug. Couples sleep this way a lot when they're in the honeymoon phase of their relationships."

"Or after lovemaking, eh," Marina said knowingly.

"A sleeping-styles doctor calls this position the Rolls Royce of intimacy."

She was babbling. Not a good sign. The alarm in her head was shrieking wildly now and she willed her thoughts away from how his thighs snared hers between their muscular strength, from how utterly and completely perfect their bodies fit together.

"A sleeping-styles doctor?" Rex unwrapped himself enough from her to prop up on an elbow to peer down into her face. "Who's he?"

"A psychologist who studies couples' sleeping language. I pulled some information up when you started discussing the subject. There are a lot of sleeping styles."

"Really?"

She nodded, any headway she'd made catching her breath lost. She'd pleased him.

She was pleased that she'd pleased him.

This was not a good thing. But for the life of her she couldn't remember why at the moment. Touching this man had scattered her thoughts completely and April didn't have a chance to dwell on this unfortunate development because Rex chose that moment to turn the floor over to her by addressing the group.

"Okay, ladies, let's try these sleeping styles on for size," he said. "Marina, my notebook is on the table. Will you do the honors."

"Absolutely."

"Tell us what other positions there are, April. Ladies, stop us when you recognize the ones you sleep in. Marina, write down the name and the style after it. Make sure you get yours and Bonnie-Jean's down there, too."

"Got it."

"First there's the Crab." April scooted away so quickly the bed frame creaked loudly. "No contact. You sleep over on your side of the bed and I stay over here on mine."

Worked for her.

"Any takers?" Rex asked their audience.

Several women shook their heads while Marina made notations in Rex's notebook.

"That one isn't so popular. I don't like it either." Rex rolled back toward her. "What's next?"

"The Leg Hug." Another position with limited contact. "Hook your leg over mine. That's it. Nothing else touching."

"My boyfriend and I sleep like that," Nikki, the career woman who worked on the road with a Fortune 500 company, said.

Then the Sweetheart's Cradle, which had April's thigh draped casually across his, just a hair's breadth below a bulge in his crotch…

The Buttocks Hug. Facing in opposite directions with bottoms pressed together. The perfect Zen position for giving each partner a sense of independence while still maintaining the intimacy through a physical connection.

"That's me and my husband." Sheila, a mom of toddlers, headed toward Marina and motioned to the notebook. "Put me down for that one. We sleep that way so the kids can climb in on both sides of the bed."

The Loosely Tethered position drew a response from Elizabeth, the nursing supervisor. This position had the added benefit of keeping April facing away from Rex while he molded around her like a spoon, almost but not quite touching and still leaving her room to breathe.

But not for long.

The Shingle, a position that robbed April of her breathing space by placing both of them on their backs with her cradled in the crook of his arm. This was a protective position, with Rex assuming the dominant spot with that same lofty confidence she'd noticed earlier when he'd taken over these offices. He took advantage of the closeness, his nose hovering just above her head, his strong arms anchoring her close.

By the time they'd reached the Pursuit, which had him rubbing up against her, molding his body around hers as he chased her across the mattress, April was so high-strung that when he said, "All right, ladies. Looks like we got them all," she shot away from him like a bolt.

She hadn't counted on Rex hanging on though, and the top of her head connected with his chin so hard his teeth rattled.

April winced, tears springing to her eyes on impact, but before she could even say "ouch!" Rex had reared back and teetered uncertainly. April wasn't the only one in the room to gasp as he rolled right off the bed.

Unfortunately the bed wouldn't let him go that easily. The dual-temperature vibrator trapped his hand before the pocket ripped away from the sheet and Rex hit the floor with a thump. The vibrator shot across the carpet and cracked against a metal heating vent.

Then all hell broke loose.

"Are you all right, Mr. Holt?" Marina asked.

No, Mr. Holt was not all right.

"You're bleeding," Bonnie-Jean said.

"And your vibrator's broken." Carolyn had retrieved the cracked apparatus and held it up for inspection.

Their resident nursing supervisor wet a napkin at the water bar and brought it to him.

Rex glanced up at April. "I just bit my lip. No problem."

But there was a problem. A *really big* one.

April Accidentally had struck again.

6

REX CRADLED the telephone against his ear and kicked the bedroom door closed. "You've got potential liability," he told Wilhemina. "I suggest you send the Fetish Collection back to Research and Development to take another look at those open pockets. Maybe they can lower them or devise some sort of flap that closes over it. As it is the items hang out now, which can be dangerous when someone rolls off the bed."

Or falls off, as was his particular case.

"What happened?" Wilhemina asked.

Tugging off his shoes, Rex recapped the day's events and his concerns. He didn't mention to Wilhemina that she'd provided him with an assistant who should have come with a warning label. The deed was done and now April was all his to deal with.

Perhaps he should say thanks.

He complimented April's work performance and left it at that. This telephone call wasn't happening quickly enough to suit his mood tonight, not when he could hear April moving around in the suite, which meant every second he was on this phone was another second he could be spending with her.

And he needed every second because today's mishap only confirmed what he'd begun to suspect last night—April was feeling the chemistry between them and it made her nervous.

Rex had big plans for the night and he was eager to get on with them. They'd just arrived back at the hotel. It was late and he was hungry and he hadn't even glanced inside the refrigerator yet. From the blips and beeps issuing from beyond the door, he guessed April hadn't either.

Juggling the phone between his shoulder and ear, he stripped off his work clothes and donned sweats so by the time he finished talking business and bid Wilhemina a good night, he was ready to join his lovely new assistant for dinner and his first lesson in Relaxation 101.

Rex found her hard at work in front of her laptop, still dressed in her skirt and blouse. She'd pulled her hair off her neck with a clip and traded her heels for a pair of slippers. He marveled that she still had the energy to stand after one very long day and made his way into the kitchen.

"Busy?" he asked.

"Just breaking down today's sessions."

"I'll give you a hand after dinner."

"No problem. I've got it under control."

She didn't glance up. Perhaps he should have been pleased with her efficiency, but he found that he didn't like being dismissed so easily. "Hungry?"

"Um, yeah," she said absently. "Not enough to stop working to deal with it though. It's getting too late."

"Tell you what. You work and I'll fix dinner. Something that won't take long to prepare."

She finally made eye contact. "Prepare? There's food here? I thought we were in a hotel."

"I leave standing instructions to have my suite stocked with groceries when I'm in town."

"Really? The staff stocks your groceries. That's rather… privileged." Her eyes sparkled almost blue in the light.

"Well, I don't know about privileged," he replied. "I

come from pretty run-of-the-mill roots, a fairly large Irish family with an Italian mother who ranks cooking right along with breathing.''

"My good fortune then.''

Pulling open the refrigerator, he inspected the contents. "How does steak and salad sound? No grill, so I can't do real justice to this London broil, but it won't take long."

"Fine by me."

She'd gone back to working and Rex retrieved the ingredients for a decent meal and went to work himself. After rinsing romaine lettuce and setting the leaves on a dish towel to dry, he contemplated April. He must have gotten used to all her high energy because right now, with the suite quiet except for the sounds of running water and her fingers tapping on the keyboard, she seemed almost subdued. True, she was working but still, there was something about her....

Rifling through the cabinet for a grilling pan, he wondered if she'd eaten today. Matthew had provided lunch for him, which he'd devoured between sessions. He'd assumed Matthew had done the same for her. But perhaps not, he thought, noticing the faint smudges under her eyes. She looked tired, though he guessed by the way she was typing away on the keyboard that she didn't plan to slow down any time soon.

"Wilhemina asked how your day went." He turned on the broiler and placed their dinner in the oven.

"Did you tell her I took out another dual-temperature vibrator?"

"No. We're one for one. Technically, I took out this one."

That got her to glance up from the computer screen and he was surprised to see her eyes narrowed. "Hopefully we won't go through any more," she said. "The company will wonder what we're doing with them if we have to reorder."

Rex chuckled. "Reordering product comes with the territory. No one will think a thing about it. Listen, April, I wanted to tell you how impressed I was with the information on the sleeping styles you provided. We're working well together."

She threaded her fingers through her hair as if she wasn't sure what to do with them and winced. "I'm glad you think so."

"I do. I'm pleased with how the day went. Especially with falling off the bed. Those pockets are a problem. I told Wilhemina and suggested she send the sheets back to R and D. Thanks to you we pinpointed the problem."

April frowned.

He opened the freezer, grabbed a few ice cubes into a plastic zipper bag then wrapped the whole in the dish towel. "Here you go." He handed her the ice pack. "Put this on your bump."

She shook her head and fine wisps of hair escaped the clip to fringe softly around her neck. "You need the ice. Put it on your hand."

He flexed his fingers to ease the stiffness. "It's just a bruise. The vibrator got me. Looks worse than it is."

"How's the lip?"

"Won't stop me from enjoying dinner," he said, recognizing the pattern. Circling the bar, he placed the ice pack on her head, not leaving her a choice. "In order of importance, head injuries make the top of the list."

She stepped out from under the ice pack. "I'm fine."

She wasn't fine. That much was evident in her prickly response. "I think I should wake you up during the night to make sure you're not concussed. I caught you hard with my chin."

"You mean I caught you with my head, don't you?"

Ah, there they were. What was really bothering April.

Dropping the ice pack on the bar, he stepped onto the rubber mat the hotel had provided during the day and slipped both hands over her shoulders. She gasped, clearly surprised and tried to back away.

Rex held on.

"Come here." He steered her toward a dining room chair, operating under the assumption that if he made her sit, she couldn't get away so easily.

"I'm not concussed."

Dragging another chair around, he sat in front of her, one more obstacle in his line of defense. "I'll take your word for it, but I'm not letting you up until you talk to me."

"Talk to you about what?"

"About what's bothering you."

"Why do you think something's bothering me?"

Now it was his turn to frown. And notice how hard she was trying not to bump knees with him. Every brush of her silk-hose–clad leg against his jetted his pulse rate a little closer to overdrive.

"Listen, April. We've got to work together. Closely, I might add. What's bothering you about what happened to-day?"

"Well, now that you mention it…was it really necessary to demonstrate those sleeping positions? Something about rolling around on a bed for an audience doesn't strike me as terribly professional."

"Under most conditions, I'd agree, but we're studying sheets."

Her full mouth curved downward, no less tempting for its frown. She had kissing lips. Full, moist and inviting. Rex hadn't thought much about kissing lately. He'd kissed his fair share, he supposed, but he hadn't thought much about those kisses, or anticipated any with the sort of impatience he felt right now.

In fact, when he dredged his memory for the last time he'd actually thought about kissing, he remembered high school, so long ago he couldn't recall who he'd wanted to kiss. But right now, he remembered clearly how much he enjoyed the ritual and added a new item to his mental list of things to accomplish.

Kiss April. Kiss her until she stopped frowning, until those sweet lips parted beneath his and she sighed.

"Even so, Rex," she was saying. "I'd rather avoid being your assistant in any more physical demonstrations. If there's a need, please get someone else."

"I could have asked Matthew."

That sweet mouth pursed. She knew he was teasing. "You could have. He'd have done whatever you'd asked."

"True enough." He clasped his hands over his knees and leaned closer. "His company is paid well to accommodate me."

"So it's settled then? You'll ask someone else to demonstrate sleeping styles or whatever else you need demonstrated in the future?"

"No."

"No?"

He leaned in a little more, invaded her space. "I asked *you* to help me because I wanted to get close with *you*."

Her mouth popped open and she sank back in her chair. Clearly he'd stopped her in her tracks with his honesty and as he'd planned she had no escape.

"Why?" she finally asked, and his cut inner lip twinged as he fought back a smile.

"Because I wanted to touch you."

She blinked.

He waited, enjoying the play of emotions across her beautiful face. April clearly hadn't expected him to lay his cards on the table.

"Seemed like the perfect opportunity to introduce some closeness between us. Since we were working and had an audience I figured you would feel comfortable. You get nervous whenever I get too close. Or when I touch you."

"Which means I don't want to get close or be touched."

Her delivery implied that any idiot should have understood that, but Rex wasn't buying into her reasoning. "Actually, I'm interpreting it to mean I make you nervous because you want to get close and be touched. Am I mistaken?"

To say she looked flabbergasted would have been an understatement. *Downright stunned* better described her expression, and when she scooted her chair back to get away, he knew he'd read her correctly.

Unfortunately she scooted back too fast and overbalanced. The chair would have gone over had he not grabbed her shoulders and pulled her back.

She stared at him wide-eyed.

He didn't let go. "I'm not mistaken, am I, April?"

Rex pushed the issue solely because he wanted to see how she'd deal with him, needed to know if she'd admit to the truth or deny the obvious. A test.

"I can't."

Avoidance. Interesting. "Why not?"

"We work together."

As if logistics affected chemistry this hot. "There's no conflict. We're independent entities, off-site and of consenting ages. I don't see a problem. You're not seeing anyone and neither am I."

She blinked, clearly unwilling or unable to accept his candor about the subject, but he found that panicked glint in her eyes very telling.

"Do you find me attractive?" he asked.

She inhaled a shuttering breath that answered his question.

"Good, because I find you attractive, too. And refreshing."

"Refreshing?"

He nodded. "Very."

"Rex, you can't find me refreshing."

"You haven't given me a solid reason why yet."

She huffed, an exasperated puff of sound that sent wispy hairs flying off her forehead. He wanted to feel those silky hairs against his skin so he leaned forward, close enough to see the sooty black lashes fringing her eyes. Close enough to see the slight flare of her nostrils when she inhaled.

The faintly floral fragrance she'd worn earlier today had faded, leaving behind only a delicate, womanly scent that was all April. He could feel the warmth of her skin beneath his hands, her sheer blouse no barrier at all.

Another breath and the moment became charged. Time stalled between them, their nearness enveloping them with the intensity of their attraction, with the chemistry that made his blood heat, made that vein in her throat throb with her racing pulse.

Rex leaned a hairbreadth nearer. He was going to kiss her. Her soft gasp told him she knew he was going to kiss her.

The question was would she let him?

The air around them stretched with expectation. The breath locked tight in his chest and his heartbeat made a wild leap as he awaited her reply.

Then there it was, a sudden softening of her mouth, an exhalation that made her sway forward just enough to let him know she'd welcome him.

He lowered his face to taste those sweet lips....

A loud crackling sound made them both jump. They

sprang apart and stared at the kitchen. It took Rex a second to realize he was hearing the crack and pop of flames.

The steak.

"Damn." He was on his feet before he'd inhaled another breath. Good thing, too, because smoke seeped through the cracks around the oven door where his London broil was on fire beneath the broiler.

That they'd missed the smoke only proved the intensity of their chemistry. Flipping the switch of the kitchen fan to high, he snatched a pot holder from the counter.

"April, get the door, would you?" he said. "I don't want to activate the sprinkler system." He didn't need to deal with a rainstorm on his office equipment. Especially when he hadn't gotten to kiss the girl.

April launched into motion as he pulled the grilling pan from the oven, coughing when he inhaled more smoke. But contact with the air immediately extinguished the flames, which turned out to be nothing more serious than a fat fire. Upon closer inspection, he found most of the meat in pretty decent shape.

"How do you feel about well-done steak?"

"I prefer it that way," she called out from the doorway, where she stood opening and closing the door like a fan.

He went to work trying to salvage what was left of their meal, waiting to see what April would do next. Would she try to buy some time before dealing with the issue of their attraction again? Another test.

She showed up back at the bar.

He held a knife above a tomato and waited.

"Rex, I won't deny I'm attracted to you," she said. "But I do have some solid reasons why this can't work."

He liked the fact that she dealt with the situation head-on, but she sounded determined and articulate, no longer breathless and off balance. The interruption had allowed her to put distance between them and catch her breath. He made a mental note not to give her too much distance in the future.

"Why don't you set the table and we'll talk about it?"

"No need. I'll eat while I work."

Shaking his head, he set the knife down and handed her two plates. "I insist you sit. You've been standing all day and I want to hear about these solid reasons."

For a moment he thought she'd argue, but she accepted the plates. "There's no room on the table."

"Try the coffee table if you can get to it." He assembled the accoutrements she'd need for their meal. "Or the bed. We can have a bed picnic. The sheets are water-resistant, so we don't have to worry about the mattress."

She managed to get to the coffee table.

"I'm not comfortable with the work thing between us," she said when she returned to the kitchen to pick up silverware and napkins. "It's important I live up to expectations on this job."

"I see." He arranged the tomatoes in the salad bowl. "But you're very competent, and I'm easy to work with. I have high expectations, but I don't expect you to read minds. I'll tell you what I need. So far you've not only met my needs but anticipated them. I don't understand your concerns about job performance."

"I told you I'm not out of my office that much," she said hesitantly, and he couldn't help but notice that she was hanging onto the silverware for dear life. "I can't jeopardize getting this job right."

Rex might not have understood her concerns or exactly why this particular job was so important, but it was. There was more going on here than he understood. Instinct told him she was dancing around the heart of the issue and if he could just get her to open up, he could figure out what the problem was, maybe even find a way to help her deal with it.

"Come on. Let's talk while we eat." He reverted back to distraction. Handing her the salad bowl, he motioned her toward the table then followed with the steak and a bottle of dressing. "I'm usually moderately proficient in the kitchen."

"With an Italian mom, I'll bet."

"She's one Italian in a family of Irishmen. It's a strange mix to say the least. Here's hoping this isn't too bad."

"The salad looks good," she said generously. "And you made enough so we won't go hungry."

In his opinion, a salad didn't constitute a balanced meal, but he kept his opinion to himself. He didn't ask if she wanted wine, just returned to the kitchen to pour two glasses. With any luck, the alcohol might have a calming effect.

Just the thought almost made him laugh. He'd never had to resort to getting a date drunk before. Technically April wasn't a date but he wanted her to be.

Sitting on the floor across the coffee table from her, Rex tried the steak, found it too well-done for his taste but not bad all things considered. She seemed to be enjoying her meal, though. "I'm glad I cooked. You were hungry."

Shrugging, she rested her fork on the edge of her plate. "It's very good despite the mishap."

"I was hoping to impress you."

She took this news by darting her tongue along her lips, a quick motion that riveted him to the way her lower lip shone, made him imagine what her mouth would taste like. "You have. I'm impressed by any man who can make his way around the kitchen."

He had some work to do disabusing her of the notion that

he was "any" man but her concession was a step in the right direction.

"So you're worried about a relationship interfering with work," he said. "What if I can convince you that exploring our attraction to each other and following its natural progression will actually improve your job performance?"

"How do figure you can do that?"

Rex leaned back against the foot of the bed, hung his hand over his knee. "Since I'm making you nervous, getting to know me better should help you feel more comfortable."

"That's one way of looking at it, I suppose. Of course, getting to know you could just make me even more nervous." She toyed with the wineglass. "It's better to be safe than sorry."

"What do you suggest we do about this raging attraction between us?"

"Ignore it. The only thing to do."

He considered her, could detect nothing at all coy in her expression, so he had to assume she honestly thought they could ignore how they felt. Forget the fact that she was already so jumpy she'd gotten downright dangerous and he'd torched a perfectly decent cut of meat in his white heat to kiss her.

"Did you know that seventy percent of couples who gave in to their attraction right away reported having better orgasms than couples who fought their attraction?"

"Are you joking?"

"It's a fact," he said stoically. "I conducted the analysis for a medical facility that studied nifty stuff like average erection angles and typical duration of orgasm."

She stared at him wide-eyed, the wineglass poised in midair, clearly not sure what to make of his statement. But he got exactly what he wanted—he'd distracted her.

"Good chemistry doesn't come around that often in my experience, April. Seems a shame to waste a good thing."

She abandoned her wineglass and crossed her legs, the gauge on her nervous meter clearly rising. "Just because we're attracted to each other doesn't mean we have to act on it."

She admitted to being attracted to him so casually that he had to force back a smile. "That's true. I'm not looking for coercion here. I'm looking for seduction, for a chance to give our chemistry a fair shake and see where it leads."

"We're two ships passing in the night. Where can it lead? A fling?"

"Are you looking for long-term?"

"No."

The panic in that *no* blew his theory right out of the water. "You don't want long-term and you don't want a fling. What do you want?"

She scooted back from the table, clearly losing her battle with the jitters. Scooping up her plate, she headed toward the kitchen. Rex recognized the stall tactic for what it was and knew he didn't stand a chance as long as she could pace.

Distraction and distance were the dynamic duo for dealing with April. But he'd pushed as far as he could right now. Whatever was holding her back—and his gut told him they still hadn't hit on the real reason yet—she would have to decide when and if she wanted to share. He was only making her more nervous by prying.

"I'll take that as an 'I'm not sure' and leave it at that," he said. "Sound good?"

To his surprise, he heard her laugh, but when she emerged from the kitchen she met his gaze with an expression that was clearly more desperation than amusement. "The truth is I'm not exactly at my best leaping into new situations. I try to avoid them whenever possible. It's safer that way."

"Safer?"

"For you."

He followed her gaze to his hand. "It's just a bruise."

"It's not *just a bruise,* Rex. It's an injury. One I caused."

"It was an *accident.* They happen."

Giving a shaky laugh, she thrust her fingers through her hair, winced. "Yeah, unfortunately they do."

The resignation he heard in her voice gave him a sharp pang of guilt for steering her someplace so obviously painful. He'd meant to convince her to explore their attraction and he'd upset her instead. "Listen, April, I'm—"

"It's not you, Rex. Really. I'm actually rather flattered that you're interested in me."

Flattered? Hell, this was getting worse by the second. "April, you don't have to—"

"I may be attracted to you but even if I wanted to get around the work thing, I can't."

With four younger sisters, Rex recognized a roll when he saw one. She was on one now and he decided he deserved whatever he got for pushing. "April, I—"

"It's me." Inhaling deeply, she looked a bit frayed around the edges. "I...I just don't do the sex thing very well."

Of anything she could have possibly said to him, *that* was about the absolute last he'd expected. Surprise made him open his mouth before his common sense kicked in. Instead of telling her that he respected how she felt and to consider the subject dropped, he said, "Really?"

Really invited an answer. He got one.

"Can't relax, can't have sex. Does that make sense?"

Whether or not she made sense wasn't the issue as far as Rex was concerned. Two things were happening here. The first was that April wouldn't be spilling her guts without a very good reason. Although he'd pushed, he really hadn't pushed hard enough for her to open up like this, which led him to the second realization—this subject hit seriously close to the bone.

She didn't seem to notice he hadn't answered her question. She was off and running—literally. Her slippers shuffled across the carpet as she paced between the dining room and sitting room. With animated hand gestures, she told him about being so high-strung that whenever she tried to get close to a man, the situation always resulted in some accident.

Exactly what had happened today.

She obviously needed to talk so he sat back to listen. Fixing his gaze on her face, he refused to give in to the urge to glance down at the gentle swaying motion of slim hips and long legs. But even though he didn't look, Rex couldn't forget how she'd felt in his arms earlier. Or how she'd seemed to melt just as he'd been about to kiss her.

There'd been an element of surprise about her that he found very arousing. She'd been so breathless, so ready. That memory of those parted lips imprinted on his brain, made his body react to the lovely display she presented, made this feel like more than wanting sex.

He could help her overcome this obstacle if she'd let him.

She wound down by saying, ''Trust me, you'll be safer in the long run.'' And as soon as she paused to draw air he was ready.

''What if I'm willing to chance it?''

''Rex, I can't.''

Perhaps she *couldn't*, but everything in those incredible eyes said she *wanted to*. That was enough for him. At least for now. ''Tell you what. I'll accept that if you'll accept my help trying to relax.''

"You want to make a deal with me?"

He nodded. "Let me tell you a story. Once upon a time I conducted analysis for a research foundation that studied oddball human ailments. Fascinating place. I acquired data about massage as a viable treatment for various maladies so the facility could meet the requirements for a federal grant. While I was there I became obsessed with massage, not so much for the health benefits, although that's definitely a part of it, but because it feels so damned good. I've got a massage therapist in every major city from the eastern seaboard to L.A."

"And what does this mean to me?"

"It means I'm very well versed in the effects of massage. But that's not the end of my story. I wasn't content to just get massages. I wanted to understand everything about them. I've studied the subject and attended a number of seminars. I even went to an international conference once." He smiled. "What this means is I can give a decent massage. I know plenty of techniques to help you relax. The question is—will you let me?"

"This won't be about seduction?"

"This will be about *relaxing*." His smile deepened. "I won't deny how much I want to touch you, but you have my word I'll be a perfect gentleman, unless you give me permission otherwise."

Finely arched brows drew together in a frown as she considered him. Beneath the hesitation, beneath the skepticism that clearly questioned his motives, he glimpsed longing.

"Will you let me try to help?"

He reached for her hand and she stared down, and he sensed that something about the sight of their clasped hands fascinated her. He squeezed, just enough to encourage, to push her over the edge to acceptance.

When she lifted those wide eyes to his, he saw the answer

reflected deep in those violet depths, knew she couldn't resist, even before she said, "You promise?"

"I promise."

But if helping her relax just happened to wear down her defenses and make her open to seduction, April had the free will to resist that.

If she wanted to.

7

APRIL STARED into Rex's face and those melting dark eyes seemed to see right through her. But he couldn't see that she was a private investigator paid to be keeping her eyes on him—a relationship that precluded any other.

But he wasn't talking about seduction. He was talking about massage and he'd promised to be a gentleman.

Could she trust him?

Could she trust herself to resist him?

The man scattered her wits. And if April were honest, she wanted to feel the way she did when he touched her. And what if he was right? What if relaxing would help her calm down enough so she could catch her nerves before the alarm in her head started shrieking and she reached critical mass?

Jeff had thought relaxation would work.

Vic had thought control.

Kenny spontaneity.

But they'd all been talking about sex and all the tricks she'd learned to contain her livewire physical impulses didn't work with sex. Arousal blinded her to the warning signals. She got nervous and disaster struck before she'd regained her senses enough to realize what was happening.

Just like today, and Rex had only been holding her....

But he'd promised to be a gentleman.

He'd also admitted to wanting to seduce her.

Gazing deep into his dark eyes, April searched for answers. She wanted to believe he could help her, more than she'd ever wanted anything before.

''What do you have to lose?'' He slipped his fingers through hers and the warmth of his skin sapped her resistance with that crazy sense of rightness.

The answer was really as simple as how badly she wanted to feel the way she felt when he touched her.

''Okay.''

The word filtered between them, oddly tame to have such bearing on her emotions, and on Rex. His face softened around the edges, his approval chasing away the last of her hesitation, his smile warming her from the inside out.

''Let's get started.''

''I'm in the middle of inputting today's data.''

''You've been working all day. You've earned a break.''

Steering her toward the bed, he motioned her to sit. He sank to his knees in front of her and then his hands were on her again, his warm fingers enfolding her ankle, sending a heat wave sizzling through her panty hose and straight up her calf. He pushed off her slipper, his hand lingering with the motion, following the arch of her foot, rounding the curve of her toes.

Then he repeated the process, his hands lingering just enough to let her sample his touch. But a sample was all it took to make April question her intelligence. Her body felt wired with a live current, ultrasensitive and primed to react.

''I'll start with your neck and shoulders,'' he said. ''Sound good?''

He was keeping everything on the up-and-up and April appreciated his effort. But she still found herself forgetting to breathe, anticipation taking a deep hold of her, yet not quite pushing her into the red zone. Her alarm was currently within an acceptable range so she inhaled deeply and nodded.

"All right then, turn around. I'll sit behind you."

Drawing her legs up, she braced herself against the sinking mattress when he sat behind her. With a light touch, he brushed her hair from her neck.

"Pull your hair up with that clip. Most of it has fallen out and I want to work your neck muscles."

He sounded so pragmatic and professional that she almost smiled. Almost. There was something so pitifully desperate about the way she longed to be touched. For a woman who'd sworn off sex, she was playing with fire. She'd already damaged three body parts today—her head, his mouth and hand—and now she was gearing up all over again....

"Rex, what if I hurt you?"

"Shh. I'm willing to risk it."

Slipping his fingers around her throat, he eased her forward until she circled her head in a slow, smooth motion that made her neck creak and her muscles pull.

"This is a handy trick to know. Easy to remember and you can do it anywhere. File this one for future reference."

Trailing his fingers beneath her chin, he directed her to deepen the motion until muscles were pulling halfway down her back, a sensation that wasn't unpleasant. "I'm going to let you go. Keep that up until I tell you to stop."

She did as he asked while his fingertips trailed down her throat, caressing the muscles there with a touch that was still slow, smooth, *safe.*

A gentleman's touch. A very skilled touch.

"You're very good."

"Thank you."

"How often did you say you get these?"

"Usually three times a week."

"Will you invite me along?"

Another chuckle, a rich burst of sound that gusted over

her hair, ruffling wisps against her cheek. "I plan to perform the service on you myself."

There seemed to be innuendo in that statement, but April found she couldn't concentrate long enough to be sure. The sound of his husky voice was dulling her wits and the steady motion of his hands lulling her senses.

"Who knew that analyzing data for a research foundation could be so rewarding?"

"The project was intensive so I tried out a variety of massages to bone up on the subject. Helps get me in the right frame of mind to work. I try to immerse myself in all my projects. Gets my brain working."

"Like trying out the different sleeping styles?"

"Yes. After I completed that project, I was hooked. I've been exploring reflexology lately. Fascinating subject."

"Really?"

"Really."

She couldn't think of a reply. She'd been degenerating into babble, which was never a good sign, but now the steady rhythm of his hands, the slow, smooth circles were making her head feel too heavy for her neck.

The man had magic hands because she'd never felt this way in her life. Perhaps it was a combination of the meal or the wine or even the late nights spent studying marketing to establish her cover, but she could barely keep her eyes open.

Finally he trailed his fingers back under her chin and he brought her movements to a stop before probing the muscles around her neck and the juncture of her shoulder blades again. "That's much better. How do you feel?"

"Drugged. Did you put something in the wine?"

He only chuckled, continued moving those magic fingers along her throat, his skin warm against hers, exploring with a gentle, persistent demand to relinquish tension, to trust him.

She did, though she could find no logic in that particular response. Then again, with her head filled with clouds, how could she possibly expect herself to think clearly?

Not part of the plan, not with this languor pouring through her, stealing her senses, making her drowsy. Her brain wasn't working right because she found her thoughts drifting off to the other women Rex used these magic fingers on. Was massage a part of his normal repertoire?

Not that the man needed maneuvers. He was so handsome, so completely personable. She'd bet he could charm a woman right out of her clothes if he wanted, just as easily as he'd charmed her into this massage.

But it drove home how little she actually knew about him. Sure, John had researched him and she'd studied the findings, briefed herself on his basics. But nothing she'd read had prepared her for the man himself. No report could have ever warned that all he would do is smile and she would dissolve into a babbling idiot. Or his touch would melt away the walls she'd been building around her emotions since her all-important decision to give up men after Jeff.

She hadn't expected Rex Holt, couldn't have known how she'd react to him if she had. And she was reacting. With each skim of warm fingers across her bare shoulders, each caress between her shoulder blades, she responded. Her senses were blossoming to awareness even as her body was slipping into a coma.

April couldn't resist, not when Rex shifted position, leaning against the sofa back and spreading his legs to pull her against him. Some part of her brain warned her to protest, but she could barely keep her eyes open. She roused only enough to do as he asked, to sink back against him until she could feel his hard thighs cradling hers, his tight stomach pressed against her back.

And all the while his hands continued to work, massaging, stroking, kneading. His touch was never intrusive, yet was solid enough to coax the tension from her muscles, to make her relax and prove that being curled up in the shelter of his hard body was exactly where she wanted to be.

THE NEXT TIME April opened her eyes two thoughts struck her simultaneously—the suite was still dark with the haze of late night and she was draped across a warm, strong male body that shouldn't be in bed with her. It took a sleepy moment to remember Rex's massage and realize she must have passed out.

Which didn't explain why he'd slipped between the sheets instead of waking her up....

They were both fully clothed, or almost. Her skirt had ridden up around her hips and he'd stripped off his sweatshirt, leaving her head nestled in the cradle of his strong shoulder, her cheek pressed against warm, bare skin.

For a drowsy moment, April savored the feel of his hard body against hers, the way her hand lightly rested on the crisp silk hairs of his chest, the way her leg fit snugly against his, the other hiked high across his thighs.

He'd covered them during the night and the water-resistant Fetish Collection sheets created a warm cocoon, a place where only this moment and this man existed, where she could linger in half sleep and enjoy the feel of his strong body.

She'd never made it through the night with any of her former boyfriends so she'd never experienced anything to rival this indolent, sated feeling that deterred her from awakening. She wanted to languish around in this dreamy state, savoring the heat of the man against her.

His chest rose and fell with deep, even breaths. His heart beat a steady rhythm beneath her cheek. He'd wrapped an arm around her shoulder and his hand rested just above her breast. She definitely wasn't awake yet because the sight of her nipple peaking through her silk blouse made her smile.

"The Shingle." His sleep-rough voice jolted the quiet.

His arm tightened around her, pulled her impossibly closer and April glanced up, into his handsome face, realized that not even sleep dimmed this man's star quality.

With his tousled hair and dark stubble, he looked much more male, far less polished and professional than she'd seen him. There was something about his heavy-lidded expression that accentuated the way her breasts were currently brushing his bare chest, the way she fit perfectly into the crook of his shoulder. The way that problematic skirt left her thigh bared.

Unfortunately, rearranging her skirt now would only let him know that she'd noticed. "What did you say?"

"We slept like shingles. What does that say about us as a couple?"

There was no *us,* no *couple.* A night spent wrapped around each other had been pure chance, an *accident.* "It says you have a big ego and a sense of entitlement, which sounds about right since you took advantage of me."

Rex only laughed. "How do you figure that?"

"I fell asleep. You didn't wake me. You just crawled in bed. Half-dressed, I might add."

"I was already in bed and I'm not half-dressed. I only took off my sweatshirt because you were getting hot."

No small wonder with all that hard body pressed up against her. She made a move to get up and found herself thwarted again when he propped his chin on the top of her head to stop her.

"Don't go," he said. "I like testing the sleeping styles with you. It's even more fun without an audience."

"You promised to be a gentleman."

"I have been, believe me."

That statement was so rich with implication that she slid her knee down his thighs, deciding she didn't need proof. "No one to blame but yourself. I signed on for a massage."

"This was part of my relaxation therapy."

"What relaxation therapy? I agreed to let you give me a massage. You put me into a coma."

"You agreed to let me help you try to relax. A massage was only part of it."

"What's the other part—sneaking a feel whenever you can?"

Before she registered what was happening, he flipped over, used his powerful body to press her into the mattress. She rolled with him, stretched full-length beneath him, his long legs bracketing hers and holding her tight.

Whipcord arms came around her and he levered himself up, stared into her face, a position that pinned her hips beneath him and drew attention to the steely length of erection that supported his earlier claim of gentlemanly behavior.

"Rex!" His name slid out on a gasp, though April wasn't sure what to say because her senses overloaded with the feel of him against her.

He smiled, his star quality on high-beam until he nearly blinded her. "Let me kiss you. I'll promise to be a gentleman and stop when you tell me to."

Stop? The man had her surrounded. He blocked out the whole world with his body, awakened all those achy places he'd aroused with his magic hands last night.

"Just one kiss, April, to see if you like it." And then he lowered his face toward her with exquisite slowness, allowing her a chance to retreat or to savor what was about to come.

Decision by indecision.

The instant their lips met, April knew this would be no kiss as she'd ever experienced one. Rex seemed to explode with emotion. His muscles gathered against hers. He tucked her into all the sculpted places of his body, enfolded her in a layer of hard, aroused male.

Perhaps it was her state of semiconsciousness or perhaps it was just *him*, but she'd never felt anything like the way she felt now. Not quite awake, but very aware, her every sense heightened, focused on this man in a way only consciousness could allow.

The steady beating of his heart. The feel of his strong muscles draped luxuriously over her. Her every breath became his as his mouth prowled hers hungrily, coaxing her lips wide, thrusting his tongue inside, devouring, demanding a reply.

She replied with the only answer that made any sense. Curling her hands around his neck, she kissed him back.

He tasted of appreciation and boldness and she threaded her fingers into his hair, unable to entertain thoughts of resistance, or common sense, or conscience. At this moment, with nothing but the night and a few scraps of clothing between them, with their mouths exploring and their hands discovering and their bodies pressed close, Rex Holt was much more than a job. He was the only man who'd ever made her feel like this before.

He traced her lips with his and then trailed along the curve of her jaw, featherlight kisses he must have known she'd welcome because she lifted her chin to offer her throat. She wove her fingers through his hair, not hindering, not encouraging, just leaving him to make his way where he chose.

He chose to nibble on her earlobe so ribbons of pleasure unfurled low in her tummy and made her squirm.

He chose to wedge his erection between her thighs so only sheer panty hose and soft cotton separated them.

He chose to prove that he wasn't the only one wanting here by stroking that hot length against her and making her ride him to feed this growing ache inside.

To a woman who'd never quite fit in, this was such a singular sensation. She felt right, as though finally, *finally,* the pieces all fit together and she was exactly where she was supposed to be. In this man's bed. In his arms.

And he must have understood the power he wielded over her, because he kissed his way down the length of her neck. He licked the fluttering pulsebeat below her jaw. He explored every sensitive inch of skin between her ear and shoulder.

And he kept trailing his mouth down.

April recognized that another opportunity to stop him approached as he nibbled his way along her shoulder, down her bare arm, hot moist kisses that sent goose bumps spraying over her skin, fed that ache between her legs a little more.

Even if she could have found the word *no* someplace deep inside, April wouldn't have spoken the word aloud. She didn't want to stop Rex from his sexy exploration, didn't want to do anything but hold her breath as he skimmed those light kisses along her ribs. She wanted nothing more than to savor this anticipation of wondering where he would nibble next....

Darting his tongue over a nipple, he dragged at the silk with that delicious stroke, fired heat right through her blouse, and the bra below. April gasped, a sound lost somewhere in his hair, but he must have heard because suddenly he was molding her breasts through her shell, cupping their weight in his hands as if he'd waited forever to touch her.

April *had* waited forever. She'd never felt such a powerful longing, had never known her breasts to be a touchstone for every nerve ending inside her. She'd never been able to lie still long enough to find out. But as Rex flicked his thumbs across her nipples, drawing them to peaks through the silk, she knew a need that made her ache.

Suddenly, he rolled off her to lie on his side, propped up on an elbow; for a breathless moment all she registered was the absence of his body, the cool emptiness where his erection had pressed so enticingly against her.

But when he leaned over her, April understood. He never slowed his trail of hot kisses as he pushed up her blouse to make way for his mouth on her skin.

Here was another opportunity where she could have said no.

She arched into his touch instead.

And he obliged her by freeing her breasts from the tangle of silk shell and sheer bra, baring her skin to his view. Her nipples puckered, but it was the expression on Rex's face and the sound of his throaty growl that pleased her most of all.

She'd always thought her breasts were a waste as they were just big enough to make shopping for anything but separates a chore. True, she'd never be mistaken for a boy, which prior to adolescence had been a problem, but given that she could never lie still long enough to let a man appreciate them, April never quite saw the point.

But finally her breasts seemed to be serving a purpose besides making her clothing hang awkwardly.

Rex skimmed his hand across both peaks then caught a hard tip between his thumb and forefinger. April gasped. He met her gaze and smiled, then lowered his face to lavish the very same attention with his mouth.

He explored with his tongue. He nibbled with his teeth. He sucked her deep inside his mouth until she squirmed. And then his other hand broke free to trail down her stomach, down, down…he brushed up her skirt, and his strong fingers zeroed in on that sensitive bundle between her thighs.

Here was the perfect opportunity to say no.

But with the pressure of his thumb right *there,* the only sound to slip from her lips was a moan. Closing her eyes, she abandoned herself to the feeling….

She recognized this sensation, so much more intense than when she pleasured herself in her bed, the only place she'd ever been relaxed enough to experience the phenomenon firsthand.

Until Rex. She needed him to keep touching her, wanted to tell him how important it was that he didn't stop working this magic with his mouth and hands. So she simply pressed her breast to his mouth, encouraging him, wanting him to feed this feeling inside her more than she wanted anything.

She wanted to experience *real* pleasure. She wanted to know what it felt like to want.

And right now she did.

It didn't matter that she was so aroused disaster should have stuck. Or that she should feel too nerved out and antsy to lie still. Or that the alarm in her head should be shrieking. Right now she felt drowsy and excited and good.

And then April came apart, just burst inside, a swell of sensation that had sneaked up on her, dragging a breathless moan from her lips, a moan that sounded just like a sob.

A *real* orgasm. Her first.

Rex propped himself up on an elbow, his smile telling her how much he enjoyed the sight of her, nearly naked and spread beneath him as he watched her come back to earth. And while she struggled to catch her breath, she took in the satisfaction on his face, the dark, heavy-lidded eyes, the chiseled features that had softened around the edges.

"I promised you a kiss to see if you liked it," he finally said, his voice a husky whisper between them. "Did you?"

She lay panting beneath him, her skin flushed, her breasts tight, her sex pulsing with the remnants of that wild explosion. A *real* orgasm. Beneath this man's kisses and his skilled hands she'd actually reached the finish line.

Had she liked it?

Her blouse was tangled beneath her armpits. Her skirt was bunched around her waist. Her panty hose had grown damp with the moisture of her pleasure and she could only blink in amazement, struck by the realization that he'd kept his word. That had been only *one* kiss, one long, unbroken kiss that had started at her lips and ended in a climax.

Had she liked it?

Like seemed too inadequate a word to describe what she felt right now. Had she ever even imagined she could feel this way?

Not once. Not ever.

He'd offered to help her relax and had given her a gift instead. Reaching up to stroke his handsome face, to run her fingers along the jaw, she was awed by the man who'd done exactly what he'd promised, and then some.

"I want to make love to you, but I'm a gentleman. Say no, April, and we'll stop. Just say no."

"Yes."

8

"No!" APRIL SAT bolt upright, shooting from zero to sixty so fast that Rex could only stare. "I mean, I wasn't expecting...I don't have any protection."

He might have laughed, but she was so close to panic on the nervous meter that he knew his amusement would push her right over the edge. Losing her to hysteria now wasn't part of his plan, not after he'd kissed those sweet lips, tasted her satin-soft skin and experienced her passion.

She was a vision against the backdrop of the moonlit suite with her wide eyes, her hair tousled around her beautiful face. Her body gleamed in the darkness, her breasts pale and quivering, her long, long legs curled beneath her. She was so utterly exquisite that he could only marvel that she was real.

And how lucky he was to get her into his bed.

He wasn't stopping to ask questions. He was running until his luck ran out.

"April, we're sitting in the middle of the Fetish Collection." Sweeping a hand around them, he motioned to the shiny black sheets, knowing that as soon as she calmed down she'd realize protection wasn't an issue.

Understanding dawned quickly and she darted her gaze to an oval pillow wedged between the sofa back and the mattress, a pillow made from water-resistant black fabric that appeared to be nothing more than a decoration to match the bedding.

The Hidden Secrets Pillow.

Opportunity knocked and Rex was never one to let an opportunity pass. "Go ahead and open it. Let's take a look."

He already knew what was inside, and assumed April did, too, but that pillow would occupy her while he stripped, tossing aside his sweats and peeling off his socks quicker than he'd ever stripped in his life.

"Oh my."

He glanced up to find her watching him with wide eyes. He wasn't sure whether she referred to the contents of the pillow or the sight of him, so he dropped down on the edge of the bed, cutting off an avenue of escape.

"So what have we got?"

A compartment had been designed inside the padding of the pillow to conceal the sexual accoutrements necessary to enjoy the Fetish Collection—lubricants, *protection* and a variety of other items designed to enhance an excursion out of the world of mainstream sex.

April held up a tube to make out the words in the faint glow of moonlight shining through the window. "We've got Happy Penis Lotion."

"Sounds good to me."

"I'll bet," she said saucily, but she didn't look at him.

Scooting closer, he brushed aside the hair from her shoulders to assess the fastening on her blouse. One button. No sweat. "Although my penis is already happy without any lotion."

Her gaze dropped straight to his lap, where his happy penis performed a dance for his audience.

Rex used the distraction to unfasten her button. "What else?"

"Bawdy Body Butter, another edible treat."

"Now that had some possibilities," he said. "Maybe I'll eat you for breakfast."

"Or maybe I should eat you."

"My happy penis is getting happier by the second."

She laughed, or at least he thought it was a laugh. Not giving her a chance to digress, he started working the blouse over her head. She needed to get comfortable. And naked.

"Lift your arms," he said and she dropped the Bawdy Body Butter onto the bed.

Had her skin not been so fair, Rex might never have noticed her blush in the darkness. But she was both pale and exquisite with her translucent skin.

"God, you're beautiful." The words just popped out of his mouth and he wasn't sorry. He wanted her to know how much she impacted him, how fascinating he found her.

Everything about her touched him in a way he'd never been touched before. His hunger was about more than satisfying a craving. He wanted her to be comfortable, so comfortable that she would joke about sex toys and let him touch her without nervousness getting in the way.

And he hadn't realized just how much until they sat here nearly naked in the moonlight.

After tossing her blouse and bra onto the floor, he reached out to stroke one of her breasts.

"You were made to be touched." He flicked his thumb across her nipple, felt the tip peak. "And kissed." Lowering his face to the tempting morsel, he ran his tongue across the tip.

April shivered, so he drew on her again, smiled when she braced back on her hands and thrust her luscious breasts out with a moan. Despite her blush, despite the bravado that belied her delightful inexperience, this woman was passion.

I don't do the sex thing very well.

Right.

Maybe she hadn't done the sex thing very well before him, but she was doing it just fine right now. He gazed at her above the swell of her breasts, found her eyes closed and her lips parted. He needed to keep her distracted with arousal, not give her a chance to think about what they were doing.

"Did you know on average it takes most women four minutes to have orgasms with manual stimulation compared to nearly twenty minutes with intercourse?"

She gave a laugh but didn't open her eyes.

He dragged his tongue across her nipple again while reaching over the side of the bed. Of course he'd placed the item he wanted in the one pocket out of easy reach. "We need to test you out against the average."

"You think?"

"I do." He ferreted out what he was looking for and the sound of metal mingled with her excited breaths as he withdrew a stainless steel chain.

"What's that?" she asked.

Giving a final flick of his tongue, Rex held up a shiny silver chain for her perusal. "Something to keep you on the edge while I move on."

"On the edge, hmm?"

"I don't want to ignore anything that gives you pleasure and I sense you get a great deal of pleasure when I pay attention to your breasts." He dangled the chain suggestively. "Am I right?"

She replied by running a hand through his hair, an unexpected touch that struck him with its tenderness.

"You're a very responsive woman. I want to help you explore this side of yourself."

Her expression melted before his very eyes. Maybe her anxiety about relaxing had stopped her from acknowledging her passion. Rex didn't know, but he was inspired to similar tenderness, an unfamiliar need to reassure.

Reaching up to caress her cheek, he ran his fingertips along her soft skin, was rewarded when she pressed a kiss into his palm, just the approval he needed. "Allow me."

He inspected the clamps, adjusted the tension. Her nipples were ripe from his attention, easy to coax into the padded ends. He let the first close, so turned on by the sight he ached.

She gasped.

"Too tight?" He searched her expression, wanted to stimulate her, and yes, distract her, but not hurt her.

"No." She shifted her hips in a way that suggested she was feeling the effects of that clamp everywhere. "Not too tight. Intense."

"Good." He applied the second, tugged lightly on the chain to gauge the effect.

Tossing her head back, graceful throat arched, fine hair sweeping back over her shoulders, she let out a sound that was a half gasp, half moan. "Oh my, my, my, my."

When she'd managed the sensation, she faced him with a gleam in her beautiful eyes and he felt a surge of satisfaction that was unlike anything he'd ever known.

This woman had the most amazing effect on him.

Rex dragged her closer to divest her of her skirt and hose. He wanted to feel skin. He wanted to explore her sleek curves and discover all the places that would make her sigh that needy sound again. That sound turned him on more than he'd ever been turned on before, made him feel as if he controlled all the secrets to pleasing her.

It was a heady feeling, one that inspired him to take particular care when he worked the skirt over her hips and down long, long legs, exposing her gorgeous body. He peeled away her hose, pressed kisses to her skin to mark the trail as they slipped down sleek thighs, over shapely calves, past slim ankles and delicate feet with pink toenails.

And then she lay before him, finally bared to his gaze, all pale curves and creamy skin, all loveliness and vulnerability that she didn't try to hide. His hunger was never more real than in that moment, when she grazed her smooth hands over his shoulders and down his back, exploring him with the same liberty he'd explored her, but with a tentative eagerness that was all April.

Capturing her mouth with his, he chased away all remnants of her hesitation, determined to prove that he wanted her more than he'd wanted any woman in his life. That she touched him in places he hadn't realized were there to be touched.

He'd had sex on the brain, a combined result of not making enough time to date and the Sensuous Collection. But this need to make love to her, to feel her body open around him was so far beyond sex that it literally sandbagged him.

With a groan, he pressed against her, wanted to ease this unfamiliar ache, could barely restrain himself when her moist heat scorched his erection, tormented him. She thrust back, one sleek stroke that promised everything. But everything wasn't an offer he could take her up on just yet. He still had enough grasp on his reason to remember protection.

Dragging his lips from hers, he reached for the Hidden Secrets Pillow, tipped the whole thing upside down until the contents spilled over the mattress. Tubes, jars and small foil packages scattered, such a variety that he needed more than moonlight to see what was what.

"We need light," he said.

"Here, I'll help." April propped up on an elbow and though he didn't want to let her go, she seemed so comfortable to be lying naked that he didn't stop her. She was caught up in the moment and he could ask for no greater accomplishment than that.

"Well, look at what we have here," she said. "Colors to appeal to every sense of style and flavors, too. Hmm. We have extra large, extra long and even ribbed for extra pleasure. Do you have a preference?"

"Not one that's extra large *and* long? Damn, we may have a problem." His delivery was so on that she burst out laughing.

"I'm sure we'll manage. But it does seem a shame to bundle him up without giving him a chance to play, don't you think?"

"He can play with his wetsuit on."

She grinned at him with a mischievous expression that lit up her eyes and made his heart beat hard.

"With all these goodies? Are you sure? One good turn and all." She reached for a jar. "Want to try some Happy Penis Lotion?"

"If he gets any happier he might never recover."

"Can't have that." Placing the tube aside, she lifted a jar and held it close to see. "Here's Coochie Coo Shaving Gel."

"What's that?" He pointed to a large jar.

"Pleasure and Sizzle, a naughty nipple cream."

He tugged the chain again, smiled when she trembled. "Looks like we have that base covered. What else do we have?"

"We're back to Happy Penis Lotion." She surveyed the jar. "An edible penis sensitizer."

"If he gets any more *sensitive*, he won't recover and neither will I." But Rex knew as he spoke the words that he was game for whatever she was. That chain dangling between her breasts prompted him to play fair. "Let me see."

He struggled to read the print of the jar that claimed to

increase pleasure, a claim he didn't doubt if April considered the stuff edible. "All right, go for it. But let's get the rest of this stuff off the bed. Except for a condom. Lady's choice."

Her hair swung forward to cover her face, in what he considered a very sexy look, as she glanced down at their paraphernalia. "We'll go with the Blueberry Blue. It's my favorite color."

"Blue it is, then. I aim to please."

"You do, don't you?"

Yes, and he'd be trying even harder now that she'd noticed.

Rex shrugged then passed her items to place on the coffee table. Once the bed was cleared, they had a bright blue condom and a jar of penis sensitizing lotion and sat facing each other ready to play.

"Sit back and make yourself comfortable," she said, motioning him back into the pillows, into the position she'd just previously enjoyed.

Reaching for the jar, she spun open the lid and gathered a dollop. She eyed his erection so purposefully that Rex laughed.

Her breasts swayed and the chain jingled as she wedged herself between his spread legs, so delightfully uninhibited, he marveled at her claim not to do the sex thing very well. Says who? He wanted to know.

Just the heat of her curves against his thighs forced him to grit his teeth to control himself. He wanted this woman. Enough to agree to wear a bright blue condom and have his penis stimulated, for Christ's sake.

The feel of her cream-slick fingers around his erection rocked him from head to toe. Closing his eyes, Rex ground out a sound that made her chuckle. And he was glad that

April found something amusing because his smile was fading fast. He opened his eyes, glanced at the jar in her hand.

Sensitizing lotion? More like *scalding* lotion.

He sucked in a breath as heat curled through him, so hot, he knew something wasn't right. This lotion was doing a whole lot more than sensitizing.

He breathed deeply to manage the sensation.

No good.

Maybe he was having an allergic reaction? He wasn't sure about anything except that winding up in the emergency room was not on tonight's itinerary.

I don't do the sex thing very well.

He couldn't handle laying that on April, and he couldn't handle explaining to a triage nurse how he'd wound up with third-degree burns on this particular body part.

"Let me see that stuff." He sounded reasonably composed, which was a miracle considering he was fighting the urge to head for the shower.

Pleasure and Sizzle Nipple Stimulator. Crème de Menthe flavor. Caution: For females only. Women will experience more pleasure than men.

Damn straight.

In all fairness, the room was dark and the jars were similarly shaped. A mistake anyone could have made. But he didn't think April would see it that way. The last thing he wanted to do was scare her off. Not after they'd gotten this far.

Fortunately she hadn't noticed a problem yet; in fact, she looked thoroughly amused.

"You find something funny about me sitting here bareassed with my dick sticking straight up in the air?"

She burst out laughing and collapsed onto the bed, sprawled like a pale goddess in the silvered darkness. Metal chains tinkled as her breasts plumped against the mattress, and the smooth dip of her waist and lush curve of her bottom drew his gaze and made his erection throb hard.

Which only rekindled the sizzle.

"Argh." He ground against the bed in agony, deciding he'd keep his mouth shut about the problem if it killed him. At this rate, it just might.

But all his noble intentions went straight to hell when she asked, "Rex, is something wrong?"

"I'm stimulated," he said, forcing a smile.

She wasn't buying it. The play of emotions across her face told him she'd put two and two together. Plucking the jar of offending lubricant from his hand, she glanced down at the label and her eyes grew wide. "Oh no."

"Oh yes." If he was going to lose her, he knew right now was the time. But he didn't want to lose her. Not when he was aching, and *sizzling*. "Either you do the honors, April, or I'm off to the shower before my happy penis falls off."

He held his breath. She would either come to the rescue or punch him. A definite possibility given the high-handed way he'd just asked her to give him head.

"I can help," she said, shimmying toward him in a sleek motion of pale curves that made him catch his breath, and sizzle some more.

But she was still smiling, and the instant her tongue stroked his burning skin, Rex didn't regret any part of the process that had landed them in this bed. His whole plan had revolved around helping her relax enough to seduce her. But April was caught up in the moment, caught up in the excitement and challenge of sex with the Fetish Collection.

When he watched her, eyes sparkling, tongue lashing out to soothe away that killer crème de menthe ache, he wouldn't have sacrificed even one damned second of the pain.

Threading his fingers into her hair, he savored the fine texture, the sexy strokes that made the sizzle cool to a slow burn. "That feels…so…much…better."

"It's going to feel even better, I promise."

That was a promise April intended to keep. This accident was a wrong she could right. She hadn't had to call 9-1-1 or drive Rex to the emergency room. That alone squelched the familiar feeling of incompetence, helped her put it behind her to accept what he offered—pleasure, orgasms and the feeling that he trusted her to do something…no, *everything* right.

This was a feeling that inspired her. Made her yearn for him so much that her sex clenched with needy little spasms. Her breasts had grown taut and the nipple clamps pinched, heightening her excitement and leaving her feeling exposed with the chain dangling against her stomach, his thigh. The ache inside grew, made her think bold thoughts about ripping open their Blueberry Blue condom and sheathing this exquisite erection….

His low growl broke the silence, startled her, and she glanced up just as he reached for her. Without a word, he pulled her into his arms. With strong hands he anchored their hips together, twined his legs through hers, pressed that hot erection into her stomach.

"God, I want you," he whispered against her lips and April thrilled to the hunger in his voice, the honesty.

Her fingers closed around the foil-wrapped condom and she pressed it into his palm, sighed when his hand tightened around hers, a reassuring squeeze. Then he opened the packet and sheathed his erection. April watched him, marveling that she didn't feel self-conscious with her legs spread, her breasts aching, *wanting*.

Sinking into her arms, he kissed her, a greedy, possessive kiss that promised her more than she'd ever dared hope for.

Then he pressed inside, and her sex unfurled around him, discovered the feel of his body filling her so completely. She slipped her arms around him and held him close, awed by the feel of their bodies together and overwhelmed by her need.

Still he didn't move, only let his lips trail from hers so he could raise his head and skim that beautiful dark gaze over her with a need that reflected her own.

He freed her nipples from the clamps, bent forward and blew on one, then the other, gentle gusts of air that brought her sensitive skin to life and a moan to her lips.

Apparently this is what he'd been waiting for because he pulled back on a breathtaking stroke that brought him almost clear out before he drove back inside with a low groan.

And that was all April knew. With his next stroke she was blinded to anything but the strength of his body arching above hers, the feel of those hard thrusts, the magic of the way he levered his hands beneath her bottom to help her create friction exactly where she needed it.

She had the wild thought that the average woman could survive this for nearly twenty minutes. She knew she'd die of pleasure long before then.

His every stroke fed the fire building inside her, and he knew somehow…knew to time his strokes to match hers…knew to roll his hips to catch the pleasure point that dragged each breath from her lungs as a sob…knew to kiss the sound from her lips, even as his thighs started to tremble….

Then she was gone. He dragged her right over the edge to a place where their breaths collided and their hearts beat together. Their hips levered against each other to capture each sensation.

Rex cradled her close and she clung to him, memorizing the way his arms felt around her, marveling that he'd coaxed responses from her body that she hadn't believed possible, that she'd abandoned all hope of ever feeling.

April told herself not to think, to simply steal this moment as hers, imprint it in her heart forever. The dawn would bring the reality of what they'd done. And along with reality would come the problems, and the cosmic irony that the only man who could make her feel right, the only man who could bring her to completion was the one man she couldn't be honest with.

9

APRIL SNUGGLED against Rex, inhaled deeply, a breath filled with the scent of his skin and their sex. Far too potent a combination for her to resist even though she'd known better than to give in to his kisses. Even drugged by his touch, she'd recognized the point where she'd chosen to place desire above her common sense.

She'd complicated both their lives in the process. Even sleepy and sated and more content than she'd ever felt in her life, she still possessed enough clarity of thought to understand the problems. *All* of them, and there were a bunch.

The biggest was that she'd repaid this man's kindness with deception. He'd been thoughtful and she'd lied about who she was and why she'd become his assistant. And she couldn't even feel guilty. She was doing her job. Penance might have made her feel better, but she just got to feel horrible for deceiving him.

Rex affected her like she'd never been affected before and her need was so singular that she couldn't have resisted if her life depended had on it.

Desperation. That's what this was.

She should be humiliated but all she could think about was how his hard body molded around hers, how her muscles ached with a delicious feeling she'd never known before.

How she hadn't wound up calling 9-1-1.

Their encounter hadn't been snafu-free, but Rex was still

in one piece, seemingly content to hold her as if he didn't want to let her go.

The night surrounded them, the darkness so filled with promise. His strong leg fit between hers perfectly. His heart beat steadily beneath her cheek. He watched her with a lazy smile, a man who'd earned a privilege and intended to enjoy it.

"You look worried." He traced a fingertip across her lips. "You shouldn't be. We're good together."

April wished. But all her concerns for what the light of day would bring were only emphasized by his tender touch.

"Let me tell you another story." Slipping a knuckle beneath her chin, he tipped her face toward his. "Once upon a time there was a businessman from a family with a hard-working Irish father, an Italian mother who liked to cook and four younger sisters. Two men against five women. An uneven balance that made for some really interesting situations."

"I'll bet." John had a similar situation with his family, and she'd witnessed firsthand the nuances of being outnumbered by women.

"This also meant that father and son had to work hard to care for the family and make ends meet, but the son was okay with that. He happened to be responsible and liked that his family felt they could depend on him."

"Sounds like the model son."

"Not quite model. Not all the time, anyway, but a son who usually made his parents proud. There's a downside though."

"Really?"

"Really." He nodded with mock seriousness. "This son grew up to be just as responsible, dependable and capable in his own life as he'd been growing up."

"That's a downside?"

"Not in school or business. Those qualities were a real asset to getting ahead, but they didn't do a thing for this guy's personal life." He pulled her closer.

"There's a twist. I'd think those qualities would have served the guy well in all aspects of his life. Most women like responsible, dependable and capable men."

"You'd think so, wouldn't you? They just might have, had the guy had sense enough to slow down long enough to find out."

"He didn't?"

"No, he didn't. He was so busy being responsible and dependable and capable that the next thing he knew, he'd been out of college for a decade, had a very successful career and no life whatsoever. He was even avoiding trips home because he was tired of listening to lectures about not making time to do anything but work."

Given Rex's upbringing, April could see how he could have easily fallen into that trap. She was ensnared firmly herself and she could completely relate to being tired of the lectures. But unlike Rex, she had a reason to hide.

"So has this guy conquered the working-too-much thing yet?" she asked, needing to keep things light, until she could think this situation through, figure out what to do next.

Thinking was completely impossible while her body was wrapped around his, still moist and tender from lovemaking, still yearning to feel his touch.

"No. But he's working on it, and he thinks he might have just fit another big piece into the puzzle."

"Really?"

"Really."

She wasn't going to ask. Something about his quirky smile warned that *she* somehow factored into his epiphany. She didn't want to know how.

But before she could come up with a way to segue from his story, he asked, "So did you get the moral?"

"I think I missed it," she admitted.

"The moral is, it doesn't matter what's getting in your way, work or not being able to relax, the result is the same. Life passes you by. Just like your boss told you."

Here was another prime example of how his interview technique ranked far beyond mere mortal levels and how she was in way over her head. With his relaxation therapy, his orgasms and his strong arms, Rex had slipped himself into the intimate places of her life. "Why are you thinking about this?"

"I like the way you feel," he said simply. "I'm not sure what to say besides that."

"Why me?"

"I like your take on life. You make me laugh."

Well, that definitely wasn't news. April Accidentally made a lot of people laugh, only, she typically didn't feel as if the trick was any accomplishment. For some reason making this man laugh felt like one right now.

She wasn't sure what to say. The conversation had gotten away from her, just as the night had.

"I enjoy being with you," he said. "And I'm a good influence."

"How do you figure that?"

It was a really good question. The man had distracted her from her job, made her chuck reason and integrity out the window and had made her forget her decision to give up men and sex.

She'd *never* met a man like him, had *never* had sex like this.

Letting her eyes flutter shut, she blocked out the satisfaction in his sleep-softened face.

"I'm not sure I want to tell you right now."

"Why not?" How much worse could this possibly get?

He was silent so long that she finally opened her eyes and looked at him, which must have been what he'd been waiting for.

"Do you realize how long you've been lying down? And you haven't been fidgeting. Miracle of miracles."

No lie.

"You're distracting me with your massages and your stories and your—" She'd almost said "And your orgasms," but caught herself in time. She needed to forget all about those orgasms and get back to business, figuring out what to do now that she'd jumped into bed with Rex and totally messed things up.

"Yes, I am." There was no remorse in that statement.

"Well, you can just stop right now." She wedged her elbow between them and levered herself out of his arms. "I'm here to do a job. You shouldn't be distracting me."

"I'm helping you, April. Don't stop me now." He raised up on an elbow. "I promised to be a gentleman and I will."

Their interpretations of gentleman were two different things, but the earnestness in his words made her melt. Or was that just desperation?

She didn't know. She only knew that when she peered down at this man with his sleep-tousled hair and heavy-lidded eyes, when she listened to him talk about helping her in that whiskey-rough voice, she wanted nothing more in the world than to let him.

REAL ORGASMS were good things or so April had always heard. The ones she'd experienced to date had certainly lived up to their press, which meant that a day starting off with not one, but *two* should have been great.

April's day had been more unsettling than great.

She hadn't so much minded Rex coercing her into a jog through a nearby park before they'd showered.

Given her metabolism, cardiovascular activity hadn't ever ranked too high on her priority list. She had a treadmill at home, positioned strategically in front of her computer, more to get her blood flowing than to keep her heart rate up. She worked off her excess energy in John's home gym three times a week, for all the good it did her when Paula insisted she sit down to a full meal before heading back to her apartment.

"Is this part of your relaxation therapy?" she'd asked.

He'd caressed her with his dark gaze and said, "Regular exercise will help, but I just don't want to go without you."

Okay. She could appreciate his honesty, even when it emphasized her own dishonesty, but her internal alarm, which had been curiously silent for so long, started blaring until Rex had dragged her into an empty office during a full slate of supervised shopping experiments.

"Did you know that kissing burns approximately two calories per minute compared to making love, which burns an average of six? I think we need to start warming up."

No, she hadn't known that and she hadn't been able to resist kissing him either. He'd just sort of grabbed her and kissed her, not really giving her a chance to do anything but kiss him back.

But her real worries began when they'd returned to the hotel, where Rex had prepared a scrumptious chicken marsala while she'd edited the day's data. They'd chatted about the shopping experiments, dined over the coffee table before Rex casually asked her, "Do you have a preference where we sleep tonight? My bedroom is larger than yours, but we could always spend the night out here with the Fetish Collection again. What do you think?"

What did she think?

She thought her head was going to split wide-open because her internal alarm was shrieking so loudly.

She wouldn't tell him that.

The man had jumped feetfirst into a fling. She'd suspected that the moral of his story had something to do with her and she'd been right. He was planning to make time to have fun and he intended to have fun with her.

The question was: What was she going to do about it?

Nothing brilliant sprang to mind except a desperate image of standing in John's office explaining, "I did what I had to do to get the job done, boss."

A melodramatic thought that only undermined her confidence, which didn't need any undermining, thank you very much. She'd been reminding herself constantly of her accomplishments on this job so far—small though they were—to pump up her confidence and balance out the mishaps. She wasn't sure what category a fling with Rex would fall under.

I enjoy being with you.

Until he found out that she'd been sent here to spy on him. He'd most likely appreciate Wilhemina's confidence and foresight in ensuring his name was kept clear of any suspicion, but finding out that she'd slept with him under false pretenses was bound to be an unpleasant surprise. Discovering that she'd been so desperate to experience passion that she'd sacrificed the honesty he deserved would hurt.

Because he cared. Not any love-at-first-sight, long-term kind of caring, but simply because he wanted to be with her right now, to enjoy their chemistry. He'd been up-front. He'd been kind. He'd seen past her nervousness, a quality that drove most people to distraction.

But instead of complaining that he'd gotten stuck with an inept assistant, Rex had taken action. He'd tried to help her relax. These were the actions of a caring man, a man who deserved honesty when she couldn't be honest.

The situation sucked, plain and simple, and with that thought riding her, April did what she always did when life got out of control. She worked.

Loading her e-mail program, she logged on to the J.P. Mooney Investigators' server through a dummy account set up as her fake West Coast Luxurious Bedding Company office. She found a reply from Wilhemina.

To: April Stevens (mailto:april@mooneyinvestigators.com)
Date: 10 Mar 2003 02:12:18-0000
Subject: Unfounded Accusations

My dear girl,
I would never presume to play God and *set you up*. Or Rex either, for that matter. However, if you two just happen to be together and things click…Auntie Wil says: *Go for it!* You know I love you and I'm tremendously fond of Rex. He's the type of high-caliber man I know Paula and John would approve. Unfortunately, just like you, Rex works entirely too much and doesn't make time for a life. You're two peas in a pod.

I won't deny that the idea you might enjoy meeting Rex did *cross my mind* when I was brainstorming how to tackle my current dilemma. Paula has been very worried about you since your breakup with that hot tub salesman. She mentioned her concerns several times in our phone conversations. Naturally, I'm concerned, too.

But please understand that my current situation at work is particularly difficult. I explained at Christmas that the future of the Luxurious Bedding Company is riding on my actions. Frankly, my dear, I'm very disturbed by recent events and the possibility of a threat to the launch. I'm new

to this company and haven't yet established my own re-
gime. At this point I want to surround myself with as many
trustworthy people as possible. You're trustworthy and so
is Rex, which translates into one problem off my desk. I
appreciate this because it frees up more of my energy to
deal with the madness of these suggestive posts and their
effect on my staff.

But I have every faith that with Rex to advise me and
you to protect us both from false allegations, things will
work out as I plan and this launch will be a success. So,
to answer your question about whether or not I set you
up...the answer, my dear, is: *Not exactly.* ;-)

Auntie Wil

April scowled at her computer monitor. According to Wilhemina, she should just ignore the fact that she couldn't tell
Rex he was under surveillance. She should overlook that
becoming involved with him would be considered a conflict
of interest if she wound up testifying in court. Not to mention the awkward position she'd be in with John. Sleeping
with the suspect? He'd consider that dicey business, no
questions asked.

But apparently Wilhemina thought all those problems
were secondary to April's love life, which left April wondering how she'd missed that Paula's sister was such a romantic. Or a raving lunatic. April wasn't sure which.

Or maybe dear Auntie Wil was suffering the same sex on
the brain as her staff.

Hmm.

April did know that she didn't need another reason to
second-guess herself. She was already worried about falling
flat on her face and disappointing everyone...then again,

like Rex had said, if it wasn't for her, he wouldn't have spotted the trouble with the pockets.

That was a good thing, she reminded herself, and clinging to that thought, she took a deep breath, deleted Wilhemina's post from her hard drive and got down to business. She had a job to do and the least she could do was keep Rex cleared of any suspicion.

When he went to change his clothes, she printed a journal report from the fax machine, which showed the last twenty transmissions he'd sent.

While he cooked dinner, she slipped into his bedroom to find his cell phone and copy down all his auto-dial numbers. She pressed redial to discover the last person he'd called had been her crazy Auntie Wil.

Nothing out of the ordinary. Nothing unusual. Corroborating what Wilhemina and John both believed—Rex wasn't guilty. And this was a good thing because April wouldn't wind up in court to testify on his behalf and no one would ever be the wiser about her conflict of interest.

Especially Rex.

Making her way back into the dining room, she slipped the fax journal report and the paper with the telephone numbers between the stacks of respondent surveys she had to edit and surreptitiously copied them into a post to John.

As Rex pulled their meal together, she sent the post and deleted all remnants of the transmission from her hard drive. Under the pretense of washing up for dinner, she went to the bathroom where she mutilated the pages with soap and water until they were illegible and she could discard them in the trash.

They ate and Rex accomplished what he'd intended last night by impressing her with his cooking skills. When she finally returned to her laptop after helping him get the kitchen back together, she was feeling full from his delicious meal, relaxed from the wine and amused by his stories of his younger sisters harassing him about his single status on his last trip home.

The man was simply too charming to be allowed and she might have talked herself into Wilhemina's take on a fling until she got slapped in the face with a blatant reminder of why she was here....

To: April Stevens (mailto:marketasst@luxuriousbedding.com)
Date: 10 Mar 2003 19:18:22-0500
Subject: Employee Incentive

Provide sex toys in the employees' break room as an incentive to increase productivity!

Studies prove that the opportunity to release sexual tension can provide a successful incentive to increase job performance. Condom dispensers and approved sanitizers located inside the break rooms will adequately meet all OSHA standards and state health requirements.

April read the post again and couldn't suppress a shudder. After last night with Rex and the Fetish Collection, she certainly couldn't deny that sex toys had provided the incentive to increase her productivity.

"Oh my," she said. "I've never seen anything quite like this before."

"What?"

"I've just been stalked by the company stalker."

Rex shoved his chair away from the table and got up, radiating an intensity she'd not seen before. He braced his arms on either side of her and leaned in to view the screen.

"Damn. You've got nearly two hundred posts here. We'll need to forward all these to Wilhemina. I hadn't counted on this problem following us out on the road, but I shouldn't be surprised since we're still connected to the network. Wishful thinking, I guess.''

"The subject of sex toys seems awfully coincidental, don't you think?''

Rex scowled harder. "How much did Wilhemina tell you about what's been happening at corporate?''

"Not much," she lied. "Just that there's some sort of stalker loose on the company server.''

"That sums it up. The place has been a nightmare. These posts just keep showing up, each one raunchier than previous. Otherwise totally normal people have gotten so preoccupied with sex they can't seem to talk about anything else." He gave a wry laugh. "Wilhemina calls it sex on the brain. I've never seen anything like it.''

"Did you get sex on the brain, too?''

Arching a dark brow, he took a step back and April turned to face him, needed to see as well as hear his response. This was a business question, an opportunity to surveil that she'd be negligent to pass up.

His answer shouldn't be personal, but it was. Did sex on the brain explain why he was interested in her?

"I was distracted. Not that I'd admit that to Wilhemina,'' he said. "And relieved to get out of there. It was funny. I never gave the product line a second thought when I contracted this project. Launching the Sensuous Collection was a challenge and I looked forward to the chance to work with Wilhemina again. I had no idea this project would test my concentration.''

"Why wouldn't you want Wilhemina to know?''

"I'm a consultant, April. My clients' confidence in my abilities is all I have to recommend me. Getting personal clouds the issue so I don't get personal on the job.''

April was intimately acquainted with nervousness and Rex showed no signs whatsoever—no excessive sweating or fidgeting. He didn't avoid making eye contact and his Adam's apple wasn't doing any weird stuff that might suggest he wasn't comfortable.

He seemed *very* comfortable in fact, standing with his legs spread, a stance that suggested he was being open and honest.

More proof of his innocence.

"We've gotten personal," she reminded him, curious to hear how he rationalized their involvement.

"We're not in the office together so it's not the same thing. What I do out on the road is my business. The research companies I deal with are my associates and the respondents I interview have no idea who my client is. There's no risk to the Luxurious Bedding Company."

Raising his hand to her face, he thumbed her lower lip, his touch sending a shiver through her that he couldn't miss. "And I'm very grateful we're not in-house together. This chemistry between us—" he traced her top lip now, invoked another shiver "—would be a tragedy to waste."

And darned if she didn't dissolve into a puddle. One touch and he scattered her thoughts, filled her head with the memory of how he'd felt on top of her, inside her.

And Rex knew. His expression softened, a combination of pleasure and satisfaction that made his features even more striking, made her press her lips to his thumb before she'd thought to stop herself. His skin was rough silk to the touch and she couldn't suppress the anticipation at the thought of the night ahead.

She was so in trouble with this man.

When he lowered his mouth to hers, a voice of sanity cried out, "You can explain away one night as a lapse in judgment and Rex won't be hurt when he finds out you slept with him under false pretenses." But the voice of need countered with, "*If* he finds out. He only wants to have fun.

Have some fun, then kiss him goodbye and he'll never be the wiser.''

Then Rex's lips captured hers and drowned out both voices.

Her arms came around his neck, her fingers slipping into that thick hair. He kissed her as though he'd been waiting forever. Tongues met and breaths clashed. He ground his thickening erection against her and she ached in reply, remnants of the passion she'd discovered last night. She wanted to experience the kind of freedom she'd felt while naked in his arms, when she'd felt aroused, and so right.

Rex seemed to be waging his own war with restraint because he couldn't settle on what he wanted to touch. His hands trailed down her neck and over her shoulders, skimmed their way down her back. He kneaded his fingers into her backside and pulled her closer, as if he might forge them together by will alone.

And when they finally broke apart, panting, Rex stared down at her with a devilish grin. ''Let's wrap this up and go to bed.''

April looked into his dark eyes, knew she'd avoid so many potential problems if she could just say no.

But she couldn't. This time she'd slip between the sheets with him by conscious choice, a decision made while wide-awake and cognizant of the potential consequences. This would be her one and only chance to experience feeling *right.* Rex's magic hands gifted her with the ability to relax and to know pleasure. And she wouldn't miss this chance.

''Yes.''

A simple word for a situation that wasn't simple at all.

Rex waited until he was certain April had fallen asleep before slipping out of bed. Not that he wanted to leave when her warm body had been wrapped around his. No way.

Leaving her satin-smooth curves had been the last thing he'd wanted to do when his legs were still weak from an awesome orgasm. But right now was the only time he could work on his computer unobserved.

In the aftermath of tonight's post from corporate headquarters and his subsequent crush to get April in bed, he'd forgotten to post Wilhemina about having Research and Development reevaluate the way they'd packaged the lotions in the Fetish Collection.

As long as the sheet set was undergoing a second look, the packaging should be modified so some unsuspecting male consumer didn't wind up wearing Pleasure and Sizzle when he was expecting a happy penis. He was surprised they hadn't thought to shape the containers differently already. It shouldn't come as a surprise that sheets were frequently used in the dark.

Good thing April had a knack for spotting the oddball sorts of problems that could land manufacturers in liability. The Luxurious Bedding Company didn't need any more negative press and he didn't need any more challenges with this project. The adventure and game sheets were providing enough.

And April.

She'd seemed more wired than usual today and he wondered if the change in their relationship status was to blame. She'd gone from a marketing assistant who'd been concerned about her job performance to the marketing consultant's lover in one day.

But Rex wanted April to smile the way she'd smiled at him in bed tonight. He wanted her warm and willing and making him feel as if he was the only man who'd ever made her feel good. For that to happen, she had to stay relaxed.

Grabbing a robe from the back of the door, Rex slipped it on and quietly left the bedroom. He decided against turning on a light in the suite. The glow from the computer monitor would be all he needed.

After booting his system, he waited for the programs to load, thinking about the exquisite woman he'd left asleep in his bed. She'd taken his breath away tonight with her unique brand of bold innocence, as arousing without nipple clamps as she'd been comfortable with them.

After he'd massaged her into bonelessness, they'd made love without any of the Fetish Collection's apparatus. He'd wanted to experience her with nothing between them but their mouths and hands, to gauge how much their of explosive lovemaking of the previous night had been influenced by the sexy paraphernalia.

The answer was not much.

Nipple clamps and sexy lotions might have enhanced his attraction to April, but his response was all about her. Only she could turn him on with a glance.

She was an intelligent, beautiful woman with a rather glib outlook on life that he found charming. He wasn't exactly sure what that meant yet, but he intended to find out.

Making love to April had impacted him in a way he'd never been impacted before. He laughed with her, felt challenged by her, which had driven home the fact that he hadn't been smiling or feeling challenged enough lately—crimes his sisters had convicted him of a long time ago.

Wouldn't his sisters just love for him to admit they'd been right? Smiling at the thought, he posted Wilhemina about addressing this latest problem and then composed another post. This one to the supervisor of the research foundation he'd contracted with several years ago.

Harold Snyder had become a friend during the years as a result of Rex's continued interest in massage. Harold was both personable and respected for his knowledge in scientific research. He shared his knowledge freely—evidenced by the fact that he'd allowed Rex continued access to the research foundation's intranet.

Hopefully Harold could offer direction in following up on a suspicion Rex had about April. She was a lovely and intelligent woman and he disliked that she shied away from contact with people, that she preferred the solitude of the observation room to being out in the conference room with him.

True, as his assistant, she needed to be behind the scenes, but Rex liked to know she was comfortable venturing out when the chance arose, maybe to try out sleeping styles again, or to help with the other hundred things that might come up during a project. And she wouldn't be unless he could help her stay in the lower digits on her nervous scale.

Contrary to what he'd told her, Rex wasn't convinced that massage alone would do the trick. Scrolling on the computer screen, he maneuvered through the foundation's Web site. He had access to areas about massage therapy, but tonight he was researching another topic, one he'd heard about only casually while under contract with the foundation.

A few items of relevancy popped up in some common areas of the site, which helped him gather his thoughts and fed his growing suspicion that April suffered from something more than being "high-strung."

The official medical term for the malady was Electro Hypersensitivity, commonly referred to as EHS. A dictionary defined phrases such as *electromagnetic compatibility* and *electrostatic discharge*. In a nutshell, people stored and emitted electricity in their bodies, which could not only adversely affect electrical equipment but create biological allergies.

He reviewed an area of the site that offered pages of clinical case histories and hosted a bulletin board where EHS sufferers who'd been treated by the foundation could connect via cyberspace to discuss their various issues and have an authority respond with medical advice. Rex scanned both, found the case histories of particular interest.

Mabel R., an EHS sufferer whose new hearing aid exacerbated her sensitivity to the point she experienced crippling lethargy while at work in front of a telephone system.

Tyrone F., an EHS sufferer who experienced episodes of sudden, almost violent "bursts of energy" upon retiring every night in his new apartment. Investigation revealed water pipes and power cables in adjoining walls where the bed was located. Water pipes carried an electric current. Once the bed was moved to another location, the manic episodes ceased.

Joe H., an EHS sufferer who absorbed electrical signals from the computer, fed enough "garbage" back into the system to malfunction both computer and monitor.

Glancing at April's unique computer setup, Rex wondered if she hadn't experienced similar troubles. She hadn't mentioned anything that might lead him to believe she was aware this particular malady existed. He continued scanning the histories.

The biological effects he read about in these cases ranged from lethargy to mania to every mood in between. Even more disturbing were the results of a study conducted by the National Agency for Cancer Study that linked EHS sufferers as more susceptible to human carcinogens.

Logging off the medical research foundation's intranet, Rex conducted a global search of the Web to find more sites of interest. What he found, though, was that Electro Hypersensitivity was an obscure topic. Other than a few oddball pages where people linked EHS to alien encounters, he found no medical sites of any particular use.

Two o'clock had come and gone by the time he'd finished surfing. Rex sent the post off to Harold, received an automated reply stating that the director would be out of the office until the sixteenth. Bum timing. He would have to cool his heels for another week.

Before shutting down his system, he logged on to the Luxurious Bedding Company server to see if his in-box would be flooded with e-mails. There were only a few new items, though, and nothing pressing enough to be dealt with tonight. Rex headed back to bed and the woman who awaited him there with a smile.

10

To: J.P. Mooney (mailto:john@mooneyinvestigators.com)
Date: 16 Mar 2003 17:42:11-0200
Subject: Checking In and Checking Up

Hello Brother-in-law,

I'm checking in with news of the investigation before I head to Florida tomorrow to check up on April. The investigation is moving too slowly for me although my security chief assures me that his people are working at the speed of light. I suppose given that we're dealing with the backgrounds of well over a thousand employees I'll take him at his word.

So far they've narrowed the list considerably by focusing on staff who have prior connections to rival manufacturers in their work histories.

The influx of suggestive posts mercifully slowed for a few days, giving us some much-needed respite around here. My network administrator, Jacqui Scott used the time to track network traffic and attempt to determine a pattern. The transmissions still appear to be originating from random terminals. The only commonality is that the posts forwarded all have to do with the Sensuous Collection. Not reassuring.

However, Jacqui has been steadily monitoring all outbound traffic and hasn't tracked a single post to a rival manufacturer or any other suspicious destination, which alleviates my worries somewhat, if not my concerns about the effects of sex on the brain on her judgment. And not only Jacqui's judgment, but that of my marketing director, Charles Blackstone.

Yesterday, I overheard her haranguing him and making sexual innuendoes through the open door of the employee break room, which convinced me that they're involved. I suppose I should be grateful that the relationship appears to be curtailed to after-hours and I didn't walk in on them going at it on the table. That God for small favors.

The latest posts contain utterly *brilliant* suggestions for making the company a more attractive place to work by providing sexual apparatus to new-hires at orientation. And the idea I'm personally considering implementing will cut down on employee absences by allotting time on the clock for sexual trysts in our newly remodeled fantasy dungeon/conference rooms. <G>

Even April has received a suggestive post through the dummy marketing assistant account you suggested I set up for her. A post about sex toys, I believe, which flooded her mailbox and gave her a chance to review the files that are being forwarded.

She is my only sanity in this madness. She's doing her job beautifully and from what Rex says, it turns out our girl has a knack for spotting potential liabilities. He hasn't stopped praising her abilities or thanking me for sending her. The man sounds thoroughly enchanted! I can't wait to see them in person.

Do not lecture me about April's reports of Rex prowling around late at night to work on his computer! I've taken enough flack from the board already and *do not* have the patience. I'm sure Rex has a perfectly valid explanation—

some research for his analysis, I'll wager. He is *very* thorough, which is one of the reasons he's so tremendously valuable to me.

I suggested tracking his transmissions but he's using his own business account, not the Luxurious Bedding Company's server. As I'm sure you're already aware that means we have no legal right to monitor his activity without a warrant. As long as April is documenting the incidents we'll be covered in the event his actions are questioned.

So hold a good thought for me, brother-in-law. My security chief needs to come up with something concrete to follow up on soon because while his people are busy investigating at the *speed of light,* I'm left sitting in my ivory tower watching the world go mad around me.

Wil

John steepled his fingers before him and smiled at his computer monitor. He'd been waiting to hear back from Wilhemina about these new reports of Rex Holt's nighttime prowling because April had been bugging him for permission to infiltrate the man's system to find out what he was doing.

When John had questioned her about why she was so hot to investigate this guy when she was doing a good job by passing along her reports, she'd danced around so much that John suspected something was up.

Do you think Rex Holt is guilty? He had asked her via e-mail.

NO! came the reply.

If Wilhemina still wasn't worried about this guy's integrity in light of this new information then that was good enough for John. Toggling between screens on his e-mail program, he replied to April's last post with an equally emphatic "NO!"

APRIL WATCHED Rex greet his first group of respondents in the Florida offices of Yodzis and Associates. They'd wrapped up their studies in Atlanta and had traveled south without mishap to continue with round two of their studies.

As always, he was oh, so handsome with his burnished hair glinting in the overhead light as he circled the conference table, drawing the gaze of every woman in the room.

And from those outside the room, too.

She couldn't help admiring the way he moved with his long strides and lean grace and when he peered through the observation window, as though he could sense her watching him, she found herself smiling, helpless to resist the impulse, even though he couldn't see her.

With each new dawn after a night spent in his arms, April found herself in over her head a little more, her emotions a little closer to the edge, her internal alarm increasing its decibel level.

Her alarm was in the red zone because this fling wasn't turning out to be as simple as she'd planned. Not only was she getting sucked in emotionally, but Rex had complicated issues further with his late-night visits to his computer.

She'd awakened the minute he'd slipped out of bed on that very first night a week ago. She'd sneaked to the door to hear the sound of clicking keys and electronic blips and beeps. She'd considered following him under the pretense of getting a glass of water just to see how he'd react to her intrusion. If he knew that she could happen upon him, he might curtail his activities. But her job was to make him comfortable so he would go about his business as usual while she watched.

So the real trick this past week had been not to jump to

the obvious conclusion—that he was conducting some nefarious business in the dead of night. Business like sending information about the data he'd been compiling for the Sensuous Collection to a rival manufacturer.

She didn't think he was guilty, but heaven forbid they were all wrong....

John had a credo he lived by and during the years he'd trained her he'd drummed that credo into her skull until she could hear his voice looping through her brain right now.

Thou shalt not become emotionally involved with thy client.

Rex wasn't her client, yet John's adage still applied—he'd just never mentioned this particular bit of wisdom in reference to suspects because he'd assumed the logic should have been obvious.

In the dark, while Rex held her in his arms and coaxed responses from her body that she'd never dreamed herself capable of, she felt so *right*. As if for once she was in the right place at the right time and had managed to do exactly the right thing.

In the harsh light of day, the right thing meant her surveillance was biased.

An image of sitting on the witness stand, explaining to an entire courtroom—with John Patrick Mooney seated in the front row for moral support, of course—how she'd slept with the suspect, which rendered her testimony inadmissible...

Conflict of interest.

The blow to the agency's reputation would be staggering, which was a horrible way to repay John for fostering her and giving her a place to live and a job and a family....

April Accidentally strikes again, wreaking havoc on everyone unfortunate enough to cross her path.

Darn good thing she'd had so much practice dealing with

her own screwups. Otherwise she'd never have been able to function under the pressure of having a fling and trying not to fall in love with a man she believed wasn't a criminal—but couldn't be absolutely sure—while living her cover and conducting undercover surveillance.

But she was doing her job. It was her *only* bright spot. She was proving herself capable as Rex's assistant, successfully living her cover. Rex was particularly pleased with her ability to pinpoint potential liabilities, and she was just as pleased that he'd managed to find such an unexpected positive in her screwups.

She was documenting to protect two people she cared about and would have the information to support Wilhemina's judgment and prove Rex's innocence in the event he was ever questioned.

In an effort to shake things up and satisfy these niggling doubts, she casually mentioned one of his late-night jaunts. She'd hoped for a simple explanation to absolve him of any suspicions, but he'd just shrugged and claimed he hadn't been able to sleep.

That explanation explained one night, not three.

The only thing left to do had been to ask John's permission to infiltrate Rex's system to find out exactly what he'd been doing. John had ultimately denied her request and she wasn't happy. He was crippling her in the one area she had any real competency, which seemed so stupid. Not that she couldn't squelch her doubts about Rex. She could, because even though she didn't know what he was doing on the computer at night, in her heart she knew he wasn't guilty.

And the result was that she had to face the fact that it wasn't so much that she thought Rex might be guilty as it was she didn't trust her own judgment about him. Like Wilhemina, she believed he had some reasonable explanation for working at night and not mentioning it. But April was afraid to trust herself.

It was a sobering truth and one she decided she had to address right away. If she didn't believe in herself, no one would. So, with a new conviction to listen to her gut instincts, she threw herself into her role, assisting Rex in a series of consumer confusion studies, blind testing and accompanied shopping experiments in the Yodzis and Associates' offices that overlooked Tampa Bay.

Rex had seated himself at the head of the table and started up a discussion about a pillow—another version of the Hidden Secrets Pillow—with an inside compartment to hold the Kama Sutra Sports Set game spinner and other sexy goodies.

When a sharp knock on the door sounded, April motioned to her Tampa assistant, a young woman named Camille, to let their visitor in.

The door opened and a familiar voice said, "Hello, April. We made it."

"Finally," a male voice added.

Wilhemina entered the room with her marketing director. "You remember Charles Blackstone." She inclined her head in greeting to Camille.

"Of course," April said, motioning him inside. "Please come in and close the door."

She slanted a glance toward Rex to see if he or his respondents had been distracted by the light, noticed a few of the womens' gaze dart toward the window. "Good trip, I trust."

Charles extended his hand and April took it, frowning when she got a shock. Charles laughed but didn't let go.

"Coming to Florida in the winter is worth a little turbulence," he said with a smarmy smile.

Withdrawing her hand, April took a step back and caught

her heel on the rubber mat surrounding her computer station. She managed to steady herself on the podium and greeted Wilhemina, who said, "It wasn't bad, thank you, April. A direct flight, which is always a pleasure."

To look at Wilhemina, no one would ever have known they were two strays adopted by the same family. She presented herself as a professional who was greeting an employee and Charles Blackstone seemed to be buying it no problem. April wasn't surprised. The man was a dime a dozen, in her opinion. His eyes roved too freely and lingered just a little too long for her tastes.

If she were picking a suspect to fit the profile of the stalker, she'd have put this man on the top of her list.

"Rex is hard at work as usual," Wilhemina commented, glancing through the window at the man of the moment. "So what do you think about him? Has he impressed you as much as I told you he would?"

Wilhemina was referring to a lot more than Rex's marketing studies, so April just said, "He's very gifted at what he does."

Then she went back to her computer to look up information on competitive lines of sex toy pillows that she anticipated Rex would want, given his current line of questioning.

Wilhemina only lifted an arched brow and April experienced a surge of satisfaction that she'd thwarted what was only the first attempt to find out if April had taken her Auntie Wil's advice and *gone for it.*

Her corporate guests observed the focus groups until Rex's schedule segued into a completion technique session. He led a small group in making up a bed with the Kama Sutra Sports Set, gauging their reactions not only to the product but to the ease of assembling the product. He invited Charles to help.

"Camille," April said. "Would you go assemble the folders from the telephone interviews that Mr. Holt wants to take with him tonight. I'll keep an eye on the equipment."

Camille left and the door had barely shut when Wilhemina got straight to the point. "My dear girl, you're positively glowing. Do I take that to mean you took my suggestion?"

April had thought she'd be prepared for this question, but darned if she didn't blush to the roots of her hair, which of course, Wilhemina took as a yes.

"Oh, my dear, I'm so thrilled for you. Rex is completely wonderful, isn't he?" She clasped April's hands, rushing on before April had a chance to deny her presumption or answer her question. "And you've been completely wonderful, too. You're doing such a thorough job. I told John he didn't have to worry about you. You'd be fine if he'd just toss you out of the nest and give you a chance to fly."

Well, if that didn't just come as a mixed bag. While she appreciated Wilhemina's confidence in her abilities, knowing John had to be coerced to give her this case wasn't exactly reassuring, given that she was proving his concerns well founded by sleeping with the suspect.

"Then you're not worried about my latest reports?"

Wilhemina squeezed her hands as though she saw right through the question to the doubt below. "I'm an exceptional judge of character. I'm not wrong about Rex. I need him to pull off this launch and I need you to satisfy the board so I can have him. I'll bet he's pulling these late-nighters to get his executive summary together." Wilhemina smiled reassuringly then released April's hands as she turned back to the window.

Rex was addressing the group, "Not only are you the chief shoppers in your households—" his voice resounded over the microphone ''—you're the people who usually make the beds....''

He was nothing short of skillful in the way he presented sheets with brightly colored couples demonstrating a variety of sexual positions. He might have been handling a stapler rather than a dual-temperature vibrator for all the distinction he made as he explained the use of the hidden compartment inside the pillow.

He worked a middle-aged mom with grown children around her embarrassment and helped a young newlywed who couldn't focus because sex on the brain kept making her crack one-liners.

By skillfully rephrasing his questions, he got the respondents to delve deeper, to honestly consider the product, to offer him the information he needed to advise Wilhemina on successfully placing the Sensuous Collection in the marketplace.

As they stood side by side and watched Rex work, April understood why Wilhemina dismissed Rex's guilt so easily and silently acknowledged that if she'd had to be tossed out from behind her computer, she couldn't think of a job she'd rather have than being Rex's right-hand woman.

NOT ONLY DID REX appreciate the Westshore Regency Hotel's convenient location to the Yodzis and Associates' offices and the airport, he liked the killer view of the downtown skyline reflected by the dark waters of Tampa Bay at night.

The suites were spacious and the accommodations five-star, which also proved opportune as he and April had enjoyed dinner with Wilhemina and Charles on the rooftop restaurant tonight. Both had been impressed with their observation of the studies today and they'd discussed at length how to factor the different consumer responses into the line's marketing, a discussion that hadn't put Rex and April back in their suite until well after nine.

And the dinner had taken its toll on April. While she'd kept up her end of the conversation from appetizers to after-dinner brandies and had shared her experience with her stalker post, she'd barely touched her plate. Now she paced the suite as though suffering the effects of a quadruple espresso.

"Let's jump straight to your massage tonight," he said. "I know we planned to stay up and catch up on work—"

She came to an abrupt halt in the dining room and spun to face him, fine hair wisping around her cheeks. "Oh, no. It's almost nine-thirty and you've got to go through those telephone interviews. That stack was huge. There must be two hundred."

"Two-hundred and sixteen," he confirmed. "Groupings of twelve. Different demographics and life cycles."

She propped her fists on her hips. "We can skip the massage tonight. I've got loads of work, too."

Rex folded his arms across his chest and contemplated her just as seriously. "*After* the massage. I don't want to break the routine when I'm finally seeing progress."

"Finally? I've been a model patient."

"At night, but the effects aren't lasting through the day. We've got more work to do. A lot more work."

April regarded him as though she couldn't quite tell whether or not to take him seriously. "Are you just looking for a reason to get me horizontal?"

"Yes."

Those arched brows drew together. "We need to work."

"We've been working all day. We can take some time to relax."

She huffed. "A compromise then. Can you give me a

massage without seducing me so I can still have time to work afterward?''

''No problem.''

''Right.'' She gave a snort of laughter. ''And you've got a bridge in Brooklyn you want to sell me, too, I'll bet.''

''No bridges. Just my hands.''

His hands were her downfall and he could tell by her expression that she knew it. But she didn't say a word, just spun on her heel and took off. Sinking to her knees before the Luxurious Bedding Company product still packed in the shipping boxes, she inspected labels and ripped off mailing tape.

''Need some help?'' he asked.

''No. No, I'm just looking for...*this*.'' Rocking back on her haunches, she gave him a prime shot of her heart-shaped bottom as she tore the plastic from some small...something.

He waited for her to turn around, noticed the glint in her eyes and the satisfied smile on her pretty face when she did.

''All right. I'll agree to the massage if you wear this.''

She held up a leather loop that reminded Rex of a small dog collar—the Take Control Cock Ring from the Fetish Collection.

''You think *that* is going to protect you from me?''

Slipping her fingers inside the loop, she gave a tug to demonstrate the ring's strength. ''Look at this baby. It could cut off the flow of the Alaskan pipeline.''

He resisted the urge to shudder. ''I'll have to take my pants off to wear it.''

''Rex.'' She shot him a look of pure exasperation. ''Your pants would wind up off anyway. I'll take my chances.''

He couldn't exactly argue the point. But what amused him the most was that April didn't seem to have a good bead on what that cock ring would actually do for him. Sure it would help him control himself for a while…but then she'd better watch out.

Apparently the Fetish Collection literature didn't clarify that point. He'd add this to his list of things to mention to Wilhemina before she left town.

He wasn't going to tell April she'd pinpointed yet another problem with her unusual gift just yet, though. Not when she looked so confident that her sexy plan would work. The Take Control Cock Ring meant he'd have her supine on the bed while he was sans trousers and that worked for him.

"Toss it here."

Shooting him a pleased smile, she took aim and fired. He caught it neatly, not a little amazed by the need that sliced through him. For a man who'd been making the most of his nights, Rex found himself more preoccupied with making love to her, rather than less.

Every day had become an exercise in anticipating the night and imagining the many ways he might relax her sweet body into responding to his. Rex couldn't ever remember being this preoccupied with a woman and was frankly amazed that she consumed so much of his energy— energy he'd normally have expended on work. Yet he didn't feel any sense of losing focus. In fact, his senses were honed and his energy level was up. Looked like making time to enjoy life was giving him an edge.

"How about a counteroffer?" he asked. "I'll wear *this,* if you help me demonstrate the Kama Sutra Sports Set."

"Rex!" She exhaled his name on the edge of a breath and popped to her feet in a movement that displayed her graceful curves in fine detail. "That'll defeat the purpose. I really need to get some work done tonight. So do you."

"We will. I'll be wearing *this,* remember?" He held up the leather ring. "Just a few moves so I can get the logistics for tomorrow's focus groups. Then I'll let you up and we'll get back to work. Deal?''

She shot her a very skeptical gaze before asking, ''An *abbreviated* massage so you don't put me in a coma and just a few moves, right?''

''Right. Think Twister. Right foot blue. Left hand red.''

''And you'll behave?''

Rex nodded, which April seemed to think implied a promise.

11

As much as the idea of a lengthy massage that wound up with a game of sexy Twister tempted April, they both needed to work tonight. Wilhemina's visit had thrown them completely off schedule because she'd insisted on going out for long social meals that precluded keeping up with Rex's intense schedule.

Rex indulged her, but he did mention that he'd never known Wilhemina to be quite so hungry before. April hoped her crafty Auntie Wil gained five pounds because the only reason she'd insisted on the meals was to scope out how satisfying the alleged fling was for both parties.

April didn't think she or Rex had behaved in any way but with the utmost of professionalism. At least she hoped they hadn't, because the last thing she needed was for Wilhemina to discuss this subject with John. The second to the last thing she needed was to be distracted by the sight of Rex pushing his slacks over his hips and down those strong legs.

But off the trousers went and he seemed completely unaware of the show he presented, completely oblivious to the way he looked standing there, adjusting *parts* to shed his briefs.

Her heart began to beat slow, heavy beats, her pulse thrumming through her veins in languid bursts, a reaction that exasperated her. She'd gone from never having a real orgasm to gorging on them. Rather than satisfying her craving, April was becoming addicted.

Why else would watching this man peel away his socks—his *socks* for goodness' sake—affect her so much? Her gaze slipped over the top of his burnished head, his strong broad shoulders, and she ached to step into the circle of his strong arms, a feeling so intense it was almost physical.

And when he lifted his dark gaze, she found her desire mirrored in the depths of his eyes. She captured his image in her memory. A memento to cherish long after the feel of his arms faded, the memory of the hundred delicious ways only he could bring her body to the brink of ecstasy and then drive her crashing home.

"Do you want to make sure it's tight enough?" He'd slipped the leather ring on and displayed what was rapidly becoming an impressive erection above that unforgiving strip of leather.

"Are you…comfortable?" she asked, sounding so much more composed than she felt.

"Comfortable isn't the issue, April. *Uncomfortable* is."

She wasn't sure exactly how uncomfortable he could be given the size of his erection. If anything, that ring of leather seemed to be stimulating rather than curtailing his reaction.

He motioned to the bed. "Go on. Sit down."

After toeing off her pumps, she slipped the jacket down her arms and tossed it over the back of a chair. She moved toward the bed, her thoughts swirling around in a mire of excitement and worry, while her body reacted to the promise of his touch and the feelings only he could evoke.

He slipped behind and speared his fingers into her hair. She tipped her head forward and gave him free rein to touch her in a position ripe for arousal….

The cock ring didn't work, plain and simple. April tried to figure out a way to let Wilhemina know so she could warn the consumer without confirming her suspicions about a fling. That leather band with its D-ring and easy-release snap should have helped Rex maintain control. Instead, he seemed inspired to new levels of craftiness to get around her defenses.

His hands were everywhere tonight, massaging, kneading, stroking and copping feels wherever he could, until her numb brain finally caught on to his game. She told him to stop.

"You like the way I make you feel," he said, very pragmatically. "So what's wrong with touching you?"

She might have smiled, had she not been fighting the urge to arch backward, thus conveniently moving her breasts directly into the line of fire of his magic hands.

"Nothing," she said. "But we can't spend all our time in bed."

"We don't. We spend most of it working." His voice echoed somewhere above her right ear, sent a shiver through her.

"Work is good. We need to work tonight. Wilhemina has us seriously behind." There was something so boneless about that statement it rendered any possible validity a joke.

"All work and no play isn't good. I told you I've finally figured that out."

"I'm delighted I prompted your epiphany, but I would hardly say we haven't been playing."

He chuckled, a husky velvet sound that cascaded through the quiet suite, through her, even as his fingers stroked those circles between her shoulder blades. "It's not enough. The more I get of you, the more I want."

His laughter should have lightened the impact of that admission, yet it only underscored the truth of his words, and how amazed he seemed by his own need.

And she ached in reply. She had nothing to offer him,

for all his kindnesses, for all his patience, for all his orgasms. Best-case scenario would be for her to successfully slink out of his life without him ever knowing she'd been spying on him.

It was such a bleak prospect that she could only close her eyes against the sadness. For the first time in her memory she felt *right*. Right when Rex's hands were on her. Right when she worked by his side with the consumer studies. Right sitting with him at dinner discussing the Sensuous Collection campaign.

She actually liked being his assistant, enjoyed working on the computer behind the scenes as Rex worked his magic. She was exceptional on the computer and she loved the challenge of research. Unlike private investigation, where she routinely ran records and databases, Rex's work provided an interesting diversion from the routine. Sleeping styles last week and pillows today. The work was never the same and she could easily see why he found it so appealing.

It was such a shame that he wasn't looking for anything more than a good time and her future didn't allow for husbands and babies.

She was thinking way too much for her own good tonight. She'd had enough practice handling her emotions, both good and bad. So why was she floundering now?

Wilhemina was the culprit, no doubt. She had sex on the brain and she'd started April thinking all sorts of romantic thoughts that were exactly what a woman who'd sworn off sex, men and families didn't need to be thinking about. She'd gotten a pleasant reprieve with the sex, but…

"Thanks." Leaning forward to escape the pressure of his hands, she slanted a glance back over her shoulder.

"We're done?"

"You said a short massage. That was great."

"You're not relaxed yet."

"I'm not in a coma yet," she corrected. "I'm relaxed enough for a few turns of Twister."

Judging by his frown, Rex clearly didn't think so, but he graciously didn't push the issue. Instead, he reached over to the night table to grab the game spinner.

"I'll take you at your word. You're sure you're up to this?"

"It's Twister."

Technically, it would be Twister with a man wearing nothing but his shirt and what looked like a painful erection. But just the sight of him, so comfortable in his odd attire, touched her in a place that had no business being touched.

"Ladies first."

She plucked the spinner from his hand and said lightly, "So you're claiming to be a gentleman, are you?"

He just shot her that dashing grin and scooted back against the sofa. "Read the directions."

She scanned the tiny printed instructions and summarized. "This game is not a brain teaser. We start in the middle of the bed and work from right to left, feet first and on up. Whatever position has the most parts on it when we're through is the position we try out. Oh, and we're supposed to follow our imaginations and add *other* body parts along the way."

His gaze dropped to his lap and he gave a wry laugh. "Really? That could liven things up a bit."

As if *things* needed any more livening.

Refraining from comment, she set the spinner on the bed between them to move this show along. She snapped the plastic arrow and waited until it spun to a stop on a pie-shaped slice of blue.

"There we are," she said. "Left foot blue."

Drawing her legs up, she aimed a toe onto a nearby blue Kama Couple, who was merrily wrapped around each other while the man pleasured his lady standing up in the Jack-hammer. She completed the maneuver without ever moving from her spot.

"All right, slick. My turn." He twirled the spinner.

Green.

The sneaky man slipped his foot right under her leg to a green Ladies' Tip-Top Thrill, caressing the sensitive back of her knee with his hairy leg.

He grinned.

She ignored him and spun again.

Blue.

She aimed for Missionary Mania.

Red.

Rex went for Posterior Passion.

After their feet were engaged, the game got interesting. Knees meant that they had to get up from their seats and really move. April wondered how long until she could insist she'd satisfied her end of the bargain.

Yellow.

She headed for another Missionary Mania to dodge direct contact with his bare thighs, but he anticipated her move.

Yellow again.

"Oh, yeah." Rex wedged his knee right between hers to reach a Bound Boy Bliss. "You should be naked."

She lifted her gaze to his, forced to lean backward slightly to avoid touching his chest in their new positions. "Forget it, buddy. That wasn't part of the deal."

He dropped a quick kiss to her lips, taking her completely by surprise. By the time she'd even thought to react, he was smiling.

"I've got my work cut out trying to get you to take time to have some fun," he said.

"Massage you know, but you're no great shakes in the fun department either."

"I'm a fast learner." He nuzzled his knee between her legs, just a casual touch that started sparks inside her. "Why don't we learn together. It'll be more fun."

"Hmm."

Her skirt had bunched up around her hips and the heat between her legs was so intense she was sure Rex must feel it right through her panty hose.

If he did, he didn't comment, just handed her the spinner. *Red.*

She leaned back on an elbow onto a Posterior Passion that put some distance between them. Rex stared down at her as if to say, "Think you're getting away that easily?" and spun.

Blue.

"Now here's a place where we can improvise. I just happen to have a body part that will reach right—"

"Rex!" April shook her head to clear the image of him aiming that erection toward the nearest blue couple but heat was already creeping into her cheeks, though why she should suddenly feel shy was a mystery. They'd just spent a week together 24/7. When she hadn't been in his arms, she'd been thinking about being in his arms.

Rex was right. The effects of his massages weren't lasting long enough, and the one she'd had tonight hadn't done the trick at all. If she'd have been on her feet, April would have tightly clasped her hands behind her back, but as one elbow was currently locked on to a Posterior Position, she'd have to settle for calling an end to this game and taking a few deep breaths.

She sat up but unfortunately Rex chose that exact moment to plant his elbow on a Bound Boy Bliss that brought him full-bodied against her. Her forehead connected with his chin so hard she yelped. He reared back, clearly startled, and overbalanced enough to skid on the slippery sheets and... Darned if he didn't slid right off the bed.

Again.

"Rex!" She peered over the edge, uncertain at the sight that would greet her, heartbeat arrested in her chest.

He'd landed flat on his back. If it wasn't for the way he winced when he stared up at her—had he bitten his lip again?—she might have laughed at the sight of his buttoned shirt and his erection still bobbling wildly in its leather ring.

April didn't laugh, though. She didn't get the chance.

Rex shot an arm toward her. Grabbing a fistful of her blouse, he gave one mighty tug and before she'd even thought to brace herself, she went crashing down on top of him.

He made a noise suspiciously like "Oomph!" and she thought her knee might have landed on something important.

"I'm sorry. Are you all—"

Simultaneously, his fingers threaded into her hair and his mouth caught hers in a kiss that sucked the air from her lungs.

April didn't get a chance to worry, or to think. She could only react to the feel of his tongue thrusting inside her mouth, to the hands anchoring her close, to the feel of his naked legs pressed against her, the rock-hard erection that was just as rock-hard as he looked.

April wasn't sure whether she'd had the wind knocked from her or if Rex's kiss was stealing her breath, but she was slammed from all sides by the strength of his passion, the intensity of his wanting and her own extraordinary need.

And the realization that once she left him she would never feel this way again.

"Make love with me, April," he whispered against her lips. "I want you."

She couldn't have denied him in that moment had her life depended on it. His hands had tightened their grip. His mouth ravaged hers with an intensity he'd never revealed before, almost as if he'd sensed their time together was limited.

In Rex's arms, nerves evaporated beneath desire, high energy focused on her need to touch him, alarm bells and shrieking sirens became surprised gasps and silken moans.

In Rex's arms, she felt *right*.

Before she could question her decision, before she could convince herself that work tonight should be priority, she surrendered to the part of her heart that wanted to leave him with fond memories and take away enough to sustain her through the loneliness she faced ahead.

"Yes."

She breathed the word on the edge of a sigh and he caught the sound with his lips, deepening his kiss with a fierceness that held nothing back, a desperate need that touched the desperation inside her.

A growl rumbled low in his throat and April tried to capture the sound in her memory, the utterly possessive demand of his mouth on hers. She wanted him with a power that melted her insides and made her ache to feel him all around her, inside her, hot, hard and thrusting deep.

When he broke their kiss to nip her lower lip, she dragged her fingers through his hair to anchor him close, each tender bite making her gasp softly against his mouth.

"The pillow," he said between tender bites.

She was so blasted with emotion and sensation that a moment passed before she could make sense of his request, to realize he wanted her to grab the Hidden Secrets Pillow for a condom.

Only when she said, "Oh," did he let his hands slip from

her hair, a motion of such obvious reluctance she knew that she must feel as right to him as he did to her.

Pulling herself up on the edge of the mattress, April forced her gaze to focus, spotted the pillow all the way across the bed. She wasn't about to try and stand so she just tugged at the top sheet until the pillow slid toward her.

Rex must have noticed how her hands trembled when she tried to pull open the zipper, must have realized that this moment had become about more than sex, more than nerves, because he sat up and said, "Here, let me."

His gentle tone caressed the raw edges inside her and she guessed he was trying to lighten the moment when he held up a red foil square and smiled. "Raspberry Romp? It's ribbed for extra pleasure."

While the name was cute, the thought of *that* erection in *that* color.... "No."

He struggled to get his hand inside the hidden compartment and finally held the pillow open to see what was inside. "This is a woman-size pillow. R and D needs to address this problem, too. We need to mention it to Wilhemina before she leaves." Dropping the pillow onto the floor, he displayed a gold foil square. "I'm wearing this one—the Goldstar, the condom of champions."

When she didn't reply, he arched that dark brow and looked mildly offended. "You don't agree?"

"Oh, no. Definitely the Goldstar." She swallowed back a laugh. "Do you wear it with or without *that?*"

He glanced down at the leather apparatus making his erection point away from his body like he'd been speared on the end of a sword. "Without, thank you."

Reaching for the snap, which lived up to its easy-release promotion by popping right open, he gave a grunt as his erection sprang free. After slipping the leather ring off, he rested his head back against the mattress and let his eyes close. "Ah, man."

The sound was such pure relief April almost felt guilty for asking him to wear the thing, especially when it hadn't done the trick. But she couldn't quite feel bad, not when he'd kissed her so possessively. Not when she gazed down at him, burnished hair ruffled over his forehead, sculpted lips parted ever so slightly around panting breaths, and knew a tenderness for this man that was unlike anything she'd ever known before.

The emotion was so rich it became a physical sensation that ballooned inside her chest, cutting off her air and forcing her to blink frantically against the sudden prickle of tears.

She lowered her head so her hair fell forward and covered her face, blinking hard as she reached for his top button. She wasn't sure when he opened his eyes, but when she pushed the shirt over his shoulders, she found him watching her, his expression as tender as this ache inside her, his need unabashedly open and honest.

Lifting his hand to caress her face, he slid his strong fingers around her cheek. "Love me, April."

Such a simple request, but one that revealed the strength of his need with such quiet pride that the tightness in her chest expanded into her throat, cutting off any hope of a reply. The tears stung her eyes again.

And he held her gaze, searching her face, staring into her soul.

She nodded.

Suddenly his hands slipped beneath her skirt, molded the curve of her bottom, up, up, to peel the hose from her waist. She rolled away so he could pull them down her legs, desperately grateful for the chance to school her reaction, to try and swallow back the knot in her throat that was choking her.

But Rex wouldn't let her hide. In barely a heartbeat, he was pulling her back into his arms and she faced that penetrating gaze that had never left her face, a gaze that saw everything.

Slipping his hand between them, he positioned the head of that steely erection against her moist skin, and April braced her hands on his shoulders, sank down on his heat, unfurling, stretching, filled with his hot length.

A series of fluttering breaths escaped her on that luscious downstroke, winning a smile from Rex, who ground up against her, just enough to make her gasp even louder....

His gaze melted as he watched her and his obvious pleasure sparked the fire deep inside her, so fierce she could only strain up to ride his hot length, to feed the needy flames before plunging back down again.

Only, this time his groan echoed in the quiet suite along with hers.

Her skirt had bunched around her waist, but he pulled the blouse free of the waistband, a frenzy of motions to drag her blouse and bra up and away. His impatience to free her satisfied some need inside that she hadn't even known needed satisfying and she could only laugh when he popped a button in his haste.

He drove into her hard in reply, the sleek strength of that stroke stealing the laughter right from her lips. Dragging the tangle of blouse and bra over her head, he freed her breasts, slipped his hands beneath them, caressing, lifting, even as he lowered his head toward her....

He pinched her nipples and there was something so erotic about his dark hands against her pale skin, about watching him pleasure her as she rode him, each squeeze stabbing straight to her sex, urging her to ride him a little harder, a little faster, a little deeper.

With every stroke her hips lifted, revealing the triangle of hair at the base of his erection. His hips rocked beneath her, meeting her thrusts, creating friction exactly where she needed it to mount a rising pressure that promised such ecstasy....

And his fingers and tongue and mouth still teased and nibbled and played, fueling the urgency...and her urgency fueled his until suddenly his hands left her breasts, skimmed down her ribs, over her hips.

His fingers dug into her bottom to increase her pace, kneading, stroking, slipping between her cleft to explore. He found that sensitive core of nerve endings and touched her with complete freedom, but applying a steady gentle pressure that mounted her pleasure as if he'd opened the spillway to a dam.

April closed her eyes and arched her back as orgasm rushed upon her, a wave of sensation so fierce that she cried out, a desperate sound that was half sob, half gasp.

He ground into her with a rumbling growl of his own climax and she collapsed against him, completely boneless and utterly spent as her body continued to contract, spasm after greedy spasm, never wanting this moment to end.

Rex held her possessively, so close that their racing hearts beat in time, their ragged breaths burst together, and April clung to him, tried to reclaim her wits, tried to tell herself that such an explosion of the senses was normal. That nothing more than unbelievable sex and her newly awakened ability to have orgasms were affecting her this way.

Minutes lengthened. Their breathing slowed. Their heartbeats steadied. The silence grew between them, yet Rex made no move whatsoever. He just held her as though reluctant to let reality intrude on this moment.

But April needed reality, a strong, sharp dose to knock some sense into her and chase away this bittersweet tenderness inside, this overwhelming sense of completion that spurred her emotions too close to the surface. She couldn't trust herself not to blink back these stupid tears that prickled at her lids, to swallow back the sadness for all the things that couldn't be.

"Did you get what you needed for tomorrow's studies?" she finally asked, far too near the edge to bear the silence any longer.

He grunted and cracked open an eye. "And then some. Maybe we should recommend this position to R and D. What do you think? We'll call it the Over-the-Edge Tumble."

Only Rex could make her feel right when she felt so wrong, could chase away sadness with laughter. She managed a weak smile. "I suppose, but once we hit the floor we were technically engaged in the Ladies' Tip-Top Thrill."

He frowned and she knew he wanted her to play the game.

"Okay," she said. "How about Hurl the Girl?"

"Hurl the Girl? More like Hurl the Guy."

"No. *You* fell and dragged *me* over the edge."

"No. You *knocked* me over the edge and I *fell* on the floor."

April couldn't believe they were sprawled out on the floor, debating the cold hard details of April Accidentally's unfortunate talents. But she wasn't cringing. She wasn't even blushing. And Rex hadn't wound up in the emergency room, either.

They were both satisfied.

A few weeks ago this simply wouldn't have been possible.

"All right," she conceded. "I confess. Your massage wasn't long enough tonight. *I* knocked *you* over."

There was no missing the triumph on his handsome face. "We're back to Over-the-Edge Tumble. I'll suggest it to Wilhemina when I tell her about the thread-count problem."

"What thread-count problem?"

"Those sheets are way too slippery. Didn't you notice how people slide right off and bust their butts?"

Only a true gentleman could turn that negative into a positive. "You're right."

"I keep telling you that." He pulled her back against him again, tucked her neatly into his hard curves and rested his chin on the top of her head in an upright version of the Shingle sleeping style. "And I've had another brainstorm. I'm heading home to Chicago for the weekend to celebrate Saint Patrick's Day with my family. I want you to come with me."

She wanted to believe that Rex extended his invitation simply because he knew she hadn't made any plans for the weekend. Or maybe he wanted to share his family. Some people equated adoption with loneliness and Rex was kind enough to feel bad about leaving her alone.

But she would have been lying. April knew Rex wanted to take her home for the weekend for the same reason he wanted to run with her every morning. He wanted to be with her.

"Sure. I'd like that."

Where Rex went, she went. That was the nature of the job.

"Good. We'll have fun. My family will like you."

He sounded so certain that she was struck by the enormity of his concern for her. In her mind, April Accidentally had been in prime form tonight, had been lucky she hadn't caused an accident that had wound up with a call to 9-1-1.

But to Rex, winding up on the floor had been an opportunity to make love, to create their own Kama position, to pinpoint a potential problem with the sheets.

April had told him the Shingle was the "regal" position, indicating a strong ego and sense of entitlement. While that was true, this position was also the most "protective" of them all.

And as she lay there, April could no longer deny that there was other no place on earth she'd rather be than lying in Rex's strong arms, feeling protected.

12

_____

"I'M NOT CONVINCED the results of that interview will be valid," Rex said as he keyed in his password to access his computer.

"Acquiescence bias?"

Glancing up, he found April hovering above his right shoulder. "Yes. That particular respondent agreed with everything I said and I couldn't seem to turn her around. I'll have to take another look at the results."

She only nodded and headed back toward her laptop.

Rex watched her go, a few short brisk steps that screamed edgy on the nervous meter. He suspected Wilhemina and Charles's arrival was to blame, because for a woman who'd just had a minimassage and been made love to thoroughly, she didn't appear to have carried away any afterglow from the experience.

He, on the other hand, was still feeling the effects of their stint with the Kama Sutra Sports Set big-time. He would much rather be wrapped around April than sitting in front of this desk facing two hundred and sixteen interviews.

His gaze trailed from the stack on the table back to April again, to the slim curves beneath her robe, the fine brown hairs that wisped around her shoulders. He could practically feel her curves beneath his hands, smell the delicate scent of her skin.

What was it about this woman that sidetracked him from work to think about everything he could be doing with her instead?

Rex didn't have an answer, but he intended to keep mulling the question until he found one. He hoped a weekend off duty with his family would give April a chance to relax. And give him a chance to figure out exactly what he wanted from her.

Sex? Definitely. More?

Wrapping up the Sensuous Collection project suddenly didn't look so good if it meant April heading back to California never to be seen or heard from again. It wasn't even looking so hot if he could see her whenever he visited L.A.

His sister Juliet, the oldest of his four siblings, had once told him that when he finally got *it*, he'd get it bad.

He had it bad for April.

The thought made him smile, and remember that today was the day Harold should have returned to his office. He was about to open his business e-mail program to see if he'd received a reply, but noticed the icon to the Luxurious Bedding Company network flashing. Double-clicking on the icon, he glanced at his in-box and knew by the sheer volume of the mail what had arrived.

To: Rex Holt (mailto:consultant@luxuriousbedding.com)
Date: 17 Mar 2003 04:38:22-0000
Subject: Personnel Training

Sexual role-playing sessions will train employees to work cooperatively in an innovative and stimulating environment!

Studies prove that sexual role-playing promotes teamwork by teaching employees to focus towards a common goal. Managers can assess their staff's ability to perform under pressure. The confidentiality clause of the P & P manual will protect all parties from personal repercussions.

"Damn." He highlighted all the posts and forwarded the lot to Wilhemina's e-mail address, chuckling at the image of her in an observation room playing a voyeur to assess her executive staff's ability to perform.

"What?" April asked.

"Another post from the stalker."

"Really?" She left her laptop and took up her place over his shoulder again.

He tilted his monitor upright and watched the play of emotions across her face. "You don't find it funny?"

"I suppose." A tiny frown had wedged itself between her brows. "It's just so strange. What kind of mind comes up with these types of ideas? What kind of person would terrorize a whole company with this stuff?"

He whistled. "That's the sixty-four-thousand-dollar question. Leah's the human resources manager and it's my understanding she has a background in psychotherapy. I know Wilhemina has been consulting with her a lot and if there was an easy answer, I'm sure they would have nabbed the culprit already."

"You're a people expert, Rex. What do you think?"

Though her expression never changed, she suddenly radiated an intensity Rex couldn't miss. His answer meant something, although for the life of him, he couldn't figure out what.

Leaning back in his chair, he folded his arms across his

chest. "A pervert might get a thrill from this sort of thing, sending the posts and watching the fallout."

"Do you think that's what's happening here?"

"No."

"You sound convinced."

He shrugged. "I've gotten my fair share of these e-mails. Pulling something like this for any length of time involves a good bit of computer expertise and even more risk. At the very least our stalker will lose his, or her, job. Perhaps even face prosecution. I don't see anyone doing this for a thrill. Whoever's sending these posts has some other reason."

She eyed him with a question in her eyes. "Really? Like what?"

"I don't have a clue. But when I think of all the files that forward from the various computers with each of these posts, cluttering up the network and peoples' in-boxes, I can't help but wonder if someone isn't trying to cover up something." He shifted his gaze to the computer monitor, thinking about all the work stored on his system. He rented Web storage and obsessively backed up his files just in case his system crashed. His data couldn't be easily replaced.

"Have you looked at any of those posts, Rex? I glanced at a few and there was all kinds of stuff. Memos to research and development. Production schedules. Inventory logs. Even someone's request to accounting to be paid for a personal day because he needed a day off from the Sensuous Collection."

"I looked at a few to begin with but now I just click Send. I don't have time."

Nodding, April returned to her laptop and slid it across the bar to work. "Wilhemina said this has been going on for weeks, but it must be really hush-hush because we hadn't heard a thing about it in my office. What do you think of the way she's handling the situation?''

That was a loaded question and Rex wasn't exactly sure what to say. On the one hand, he didn't mind sharing his opinion because he trusted April, but on the other, she did work for the company. Given her concerns about her job performance, he didn't want to raise doubts about the integrity of her upper management. He decided on honesty.

''I don't understand what the problem is. I'm no computer guru but it seems to me if someone is sending something over the network there should be a record somewhere. I realize it's impractical to monitor every transmission but impractical shouldn't mean impossible.''

He cleared his in-box then closed the e-mail program. ''This company isn't some mom-and-pop business without resources and Wilhemina doesn't strike me as having a lot of patience for mysteries. She's a sharp businesswoman.''

April tapped out a quick series of keystrokes. ''What do you think the problem is?''

''I get the impression that there's more to this situation than she's letting on. I could be wrong, but I just get that feeling.''

His answer seemed to content April and they fell back into silence again. Opening his business e-mail program, he scrolled through his in-box, prioritizing as he went. Bingo. There was a post from Harold. He opened it.

Good to hear from you, Rex. I'll be in the office late catching up from my trip. Give a call or log on to my private chat room and we'll talk about EHS.

He glanced over at April and decided a phone call was out of the question. Logging on to the Internet, he maneuvered to the research foundation's chat area, instead.

Harold was as good as his word. He responded instantly to Rex's greeting. His message popped up on the screen:

Have you gotten that Ph.D. in massage therapy yet?

Rex smiled, envisioning the debonair director, a man in his mid-sixties who walked between the worlds of research science and business with an understanding of both that Rex admired. Harold Snyder was most at home in his lab but he understood what it took to operate a large research foundation, to be at the whim of federal grants and private funding. He wore a business suit just as comfortably as a lab coat.

They exchanged pleasantries and then Rex got straight to the point.

I suspect my assistant is suffering from EHS. I've been researching online and not coming up with much information.

Glancing up at April to make sure she was occupied with her own work, he found her frowning down at her laptop screen, not paying attention to him at all. Good. He fixed his gaze on his monitor as Harold's reply appeared.

No surprise. There's not much information out there. This foundation is the leading source of research analysis on the topic and as you know, we're a private institution. Tell me more about her specific symptoms. Maybe I can help with a diagnosis.

Rex went on to describe the way sparks flew whenever April first touched bare skin, her unique working arrangement and her exhaustive energy level.

Harold replied by explaining the EHS basics.

Humans are dependent on the electrical and magnetic forces of nature. Electrostatic electricity is believed to be relatively harmless, but when it accumulates in a body, it can cause a wide range of reactions, from irritability, clumsiness, fatigue or mania in people whose systems overreact to this electricity.

We deal with the effects of electricity constantly. Think about electronic-equipment processing plants. Operators on assembly lines wear antistatic wrist straps. Computer techs ground themselves before working on systems. When you understand this, you won't find it so strange for that balance to be occasionally off in a human body. We haven't yet determined which field—the electric, magnetic or electrostatic—is most severe in producing adverse biological effects, but our observations so far lead me to believe that all three can have subtle, yet profound effects on an individual's health. Think of EHS as an allergy.

An allergy perhaps, but one that could be treated in a world that relied on electricity?

What can offset the symptoms?

To Rex's profound good fortune, Harold proved more knowledgeable on the subject than he'd had the right to hope.

The solution could be as simple as moving the sufferer away from the source of electricity—or to a comfortable distance as Harold suspected April had done with her computer system.

There were also detection devices available like gauss meters and electric field detectors to test for electromagnetic radiation that triggered symptoms in EHS sufferers.

Demand switches were another type of device that proved helpful at controlling symptoms. This switch could be installed at the meter board in a sufferer's home to control the supply of electricity to the various rooms.

Aligning the body's magnetic fields was another area currently being studied. Though this research was still in the early phases and Harold warned against crackpots out to make a buck by selling expensive mattresses and jewelry that may or may not have an effect, he believed there was merit in their findings so far.

We deal with a reputable firm that makes electrostatic devices for electrical circuitry manufacturers. I'll have my assistant forward the information to you. Get in touch with this guy and tell him I sent you. But the place to start is to ascertain your assistant's symptoms and how severely she's reacting. Bring her to the foundation the next time you're in Phoenix. We have the equipment to test her specific sensitivities. You'll be able to proceed from there.

Rex agreed and was already mentally calculating how he could rearrange their schedule to allow for a few extra days during their Phoenix run.

After thanking Harold and agreeing to take him up on his offer, Rex logged off the chat and sat back in his chair to absorb everything he'd just learned.

"April, what happens when you sit in front of your computer?" he asked.

She shot him an absent glance, jiggled the mouse impatiently. "I try not to."

"But when you do."

She shrugged. "I sort of melt into the chair. Within an hour my muscles ache and my head gets foggy and I can't think."

"Getting up and moving around doesn't help?" He already suspected the answer.

"Not enough to offset the effects once they start. If I stand, I don't have any problems. I feel great. So I stand."

Which confirmed Harold's suspicions about distance and

left Rex debating his best approach to convincing April to explore her unique symptoms.

And letting him be with her when she did.

To: J.P. Mooney (mailto:john@mooneyinvestigators.com)
Date: 18 Mar 2003 23:34:01-0000
Subject: Mission Accomplished

Dear Brother-in-law,
I've listened to Paula complain about you working seven days a week for so long that I'm just popping online on the chance that you'll be in for a few hours in the morning while I'll be sleeping late to recover from the effects of too many rich meals. Don't bother asking Paula to call and interrogate me because I'm unplugging the phone.

I just returned from Florida and I do wish you could have seen April. You would have been amazed and so proud. She works behind the scenes while Rex conducts his focus groups, researching on her computer—that crazy setup traveled with her!—and running interference with the local marketing researchers. She's *flying*, John! I don't know what else to say. She is more self-assured than I've ever seen her and handles herself so beautifully that I'm convinced we did the best thing by nudging her out of the nest.

I admit I was wrong about one thing, though. I told you that Rex would have her eating out of his hand but it appears to be the other way around. ;-) The man is completely enchanted by her. Even my marketing director who made the trip with me noticed how amazing these two are together.

That's the good news. Now for the not-so-good news. My security chief is still going through the motions and coming up with lots of possibilities and nothing concrete. I know you said an investigation of this size takes time, but I don't have much. April has given the board Rex's nighttime computer excursions and they've latched on to this like a dog with a bone.

They've used this time that I've been away to brainstorm and have called a meeting for the crack of dawn on Monday, where I'm sure they'll try to strong-arm me into bringing in another independent consultant. I intend to stall, but I don't know how much longer that particular tactic will work. The natives are getting restless but I have to admit that this two-day break from the madness was welcomed even if it did jeopardize my position.

This trip also enabled me to spend some quality time with my marketing director and pick his brain about what's going on between him and my network administrator. I wanted to know if their involvement predated my arrival or was a result of sex on the brain. Unfortunately, I'm still not sure, but Charles's attitude about Jacqui surprised me. He was very free with his opinions about all the executive staff, most of whom he respects—even my VP of sales, who by his own admission gets under his skin. He wasn't very complimentary about Jacqui, though. I even sensed a little hostility.

I know what you would say, John, with your suspicious mind, and I agree. Charles may very well be blowing smoke to throw me off the scent. I can't say for sure, but I did consider it, which proves that your private-eye skills are rubbing off on me.

Wil, who wants *all* your fingers crossed on Monday morning

John reached for his coffee mug with a smile, contemplating Wilhemina's latest update. Her private-eye skills? She wished. She was a sharp cookie but she had a long way to go before he'd hire her. To her credit though, she had nailed several things cold. Paula wasn't happy that he'd gotten up early this Saturday morning to come into the office and this wasn't the first time in thirty-five years that she'd voiced her opinion.

Too, he would have cautioned Wilhemina to look past her marketing director's obvious reaction to her questioning. She'd taken on a bizarre situation with this new company of hers and couldn't take anything for granted—which, according to her had been the whole point of taking the job.

And he was feeling much better about April. About work, anyway. He refused to speculate on what she and Holt might or might not be developing in *that* department. He refused to be sucked into agonizing about what she was doing with this guy. That was Paula's department. He hadn't crossed the line with his own daughters and in all the ways that counted, April was his daughter, too.

If Holt could get her to enjoy working out from behind the computer then John owed him one. It was that simple. He just wanted to see April happy.

He knew she'd be happy if he would allow her to start investigating and after reading this post, he was tempted. She was top-of-the-line on the computer and he didn't doubt that she could figure out exactly what was going on—both with Holt and the network stalker.

But according to this update, April was conducting herself very well in the field. She was proving herself very effective at inside surveillance and as far as John was concerned that was much more important than giving her a reason to get back behind the computer again. She needed to build her confidence and he didn't want to pile too much on her shoulders.

Wilhemina hadn't asked him to investigate anyway. She was giving her people a chance to deal with the situation and he understood why. As the new kid on the block, she had an opportunity to see what they were made of. She'd covered her ass by putting April in place and he knew his sister-in-law too well to think she'd miss the signs of a sinking ship.

He'd wait to see what happened at her meeting Monday morning. If things didn't go well, he'd reevaluate. But John didn't think he'd need to. Wilhemina didn't need April's help or his crossed fingers to bully that board into what she wanted.

13

APRIL'S FIRST CLUE that Saint Patrick's Day was a well-loved holiday in Chicago came while disembarking the plane. In the blink of an eye, the world transformed from the whitewashed, serviceable decor of an airplane interior to a lush landscape of green. And that was just at the gate.

"Wow. Is there some sort of mandatory dress code to be in this city today?"

Rex gazed down at her, the warmth in those deep dark eyes winning a tingly reaction no matter how hard she tried to control herself. "I can't believe you don't own anything green."

"It's a wretched color on me."

His smile deepened. "I find it hard to believe you'd look wretched in anything when you look so good in nothing."

"Rex!" she said, not believing the man would say that within earshot of an elderly couple.

She didn't have a chance to dwell on whether or not he'd been overheard because they no sooner stepped into the terminal when a small crowd rushed them and she didn't need introductions to recognize the Holt family. Rex was the spitting image of his father, sans the silver hair and bright blue eyes.

The group cornered them between the gate and the attendant's desk, greeting them noisily, introducing themselves and pressing in to hug Rex as if he was the president arriving for a national holiday.

April shook hands and smiled a lot, with a complete sense of unreality. Somehow seeing Rex's family—his dad, mom, sisters, brothers-in-law and nieces and nephews—made him seem more real than he'd been when she'd had him all to herself.

Until this very second, Rex had been the man who could coax miracle reactions from her body, the man who could make her forget her common sense and long for the impossible. He'd been almost too good to be true, a figment of her imagination. Until now when she saw how very real he was.

He had a whole family who loved him.

He introduced her to everyone and as all his sisters, with the exception of Betsy, were married, she had her hands full sorting out which husband belonged to which sister.

"So what warranted the welcome reception today?" he asked while greeting the cluster of small children who gathered around his knees to beg for lollipops.

Uncle Rex didn't disappoint. He produced a handful of the treats from his briefcase, the cheek-filling kind with bubble gum in the middle, and earned squeals of appreciation from the little ones and scowls from his sisters.

"No, you may not open that now, Carson," Theresa, his second-to-youngest sister, told her son.

Juliet held the distinction of being the oldest sister and scowled as if she'd had a lot of practice. "I'm sending your nephews in the car with you, Uncle Rex."

He just laughed.

"Of course we'd come welcome your plane," his mom said. "You brought home a friend."

Gina Holt was a beautiful woman whose youthful olive skin made her appear more like a sister to her daughters than a mother. She clearly adored her only son and held him at arm's length to check him out before she hugged him. "I'm so glad you made it home for the holiday."

"And with a *woman* friend," Betsy said.

Gina shot her youngest a dark glance then hugged April as if she'd been missed as much as Rex.

"You're lucky your grandparents didn't show up." His father laughed. "They'd be here if Grandpa didn't insist on hearing the Rovers practice this morning, trust me."

His dad was what April had always thought of as dark Irish, tall, black-haired—though there was now more silver than black—fair-skinned with bright blue eyes that twinkled.

It was no mystery where Rex had gotten his charm. Shawn Holt laughed loudly, interacted with his wife and daughters easily and seemed genuinely pleased to see his son. Very different from the way John interacted with his girls, although something about that king in the middle of his all-female court held distinct similarities. Not to mention explaining Rex's own rather regal sense of entitlement.

"Have you ever been to the Saint Patrick's Day parade before, April?" Deirdre, the tallest of the sisters, wanted to know.

"Have you ever even been to Chicago before?" Juliet asked. "We want to know all about you, so come with us."

Rex retrieved her carry-on bag and arrangements were made for the brothers-in-law to drive the cars around to baggage claim. Giving her a smile of reassurance, he disappeared with his parents to retrieve their luggage and April found herself herded toward the bathroom to tend Juliet's infant's diaper.

The sisters were a hoot, so much like John and Paula's girls that she felt at ease as they interrogated her, conversing between the stalls, the sinks and the diaper-changing area as casually as if they were in the privacy of their homes.

"So who are you, April?" Juliet asked. "We want the scoop on why Rex has brought you home. Are you dating?"

"I'm his assistant on his current project," she replied, unwilling to get into the details of their relationship. She had no idea what Rex had told his family and since maintaining family relations didn't comprise a great deal of her past experience, she hadn't thought to ask.

"Would you hand me that?" Juliet pointed to the bag on the floor and April did, smiling as Juliet hung on to her squirming baby, fished out a diaper and ointment while managing to keep her curious gaze on April. "You're just his assistant?"

Deirdre emerged from the sink area, drying her hands on a paper towel. "Betsy wasn't kidding. Rex has never brought home a friend for Saint Patrick's Day."

"It's our biggest family holiday, if you can imagine," Juliet said.

"Rex told me."

"Well…" Deirdre prompted.

What to say…what to say? She and Rex weren't dating; they were sleeping together. She had no idea what he would have told his family. She saw no choice but to keep her explanation light. "I hadn't made any plans to head home for the weekend and he felt bad about leaving me behind at the hotel alone."

"Your family doesn't celebrate Saint Patrick's Day?"

She just shook her head, not wanting to get into interpretations about what constituted family. She celebrated most holidays with the Mooneys. For all that John Patrick Mooney was Irish, Saint Patrick's Day wasn't one of said holidays.

Juliet handed off her son's diaper to his Auntie Deirdre for disposal. "Where's home?"

"Los Angeles." An outright lie.

"How long ago did you and Rex meet?" Theresa called from the sink area, where she was helping her preschool aged daughter wash her hands.

"Just a few weeks ago when I was assigned to the project he's currently working on."

"The sheet project?" Juliet asked, illustrating that while Rex may work on the road, he remained in touch with his family enough for them to know the particulars of his business life.

She nodded, interested.

"So you and Rex spend your days doing what...talking about what to do on sheets?" Betsy appeared, tossing a paper towel into the trash and retrieving several more for her young niece, who emerged from the sink area with Theresa.

"In a manner of speaking. We're collecting data for the launch of a new product line," she coached, hoping to continue the conversation. Here was an opportunity to find out what Rex had said to his family about the Sensuous Collection.

"Oh, we know all about this product line," Deirdre said, returning the diaper ointment to Juliet's bag.

"Made for a rather entertaining conversation over Sunday dinner when he first contracted the project," Juliet added.

"I can imagine. It's rather unique. What did he tell you?"

By the time they caught back up with Rex and his parents at baggage claim, April had learned that Rex hadn't shared anything pertinent about the Sensuous Collection launch other than the details of the line itself, which had apparently entertained the Holts from appetizers through dessert.

Pleased with what she'd learned, April imagined the sisters were equally pleased. They were relentless in maneuvering her into neat little corners so she had no choice but

to answer their questions or look like she had something
to hide.

Family inevitably came up.

"Adopted? Wow!"

"But your parents died? That's so sad."

*"How wonderful that you became part of your boss's
family. They sound great."*

The sisters had been no less determined in the pursuit of
information than their older brother demonstrated on a daily
basis with his finely honed information-gathering skills.
April decided this talent must be a Holt family trait. But
when she saw Rex, standing out in the crowd with his striking good looks and charming smile, she couldn't help but
think that information-gathering wasn't his only gift.

He looked relaxed in a way she'd never seen him before.
The man was in his element, unguarded almost, a distinct
difference from that almost-regal, always-on-edge person he
projected to conduct business.

This Rex was a son, a brother, a man about the business
of enjoying himself with the people he cared about. There
was an intimacy about the way he interacted with his family,
absently taking his mom's elbow to guide her through the
door to where his dad waited with the car, holding his infant
nephew while Juliet strapped her older son into his car seat.

She watched him curiously, glimpsing a man who might
be so focused on work that he didn't make much time to
have a life, but one who knew how to enjoy himself when
he did. And now that he realized he wanted to kick back
and make more time to have fun, he'd need a woman to
enjoy that time with. And when he found the right woman,
he'd probably want to raise a family as wonderful as his
seemed to be.

Fortunately April was distracted from her thoughts before
she got to really angsting about all the reasons she could

never be that woman. Rex directed her to his parents' car and she settled in beside him for a grand tour of Chicago. From city history and trivia to landmarks like Rex's elementary school and the ball field where he'd played Little League, she glimpsed a view of his early life until their day of celebrating kicked off at nine o'clock mass at Old Saint Pat's Church.

They met up with his grandparents to attend the service and afterward made their way to the riverbank of the Chicago River for a bird's-eye view of the river's transformation into an Irish-green phenomenon, and a performance by the Shannon Rovers Irish Pipe Band.

Rex's grandfather was a retired band member, an elderly man who'd passed along his charm to his son and grandson. With his twinkling blue eyes and dashing smiles, Scully Holt clearly still reigned as the patriarch of the Holt family. His wife Anna smiled good-naturedly at her husband's loud welcomes and hugged all her great-grandchildren warmly.

"So you're Rex's young lady?" Scully asked her.

April caught sight of Betsy elbowing Rex from the corner of her eye, but Rex didn't pay any attention, his gaze was fixed on April as he said, "Yes she is, Grandpa."

Well, there, that answered the question about what Rex had told his family.

"And you've never been to Chicago before, young lady?"

"No, sir."

"Are you Irish?"

"I am today," she offered, hoping to sidestep the particulars of her upbringing. The sisters had already picked her brain enough for one day.

No such luck.

"Grandpa, April was adopted, so she might be just as Irish as you are," Betsy said.

Clearly Betsy thought this tidbit was something special so April forced a smile and stepped into the suddenly awkward silence to deflect the inevitable questions. "I can choose to be whatever I want. And today, I choose to be Irish. Seems like a good day for it, don't you think, sir?"

Scully pierced April with a searching gaze and she knew those sharp blue eyes were assessing her character. Rex took a step closer. A reassurance, April supposed. But amazingly, the alarm wasn't shrieking in her head and she didn't have to assume the stance to stand still. In fact, she didn't feel nervous at all beneath Scully Holt's gaze and when his wizened old face split into a grin, April felt as if she'd made the cut.

It was a very good feeling.

"It's not only a good day to be Irish, little lady. It's the *best* day." He shot his grandson a sharp look and gave a snort of what she assumed was laughter.

Without another word, he linked arms with her and his wife and escorted them both toward the riverbank where they could get the best view of the band on the south bank. April sensed Rex staring after them with a smile.

By the time Rex had maneuvered his way to her side again the crowd was cheering so loudly in anticipation of preparing the Chicago River for the holiday that she had to raise her voice to be heard. "I thought you said this river was going to turn green. That's orange."

Rex leaned close, his head bowed over hers, but never taking his eyes off the river, which grew more orange by the second. "Just wait."

And then it happened. Orange transformed to a bright Irish green before her very eyes. "Wow."

"There you go. A Saint Patrick's Day miracle."

"All right. I'll bite. How do they do that?"

"Leprechauns," Scully replied before Rex had the chance. "Homesick for the greens of Ireland."

April could almost believe him. With the bagpipes playing and the whole world looking as though the sky had opened up and rained green, she felt a definite magic in the air.

Or maybe the magic had to do with the company of the man wedged against her, his hand casually wrapped around her waist, so that even through her coat, her skin tingled with his touch.

His father said something that April couldn't hear, but Rex laughed, the chiseled lines of his face softening, the dark eyes he'd inherited from his mom sparkling with amusement.

That look made her sigh inside, made her imagine what it would be like to have her own family. A family a lot like this one, she decided, one that liked to have fun.

But longing wouldn't change her situation or the fact that she only had these precious moments with Rex. She needed to savor his smiles, savor her temporary place in his life, savor this unfamiliar feeling of contentment. She only had *now*—this man and his smile, his family and a leprechaun's miracle.

And she was determined to make the most of her time and every time her thoughts strayed, she only had to glance at the river—which only stayed green for four or five hours, another fleeting miracle—to be reminded to enjoy the moment.

Fortunately the Holts made enjoying the moment easy. They hurried her away from the river to find a spot along the parade route, where the kids took turns sitting up on the adult's shoulders for a bird's-eye view of the floats. Even Uncle Rex lent his shoulders to the cause, much to the delight of his nieces and nephews who shrieked and waved at two fifteen-foot high shamrocks and a thirty-five-foot high leprechaun.

After the parade, they congregated at the Irish club to enjoy corned beef and cabbage, *boxty* with applesauce and mugs of green beer. April, who hadn't worn anything green, found herself the recipient of a bowler hat, a half-dozen shamrocks, or *seamógs,* in assorted sizes, including one that had been painted on her face by a children's artist, after the nieces and nephews insisted Uncle Rex buy one for Miss April, too.

This ethnic celebration could have taught an Irishman like John Patrick Mooney a thing or two about celebrating. She liked the Holt family's pride in their heritage, something a person unfamiliar with her own history had no experience with. Every one of the Holts proved very generous at sharing their pride, though, and April couldn't remember the last time she'd felt so comfortable with anyone except for the Mooneys.

She liked to think that Rex's massages were doing the trick, after all, but found it more likely that the Holts were just easy to be around. Even Rex. Comfortable with his family in a way she'd never seen him before, he stuck close, always aware of her needs or to answer her questions, yet never overbearing. He treated her as if he expected her to have as much fun with his family as he was. And she did.

She liked this side of him, enjoyed the camaraderie he shared with his family. On the road he'd been focused on work, and she was reminded of his admission that work typically superceded everything in his life, how he'd been accused of not making time to have fun.

She suspected part of the trouble was the nature of the work itself. Being out on the road was an isolated business. She didn't really travel often and was definitely no social butterfly, but even she had her handful of friends that she interacted with at work or with the Mooneys.

Rex claimed to have friends, but they'd been together around the clock for the better part of two weeks and she hadn't seen one.

The lone ranger.

Who'd said that? Charles Blackstone had, and he'd been right. Rex was the lone ranger and she'd never noticed how much until she'd seen him surrounded by the people he loved.

But he'd identified the problem and now all he needed was a woman in his life to give him a reason to slow down and make more time to enjoy himself. Preferably a woman who could share his work so he wouldn't be alone in hotels for those long stretches. And definitely a woman who didn't mind that high-handed attitude he got while he was ordering everyone around.

A woman a lot like her.

Minus all the baggage.

When the afternoon waned and the children began passing out from exhaustion, April's hosts headed back to the house Rex had been raised in, a neatly kept home in a quiet residential neighborhood. The sisters all headed back to the bedrooms to settle the little ones.

April offered to help Gina out of the kitchen and Rex insisted he needed to supervise the preparation of the Tipsy Cake, which was a very sweet, very alcoholic Irish treat that his Italian mom needed help with.

"Don't be ridiculous, Rex," Gina said with a scowl. "Everything is already made. All I have to do is whip cream and brew coffee and I think I can handle that. Go wait for Grandma and Grandpa and keep them in there with you or else I'll be tripping over them, too. This house is too small. I'm telling your father I want to move."

"You do that, Mom." Rex kissed the top of her head and escorted April from the room. "She has been saying that since Deirdre was born."

"Hasn't found anything yet?"

Rex shook his head. "I don't think she's ever looked."

He motioned to the couch and sat down beside her. She wanted to melt back against him, but positioned herself on the edge suddenly awkward as they were alone for the first time since their arrival.

"It must have been fun growing up with your family." She took a stab at polite conversation.

"They're a crew. That's for sure. Noisy," he added as Juliet's oldest son cruised down the hallway, yelling after his cousin at the top of his lungs.

April laughed. "The size of the house wouldn't make any difference. John's house is just as noisy on the holidays."

"Do you spend them with his family?"

She nodded, struck at how little Rex knew about her in some regards, when in others he knew more than any man had ever known. Where to kiss her to make her shiver, or sigh, or climax.

Yet he'd missed a few important basics like the real reason she'd become his assistant. He'd welcomed her into his home, introduced her to his wonderful family, while she'd crossed the line by becoming his lover while she was spying on him.

"So John has a big home." Rex leaned back into the corner of the leather couch, hooked his hands behind his head and got comfortable. "Tell me about him."

"He reminds me of your dad with all these women around."

"It's always been interesting."

"I'll bet."

When she stifled a yawn, he asked, "Tired?"

"We got an early start."

Rex had intended to fly out of Tampa after a late dinner with Wilhemina and Charles last night. When he couldn't arrange her a seat on his flight, he'd rearranged his plans to get them both out of Tampa at 4:00 a.m. the following morning, which meant arriving at the airport at two.

"Turn around and come here." He slipped his hands over her shoulders, tried to pull her back against him.

"Not here, Rex. Anyone could walk in."

"Trust me. They take numbers around here for one of my massages. Even the kids. They're all just being polite because you're here and my mother threatened them."

"Why did she threaten them?"

"Because she likes that I brought you home to visit and she wants everyone to behave so they don't scare you off. Come sit here, so she knows I'm doing my bit to make you feel welcome. She says I have magic hands. Let me use them on you."

Magic hands. April had made the very same observation herself. And she wouldn't deny him. She needed his hands on her, so she wouldn't be able to think. He'd distract her from thinking about how his family wanted to make her feel welcome, about how much she wanted them to like her.

His magic hands chased away all her thoughts. That slow, steady motion worked the tension from her muscles, made that now familiar languidness creep into the edges of her brain. Her breathing slowed. Her body melted against his.

But his magic hands worked only too well. April couldn't think, but she could feel. And as she sat in Rex's childhood home, surrounded by his family, she felt like she belonged.

FOR A MOMENT Rex couldn't figure out how he'd gone from giving April a massage to being jarred awake by his grandfather's comment about how nice it must be to sleep whenever and wherever the mood struck.

He opened his eyes to find April stirring against him, her face against his shoulder, her arm tossed casually across his middle and three generations of Holts and sundry in-laws crammed into the living room watching them.

He knew the exact second April awoke, because her entire body tensed. Only, Rex had learned an important lesson. This time when she bolted upright, he neatly dodged her head, saving them both the pain and embarrassment of a public collision.

"Time for dessert?" she asked, husky-voiced from sleep.

Rex noticed a number of smiles, but his mother simply said, "Yes it is, dear. I hope you're hungry."

She took April's arm and led her through the crowd, shooting a scowl at Betsy, who'd opened her mouth, presumably to make some remark about them falling asleep together. Betsy returned the scowl but kept her mouth closed.

Another Saint Patrick's Day miracle.

Rex watched his family escort April into the dining room, feeling no particular rush to follow. She'd been holding her own all day, seemed more calm and comfortable than he'd hoped. He was a good influence on her, Rex decided.

And April was a good influence on him.

They each brought something to the table and as far as Rex was concerned that's exactly how a relationship should work. He hadn't found this with any woman he'd dated before. Admittedly, he hadn't spent much time looking, but he'd dated his fair share of women and he recognized it when he found it.

He'd found it with April.

When he finally made his way into the dining room, Rex saw that April had been placed in the seat of honor by his dad. He was struck by the sound of her laughter, the way her incredible eyes sparkled and her beautiful smile lit up the room.

"Grandpa likes her, Rex." Juliet appeared beneath the kitchen archway and pressed a mug into his hands.

This was no small accomplishment and he took a swig of coffee, contemplated his dad and grandfather who were talking over each other with their separate versions of the Saint Patrick's Day celebration the year Juliet had been queen of the parade. A celebration that had seen three hundred people crammed onto their property, along with the Shannon Rovers, a troupe of Irish dancers and the mayor.

His mother and grandmother rolled their eyes good-naturedly but his sisters tried to interject reality into the tale.

"Dad, you couldn't get three hundred people in this house if you had a crane lift off the roof," Deirdre scoffed.

"The mayor spent most of his time in the kitchen with Mom and Grandma, sneaking spoonfuls of *brim brack*," Theresa added.

Through it all, April laughed, so beautiful he was content to stand there and watch her. His entire family, from his grandparents to Betsy, had welcomed her in their own way and she'd gotten past her nerves to respond with the warm charm that was hers alone, a charm that made it impossible not to like her.

"I like her, too," Juliet said, before going to sit on her husband's lap to join the fun.

As he watched her go, April lifted her gaze to his, a dazzling look that reflected her good mood and singled him out as if he was the only person in the room.

They might not have discussed their feelings, or their relationship or what the future might hold, but the tender look in her eyes told him everything he needed to know.

And Rex knew exactly what he wanted from April—a future of celebrations where she sat at that table by his side.

14

To: April Stevens (mailto:april@mooneyinvestigators.com)
Date: 21 Mar 2003 10:02:54-0000
Subject: Well-Earned Praise

Brava, April!

A job very well done! I just posted John to sing your praises and wanted to jot you a quick note of thanks. You provided me with enough documentation about Rex's activities so I was armed to take on the board at our meeting this morning.

They latched on to his unaccounted online activities as a cause for concern but I was able to counter with the surplus of proof you've provided that he's conducting business on the up-and-up. Bottom line is they don't have enough evidence to get a warrant to access his business files so they were just trying to bully me into submission. Thanks to you, I was able to sidestep this latest obstacle and buy both Rex and me some more time to do our jobs.

You're a dear and I appreciate all your help! And it was so very lovely to see you outside of Paula and John's house. I'd like to make the effort to do this again once the dust settles after the launch. What do you say?

Auntie Wil

What did she say? April said this was plain stupid. Sure, she'd provided enough documentation about Rex to arm

Wilhemina against the latest reports—reports she'd also provided that happened to throw suspicion on Rex's credibility.

April said this situation sucked, plain and simple.

She'd just spent two of the most glorious days as a guest in the Holts' home, squeezing incredible orgasms into a very tight schedule of family events and pretending that she actually *belonged*. Now they were back on the road—Denver this week—and reality was crashing down around her ears again.

Wilhemina had only meant to thank her but how was April supposed to feel good about compromising Rex's credibility? She'd known questions would arise when she'd sent the first report, of course, but it felt even more horrible now that she'd gotten emotionally involved with not only this man, but his family.

Thou shalt not become emotionally involved with thy client.

She should have listened. Could she have listened?

No. Traveling the straight and narrow—had she been able to—would certainly have been the easiest road to take. But even now, knowing she'd leave after their fling, knowing her work had lost all credibility because of her choice, April couldn't regret what she'd shared with this man.

The only thing she could have done was to have refused this assignment. But she hadn't, which meant another hard truth to face—John and Paula were right, she'd been hiding from life, avoiding the types of situations that required her to get out and face situations that might require her to stand up and say, "No."

Then again, if she'd stuck to her guns she would've never met Rex, would have never known orgasms, would have never glimpsed exactly what she'd want her happily ever after to be if she were anyone but April Accidentally.

And now here they were, back together 24/7, without the benefit of that delightful family to sidetrack her from the fundamental truth that she'd gotten involved with this man when she shouldn't have.

She'd come to him to do a job and the kicker was that she was actually doing it more competently than she'd ever dreamed possible. Instead of feeling good that she was managing the job without screwing up, she felt like she was screwing up her whole life and any possibility of a happy future with this man.

Not that there was much of a possibility for *that*. Rex hadn't said he was interested in anything more than a good time.

But she could dream about all the things she'd sworn out of her life forever—orgasms, a man to love, her very own family and a happily-ever-after. With Rex.

Just as long as she didn't forget that she would be leaving after their fling.

A knock on the door jolted April from her thoughts.

"Are you expecting anyone?" she asked Rex, who was still in the process of setting up his peripherals.

He peered around a table leg. "No. Grab it, will you?"

April nodded, already heading toward the door to find a young, spiffily uniformed hotel clerk with a package.

"For Mr. Holt," he said.

She accepted the brown box, tipped the clerk and walked back into the dining area. "A package arrived for you."

"From StaticSaver Industries?"

She glanced at the return address. "Mmm-hmm. Something you're expecting?"

To her surprise, Rex shimmied out from under the table, a vision of firm butt and sculpted thighs that his dress slacks molded to muscular perfection. "About damn time."

"Here you go." She handed him the package, curious. "What is it?"

"A surprise. Come sit with me while I open it."

Without waiting for a reply, he led her into the sitting room and pulled her down on the sofa with him. He sliced through the packaging tape with a Swiss Army knife and scattered foam peanuts all over the sofa and the floor. Grabbing the box, she held it steady before it tumbled off his lap and they had an even bigger mess.

"Rex, what is it?" she asked again.

He didn't answer. He was too busy fishing out the contents and tearing off the plastic to inspect…

"What are those?" They didn't look like any kind of wristwatch she'd ever seen, and why on earth would he need two?

"Perfect."

"They are?"

"Yes." He lifted his gaze at her, seeming awfully excited for a reason she hadn't figured out yet. "They're StaticSaver wrist straps. Not half-bad-looking, either. What do you think?"

"Are you planning on taking up computer repair so you need to be grounded?"

"No. I ordered them for you."

"If you're planning on having me work inside your machine, I'd seriously rethink that. I'm not very good at—"

"No, April." He slid off the sofa and sank to his knees in front of her, an unexpected motion that made her stare as he dropped one of the wristbands into her lap and proceeded to grab her arm. "I don't want you to work on my computer. I want you to wear these and see if they make any difference in how you feel."

She stared down at him, at the wristwatch-looking band

he was fastening on her, not understanding what he wanted and not quite sure what she'd missed.

"How do you think they'll make me feel?" she asked.

"Calmer."

"Really?"

"Really."

Sitting back on his haunches, he met her gaze, the warmth in those dark eyes seeming wildly out of sync with the moment, with the funky-looking gifts that so obviously pleased him. But the caring in his expression touched the raw edges of her heart, and she found herself holding her breath, waiting expectantly.

"I mentioned the project I conducted that got me interested in massage, remember?"

She nodded.

"That research foundation studies all sorts of stuff. I acquired data about massage as treatment for various ailments so the foundation could meet the requirements of a federal grant. One of the other areas of interest they study is Electro Hypersensitivity. I didn't know much about it but what I did know got me to thinking that you might have it."

April could only stare, so surprised she wasn't sure what to think, let alone what to say. "I don't understand."

"Did you notice how sparks fly every time we touch?"

His grin might have lightened the moment had her brain not been racing, attempting to comprehend the implications of what he was saying.

"I didn't put it together right away," he went on. "You shocked me that first night in Atlanta when you handed me your computer cable and I remembered that the same thing had happened when we'd been introduced at corporate headquarters. I figured you were one of those 'electric people.' You know, the ones who can't wear watches. I've been having our hotels provide antistatic mats to offset the effects around the equipment and it seems to work. You were on the mat the first time I tried to kiss you and we touched without a shock. And we seem to do okay if you touch me through my clothes first.''

She must have looked stunned, because he smiled. Grabbing the remaining wristband, he fastened it around her wrist, telling her all about the scientist who ran the research foundation and how they'd discussed her symptoms and believed it possible that she suffered from this EHS.

She wasn't absorbing a tenth of what he was saying because she was still stuck on the fact that he'd been researching this ailment, which likely explained why he'd been sneaking out of bed at night to use his computer.

To help her.

''You told me you were high-strung but that may just be a symptom,'' he said. ''Harold invited us to the foundation so you can be tested. We'll find out either way. If you do have EHS, there are devices to help minimize the effects, like these wristbands. What do you say? We can work it in while we're in Phoenix.''

What did she say? She couldn't say a thing. She didn't even know what to think. His every word was playing through her head in slow motion as she tried to comprehend that this condition might explain her nerves and her accidents.

''I suppose that explains why my family blew through vacuum cleaners while I was growing up,'' she finally said, shooting for casual and failing miserably. ''My parents had the house rewired. Would have been a lot cheaper to give me another chore. I hated vacuuming anyway.''

Her laugh sounded more like a sob. She couldn't get past the fact that Rex had cared enough to research her symptoms, to formulate a game plan and buy her antistatic wristbands.

No man would do this without caring, and not a little.

But Rex couldn't care for her because she was leaving when her job was done, she was slipping out of his life and leaving him with fond memories and a smile and no knowledge of why she'd really come. She was slipping away right now before she dissolved into a puddle before his eyes.

Rex wouldn't let her get away. Sliding his hands up her thighs, he held her down when she tried to scoot from under him.

"What's wrong?" Those dark eyes searched her face, the concern she saw there so much more than a man who wanted a good time. "I thought this would be a good thing."

"It is."

"Then why do you look like you're about to cry?" Rex recognized tears when he saw them and he was more than a little surprised by her reaction.

She tilted her head so her hair fell forward to hide her face. "It's just…you've been so…thoughtful."

Obviously thoughtful wasn't a good thing.

"No big deal, really. Ordered online. They weren't that expensive. Will you come to the foundation to be tested?"

She nodded, but even though she avoided his gaze, he couldn't miss the two fat tears that rolled down her cheeks.

"April, what is—"

"Thank you." She pressed a kiss to the top of his head then pulled away and shot to her feet so fast she knocked him off balance.

Rex fell backward and watched in amazement as she disappeared into the bedroom.

Okay. Apparently he'd touched a nerve. Unfortunately, he wasn't a mind reader and there was a lot more going on here than he understood. What bothered her about his buying her wristbands? He hadn't actually thought of what he'd done as thoughtful. Practical, maybe. He'd had a suspicion so he'd followed up on it. What about that bothered April?

He didn't have a clue so he followed her into the bedroom, found her leaving the bathroom.

She gave him a watery smile. "I'm sorry. I'm okay. Just getting hormonal."

Hormonal?

True, they'd been together around the clock for weeks so hormonal had been bound to happen eventually. But her explanation came at him sideways. His sisters usually went into attack mode if anyone even hinted at PMS as the cause of anything other than the source of their superhero femininity.

Despite April's reassurance, Rex would have bet money that that there was a lot more than hormonal going on. She looked pale and worried and he had the almost overwhelming urge to wrap his arms around her and tell her everything would be all right.

Unfortunately, he couldn't do that. Not only was he uncertain what was really bothering her, but she'd retreated, emotionally and physically, and was hitting the double digits on the nervous meter if the way she mutilated that tissue was any indication.

"Massage time."

"Thank you, but I couldn't possibly tonight. You've given me a lot to think about. I was hoping to get online and do a little research."

Again, Rex was struck by the impression that there was a lot more going on here. "I've already researched online and trust me there's not much there. I'll send Harold a post, though, to ask if he wouldn't mind you surfing the foundation's site. But I do think we need to talk about what's happening between us, and you'll be more comfortable if you're relaxed."

"What's there to talk about, Rex?" she asked. "We're great. We don't need to talk. We need to work."

He frowned. That was panic in those beautiful eyes.

She forced an unconvincing smile. "We've got to go over tomorrow's schedule for the Rodeo Collection. Come on. I want to try out my new wristbands."

She swept past without glancing up, but then she didn't have to. The trail of mutilated tissue pieces she left in her wake told him everything he needed to know.

April was comfortably ensconced in front of her laptop by the time he'd left the bedroom, puzzling through his next move.

Buying her lame explanation didn't even make the list.

He glanced from her to the pullout sofa in the sitting room, presently displaying the sheet set of the week—the Rodeo Collection.

Rope 'Em and Ride 'Em With Supple Leather Sheets Made From Doeskin, Calfskin and Suede.

Rex went straight for the storage pockets.

Though April presented a casual, I'm-just-working demeanor, she was clearly still on hyperalert, because he hadn't gotten within five feet of her before she knew he was there.

Turning around, she must have recognized that trouble was on its way because her eyes widened just as he covered the last few feet between them, slipped his arms around her and swung her up into his arms.

"Rex!" She clutched at his neck to steady herself, but he didn't reply as he sidestepped the love seat and deposited her unceremoniously in the middle of the pullout bed.

She bounced once, all sleek curves and panty-hose-clad legs, before attempting to roll off the other side.

But Rex had anticipated that move and was ready. He launched himself on top of her and pinned her down. "You can lie here and subject yourself to a massage of your own free will or I'll make you. Your choice."

He reached beneath a pillow and dragged out the leather apparatus underneath.

Fit to be Tied Restraints.

"It's my turn to play with the toys," he said. "I insist we talk and I want you to be comfortable."

She bucked wildly and he dodged the top her head, which almost caught him in the chin.

"Comfortable? You absolutely may not restrain me."

"I wore your cock ring without a debate, sunshine, so buck up and deal with it. I want to know what the problem is."

"Rex!" She showed no signs of yielding.

"Restraint it is, then."

April put up a good fight, but Rex had seven inches and a hundred pounds on her. She never stood a chance. He slapped those restraints right on top of the wristbands and secured her arms to the bed frame. As she was lying face-down, he didn't bother with her legs, just sat on top of her and began to massage her back.

Her muscles were as tight as his fishing line the last time he'd hooked a marlin. "I won't let you up until you talk to me. What's bothering you?"

"Nothing."

He not only had the advantage of size but he had the advantage of patience, too. He wasn't the one with a problem sitting still. Waiting her out wouldn't be tough. So he focused his attention on kneading the tension from her muscles, on freeing her blouse from the waistband of her skirt so he could slip his hands beneath and add the warmth of his skin to his efforts.

Soon her muscles grew more pliable beneath his touch,

her rapid breathing slowed. He took another stab at conversation.

"So what is it about me being thoughtful that bothers you?"

"I thought we were just having sex." Her hair and the mattress muffled her voice but the panicked edge was gone, confirming that his massage was taking effect.

The key word here was *sex* so Rex pursued that line of questioning. "Is sex all you want from me?"

She nodded, landing a punch to his solar plexus without ever lifting a fist. "We agreed to explore our chemistry but you're not playing by the rules."

"What rules?"

"The fling rules."

Okay. Now they were getting somewhere. "How have I broken the rules?"

"You invited me home to meet your family, and now you've given me a present."

"April, I wanted to explore our attraction to each other and see where it led. I didn't know where we would end up. I just knew I'd never wanted a woman as much as I wanted you. The way I *want* you."

His admission filtered off in the quiet, empowered by being spoken aloud. He had to force the next words out. "If you don't feel the same way then we'll deal with it, but I want to know."

Raising her head from the mattress, she blew the hairs from her eyes with an exasperated breath and finally stopped hiding. "I wouldn't trade a minute of the time we've spent together."

"I hear a *but*."

"But you said you just wanted seduction."

Though she'd raised her head to look at him, the restraints held her from fully turning, so he could only see half her face. What he saw in that half made his teeth clench in frustration.

The panic was back.

Rex probably should have cut his losses and shut his mouth, but he needed to understand. ''I did want seduction. But now I want more.''

''I can't.''

''Why?''

''I don't do the relationship thing.''

''You also told me that you didn't do the sex thing, but you do it very well. We have something special.''

''No, Rex. No.'' She tugged at the restraints. ''I don't want to have this conversation. Let's just enjoy our fling.''

He slipped his hands down her ribs to her waist, needing touch to anchor him. ''You don't want to talk about how I feel about you. You don't want to talk about where our relationship can go. What do you want to talk about?''

''I don't want to talk.''

''You just want sex.''

She didn't answer, which told him she wanted something more than sex but wasn't willing to tell him what. And knowing that didn't dull the raw edge from the way he felt.

Sliding his hands beneath her blouse, he stroked her skin, needing to feel her warm and real and responding. Was it possible that he'd read her wrong and she didn't feel as strongly about him as he did for her?

On a gut-deep level, Rex knew he wasn't wrong.

''What's your problem with relationships?'' he asked. ''Does this have something to do with the accidents you had?''

''I swore off sex, and relationships. I can't handle it.''

''I understand, April, but we're way past that. We've been sleeping together for weeks and I'm still in one piece. We might even be on to a way to solve the problem permanently. What's the matter?''

''Rex, being with you has been wonderful. I had no idea I could ever feel this way. I've never…I mean, I never did this before…you know?''

No, he didn't know. He'd guessed she wasn't terribly experienced, but he would never have missed *that*. He was thirty-two years old for Christ's sake. He'd made love with enough women to know…

Unless he'd had a worse case of sex on the brain than he'd realized.

''April, you're not telling me you were a virgin, are you?''

''No!'' She bucked hard, trying to throw him off.

''Then what haven't you done before?''

Her only reply was a blush that stole through her so hot that he could feel her skin singe his hands. Even though he could only see half her face, he recognized her mortified expression. And then it hit him.

''You never climaxed before?''

She buried her face in the mattress and groaned, which was the only answer he needed.

That certainly explained why he always felt as if he was the only man in the world who'd ever pleased her. He had been.

And along with that realization came a profound sense of satisfaction. He'd been the only man to coax those soft sighs from her lips, to tease her exquisite body until she melted against him, boneless with contentment.

But something still wasn't adding up. He was missing an important part of this equation, and April, with her face buried in the mattress, didn't look likely to help him solve the problem any time soon.

In Rex's mind there was only thing he could do—prove

to her she was wrong. She might have given up sex and relationships, but that was before she'd met him.

He unzipped her skirt.

"Rex!" She arched back against him, resisted as he pulled it down, dragging her panty hose along for the ride.

"Tell me you don't want me, April. Tell me to stop. I'll be a gentleman."

Some dim part of his brain warned he was taking a huge risk here, that he should let her up, but he also knew too much was at stake. He wanted April. He wanted her to want him.

There was only one surefire way to make her respond.

"Tell me to take off the restraints so you can get up and walk away."

She made a sound that might have been a sob.

It definitely wasn't a no.

Dragging the tangle of clothing from her feet, he freed her beautiful long legs, worked his way along their sleek length with his mouth and his kisses.

April moaned, a low, needy sound that made a lie of her explanations. The way she arched into his touch, the way she sighed out her need proved that she wanted him. That this was much more than sex.

The need to hold her, to feel all her soft curves molding his body, hit him hard. Rex slithered up her back until he was pressed against her full length, his cheek pressed to hers, his erection cradled against her warm bottom. He unzipped his trousers and freed himself, unwilling to let her go long enough even to undress. He didn't want to give her a chance to regroup, to come up with new arguments that might convince her not to take a chance on him.

"Tell me to stop."

He didn't recognize the gravel-edge voice as his own, hadn't known he could feel desperate. And he waited, hoping she didn't issue the words that would test his restraint and take away any hope for their future.

"Oh, Rex." She gave a raw sob.

It wasn't a no.

Positioning his erection between her thighs, he ran his hands upward along her outstretched arms, skimmed right over the restraints to twine his fingers through hers. He sheltered her with his body, needing to comfort as much as he needed comfort.

Pressing his cheek to hers, he inhaled her scent, faintly floral and all woman. He whispered against her ear, "I love you, April. You might not want to hear it. But I do."

She gave another broken sob and he sank deep inside her, one reckless stroke that made them one.

APRIL SLIPPED OUT of the bedroom after Rex had finally fallen asleep. He'd assaulted her with orgasm after orgasm, as though he'd wanted to prove to her that there would never be another man who could make her feel the way he did.

But he'd had nothing to prove because April already knew.

And afterward he'd been so gentle, massaging her wrists where he'd restrained her, cradling her in his strong arms and telling her they'd figure everything out tomorrow that her heart just broke.

She couldn't be honest with Rex so she'd hurt him, instead. He hadn't deserved to be hurt.

He loved her.

In the space of a few weeks, April had found everything she'd ever wanted from life—a wonderful, thoughtful man with a fun, loving family—and orgasms she'd only dreamed about. And as she'd lain in his arms, listened to the sound of his heart beat beneath her cheek, she finally acknowledged what she'd been denying for too long. She loved him, too.

She wanted a future with this man. She wanted to start over again without a lie between them.

She wanted to stop hiding from life.

She wanted to take a chance that Rex would understand and forgive her once he found out that she'd been making love with him while keeping her real identity a secret.

And taking that chance meant she had to clean up her baggage and clear the problems out of her way, starting with…her job. Yet she wouldn't trust Rex's reputation to anyone else, which meant she only had one choice.

She had to clear his name off that suspect list once and for all.

Taking great care in making her way across the dark suite, April powered up her laptop and logged on to the Web site of her adoption society. If Rex happened out of the bedroom, she wanted some cover. Then she went to his computer, sat down and booted his computer. His files were password protected. A necessary precaution since he networked his assistants to his system.

Even without J.P. Mooney Investigators high-tech resources, April could still access Rex's system. She wasn't just going to sit here and wait until in-house security got on with their investigation.

She was just going to take a peek.

Standing over his shoulder one day, she'd caught that his password began with an *R* and ended with two *T*s, but from there she was on her own.

She could only hope his password was a variation of something familiar in his life because she didn't have the time or the resources to crack an eleven-digit password.

April squelched her guilt as she went to work, starting with the obvious—family names, mother's maiden name.

This would stop her investigation cold if she couldn't figure him out enough to narrow down the possibilities.

She came up with nothing.

Okay, how about not so obvious? College, high school, neighborhood in Chicago where he'd grown up.

Still nothing.

Twenty minutes passed and April still hadn't hit on the right combination. Finally losing her patience, she got up from his machine and headed back to her own, pulled up the J.P. Mooney Investigators' server to access the file on Rex.

She scrolled through the documents, looking for anything that would inspire a brainstorm. She wasn't only an investigator but the man's lover, for goodness sake. What password would he consider individual enough to protect his all-important work?

Think, April told herself. But they hadn't had enough time together for her to have knowledge of his favorite song or movie. They'd never discussed his religious or political views.

His parents. Shawn, heavy equipment operator, and Gina, homemaker. Married 1969. That meant they were about to celebrate their thirty-fourth anniversary. Frustrated, April went back to his computer and tapped out the words *thirty-four* already knowing it wouldn't work.

Nothing.

She exhaled sharply, resisted the urge to snarl at the dialogue box that kept denying her access. This was stupid. She was getting nowhere and wasting valuable time.

I've already researched the subject online, he'd told her.

She had to see it with her own eyes, had to be able to *prove* it, even though she already knew the truth in her heart.

Back to his report. She scrolled through the screen with

his data again, flipped to a page and waited for some digital images to load. Perhaps there would be some clue there.

A scanned newspaper clipping about a very handsome young Rex as the captain of the high school football team.

A photo of Rex with a shaggy black-and-white dog, a strange mix between a black lab and sheepdog. They were both standing in a forest stream and Rex held a fishing pole. On the bottom of the image were scrawled the words Rex and Ralph the Mutt.

April gave it a whirl. She typed Ralphthemutt, all one word, using his keyboard. Sure enough, she'd no sooner hit Enter than the screen collapsed and she was staring at Rex's desktop.

The dog he'd grown up with, which only underscored what a sentimental man he was.

And made her heart ache more.

But adrenaline saved her, fueled her efforts even though she was physically exhausted. Maneuvering easily through his files, she scanned his organizational system for his work on the Luxurious Bedding Company project, the data she'd been inputting for the past few weeks, his remarks on the supervised shopping experiments he'd conducted in Tampa.

Rex was organized and meticulous, keeping several copies of his work updated in different places on his hard drive and then backing up the drive to the Web and CD. Given that this information was the crux of his work, his thoroughness didn't surprise her.

She glanced at the Web sites he had bookmarked in his Favorites folder, popped into his Recent History folder and found an accounting of every site he'd surfed in the past week.

No visits to any rival bedding manufacturers. In fact, not much activity…she double-clicked on his temporary Internet files, and *bingo,* his temporary folder overflowed with files.

Only a man who didn't have anything to hide would leave such an obvious clue to his online whereabouts. And as she scanned the names of the sites he'd visited, most of which were pages to the research foundation he'd told her about, April knew exactly what kind of man had left this trail.

A man who'd said he wanted to help her.

For the first time in weeks, April felt focused. She knew what she had to do. The idea gathered speed in her head as she thought about how she'd been surveilling Rex to see if he was involved in anything nefarious, how in-house security had been investigating him and the company employees.

She forwarded a copy of his browser history to the J.P. Mooney Investigators' server for safekeeping, erased all evidence of her transmission and powered down his system. Retrieving her cell phone, she hid in the bathroom to make a call, not caring that it would still be well past bedtime in the time zone she dialed.

The phone only rang three times before a groggy voice answered, "Hello."

"Wilhemina," she said. "This is April. I need to access your network. The same permissions your system administrator has. Will you authorize security to give that to me tonight?"

"What's happened, my dear? What have you found?"

"Something that will lead me to your stalker."

It was an outright lie. April didn't have anything more than the firmly rooted belief that she could find the evidence that she needed. It was enough. She was done second-guessing herself. She would be able to find what she was looking for.

She *knew* it.

"If you arrange access for me now, I'll have something

concrete before your alarm goes off to wake you up for work.''

To Wilhemina's credit she didn't miss a beat. ''Done, my dear. Just give me time to make a phone call. Does this have to do with Rex?''

''Yes. I've found out what he was doing online and it has nothing to do with rival bedding manufacturers. I've forwarded the evidence to John. I'm afraid it won't be admissible.''

''We won't need it in court, just for the board. I promise,'' she said confidently. ''Just out of curiosity, does John have any idea what you're doing?''

''Not yet.''

Wilhemina laughed, a delighted sound that told April she understood the significance of that statement completely. ''Go for it, my girl.''

''I'll be in touch with your security people through the night. I might need access to their investigation. Will that be a problem?''

''Not at all. Do what you need to do. I'll be waiting to hear what you find. And, April?''

''Yes?''

''Good work.''

''Thanks, Auntie Wil.''

April disconnected with a smile and headed back out to her laptop to await Wilhemina's access. It had been that easy. Wilhemina hadn't even questioned her stepping into the investigation. She believed that April could help.

John, on the other hand, would likely fire her the instant he found out she'd disobeyed his orders. But she'd have to worry about that later. Right now she had a stalker to track and a man's name to clear. The man she loved.

15

REX AWOKE to find dawn paling the sky beyond the bedroom window. The restraints were still hanging from the bed frame where he'd left them after freeing April. He'd fallen asleep with her wrapped in his arms like they had every night since their first in Atlanta. He'd enjoyed waking up to the feel of her warm body curled around his, her cheek resting on his shoulder, her fine hairs teasing his nose every time he inhaled.

This morning he awoke alone.

He didn't hear the shower running and the bedroom door was shut. Given the events of the previous night, Rex wouldn't take her mood for granted. Slipping out of bed, he dragged on sweats and headed into the suite.

He hadn't made it into the kitchen to put on a pot of coffee when he noticed her laptop missing from the bar. A look around revealed her luggage piled high in the hallway.

Disbelief stopped him in his tracks. His mind was gearing up and he just stared, trying to register, yet not wanting to accept the implications of those packed bags.

He hadn't convinced her to take a chance.

Even after last night, after loving her until he hurt, after baring his soul, he still hadn't convinced her.

"April?" Defiance spurred his voice past a tight throat.

She emerged from the bathroom, dressed in her traveling clothes—comfortable jeans, sweater, sneakers. She looked pale and drawn, the slight droop of her shoulders making him guess she hadn't slept much.

"I showered out here so I didn't wake you."

"You're leaving." Not a question that needed an answer but a statement.

"I've got to go home, Rex. I need some time to sort things out before we can make decisions about the future."

"How long?"

"I—I don't know."

"What about us?"

She spread her hands in entreaty. "I don't know."

He didn't either. He might have an ability to read people but he wasn't a mind reader. Her beautiful violet eyes were shuttered against him, her expression so reserved she seemed to be holding it together by sheer will, an expression that emphasized the miles of distance she'd thrown between them.

"I need some time to think and to straighten some things out."

"What things?"

"I can't tell you right now. I promise I will, but I can't just yet."

Was she telling him the truth or simply making an excuse to get out that door?

He honestly didn't know, but believed her capable of either. She'd been confused last night, conflicted. He'd wanted to calm her fears, but was too emotionally invested himself to focus on her. He'd pushed. Maybe too hard.

Something about the way she stood so tense—a hundred and ten on the nervous meter—told him that backing her into a corner right now would only send her out that door even faster.

A wild urge to restrain her again hit him, to tie her up

until he could convince her to stay. But the night had passed and in the blinding morning light, he couldn't use the Fit to be Tied Restraints to avoid facing the truth.

Their relationship was only beginning. He didn't have much more than sex in his arsenal to convince her to tackle whatever was holding her back.

Sex obviously hadn't been enough.

She'd shuttered her heart tight and he stood there without massage, without sex, without any way to reach it. And that look of inevitability she couldn't quite hide told him he'd never stood a chance anyway. Her mind was made up. She wouldn't stay.

So he stared at her, unsure of what to do next. Did he simply let her walk out that door, and out of his life?

"Wilhemina will be sending Charles's assistant to help you," she said. "She'll have him here in the morning. Will you be okay until then?"

He'd expected to work this project alone all along and found her concerns ironic. Why was she worried? For herself, because she didn't want to feel guilty for leaving? Or for him, because she cared?

A knock on the door ended any chance to pursue the answer.

April moved past her bags and pulled open the door.

A bellboy stood in the hallway, spiffily uniformed and totally unaware of the intensity of the encounter he'd just walked in on. "Someone called for bags to go down."

"These here in the hall, please."

Rex's mind raced for some argument, something to stop what was happening. As soon as that bellboy finished loading that cart, he'd leave, and April would go right behind him, along with any chance to convince her otherwise.

All he could come up with was a solid understanding that

he wouldn't accept this. She may walk out that door, thinking she was off the hook, but *they* weren't over. Not by a long shot.

"I'll be right down," was all April said as she tipped the guy and partially closed the door behind him.

Then she turned to face him. Again, he got that sense it was taking everything she had to hold herself together. All his questions evaporated, all the uncertainty, and, yes, the hurt. He knew what to do.

Covering the distance between them, he reached for her and wrapped her in his arms before she could back away.

Instinctively, she molded against him, just like she'd done so many times, her body fitting against his in all the right places, warm, yielding, perfect.

She might walk out that door, but he knew she hadn't bargained on just how determined he could be.

Stubborn, his mother always said. Like his father and grandfather. An Irish thing then.

She pressed a slip of paper into his hand. He glanced down at it, read a telephone number with a Dallas area code.

"It's my cell phone number. As soon as I get everything straightened out, I'll call you, but…but I wanted you to have my number if you needed me."

He heard the tears in her voice, didn't understand what the problem was, knew it was big. "April, if you can't make it back for the Phoenix run, you have to promise you'll make time to go yourself. Soon," he whispered into her hair, promising himself that he wouldn't have to wait long until he could hold her again. "Harold has your name. All you have to do is call him and tell him I sent you."

Nodding, she broke away. She forced a smile but he saw the glint of tears in her eyes, knew she was coming apart. She knew it, too, apparently, because she grabbed her coat from the back of a dining room chair and headed toward the door.

But she didn't leave. She paused to look back at him. Just a glance, to capture his image maybe or reassure herself that he was really going to let her go.

Those tears still shone in her beautiful eyes. "Rex, I'm sorry to run off like this. I'll call."

"I'll wait."

She lifted her hand to open the door and her sweater pulled back from her wrist...

She was wearing the wristband.

Rex stared into her face, no less beautiful for its guarded expression, and knew.

She cared. The walls she'd thrown up and that wristband only proved how much.

"Take care of yourself, okay?"

"You, too," he said.

Then she walked out the door, as changed from the woman who'd walked into his life only a few weeks ago as he was from the man who'd gotten shocked when they'd first shaken hands.

REX STOOD in the reception area of J.P. Mooney Investigators, Ltd. biding his time while he awaited his eleven o'clock appointment with the owner. The offices were like a thousand others Rex had been in during his career—upscale, well-appointed, professionally designed to make clients feel welcomed and confident in whatever services the firm offered.

With one important distinction—April worked here.

An eventful week had passed since she'd left him in Denver and his research had yielded up some interesting facts about what had been taking place behind the scenes of the

Luxurious Bedding Company and led him right back to Dallas, where he'd first met her.

After gathering enough information to get a rough idea of what was going on, he'd confronted Wilhemina, who'd answered his questions and given him a few more pieces to the puzzle. Now he'd come to John Patrick Mooney for a few more.

An administrative assistant opened the office door. "Mr. Mooney will see you now."

"Thanks." Rex inclined his head at the pleasantly smiling woman as he passed and entered the office.

The man who sat behind the desk, so at ease—or displeased maybe—that he didn't stand to greet his visitor, measured him as shrewdly as Rex measured him.

"So you're Rex Holt," he finally said. "Awfully ballsy of you to show up after you cost me my favorite investigator."

"I did, sir?"

John Patrick Mooney motioned toward the door that was closing behind him with a thick finger. "She walked right through that door, dropped her resignation letter on my desk and thanked me for eight good years. Said she was going into business for herself."

Leaning back in his chair, he hooked his hands behind his head and stared Rex down with a very no-nonsense gaze. "Do you mind telling me what you did to her, Holt?"

Rex decided right then that he liked John Patrick Mooney, not only because he could hear echoes of April in the man's dry wit, but because he got straight to the point.

"I made her fall in love with me, sir."

Mooney exhaled heavily. "I knew it. I've got four daughters. I've seen the look."

Rex could empathize. With his sisters, he knew firsthand that falling in love could be an event.

"Wilhemina told me to expect you, so sit down."

Rex sat in the chair in front of the desk and faced Mooney squarely. "Wilhemina explained that she hired your firm to conduct inside surveillance while I was out on the road. Unfortunately, until her security people officially close their investigation, she can't tell me anything else without conflict of interest so she sent me to you for some answers."

"What do you want to know?"

"You sent April, sir. Why?"

"That's a personal question."

"I have a personal interest in her."

"I thought you wanted to know about how our end of the investigation wrapped up?"

Rex knew that his answer counted, that John Patrick Mooney would base his decision to be forthright on whether or not Rex produced a satisfactory answer. "I do, but only because I need to understand the part April played in it."

"And what the hell difference does that make?"

"It may be the difference in whether or not she takes a chance on me." He could be equally forthright. "I'm in love with her. I need to understand what's holding her back from getting involved in a relationship with me."

"You're that sure she has it for you?"

Rex smiled. "I have four younger sisters, sir. Trust me, April has it bad."

Mooney snorted. "All right. I'll fill in the blanks. To make a long story short, April went rogue. I sent her to do an inside surveillance job. I'm sure Wilhemina told you that this was just a precaution for the both of you. You were never a serious contender as a suspect."

Rex nodded.

"April went in to watch you, to see who you interacted with and make sure you didn't contact a rival bedding manufacturer while you were on the road with the company secrets. She wound up in such a crush to prove you were innocent that she solved the damned case."

"Industrious of her." He couldn't contain a smile.

"Yes, it was, wasn't it?" Mooney steepled his hands before him and frowned. "She asked me to let her investigate, told me she could find a trail to who was sending the posts on the computer. I'm sorry to say I refused her. Wilhemina didn't ask us to investigate and I was afraid to pile on too much responsibility. But it turned out all she had to do was get inside their network to figure out what the idiots in security couldn't."

"And that was what exactly?"

"No *person* was stalking the employees with those posts and covering up corporate espionage. There was a worm running loose in the system. A damned computer virus type of thing. Who'd have guessed?" He shook his grizzled head, and Rex saw what appeared to be Mooney's first smile of their acquaintance. "Leave it to April."

She certainly had a gift, one that Rex suspected she didn't fully appreciate. "Wilhemina wasn't free to share how that worm got into the company network as it apparently involved several of her employees. How much can you tell me?"

"I don't have any conflict issues. Wilhemina's marketing director was surfing porn sites at work."

"Charles Blackstone."

"Right. He picked up something from one of the sites— one of those new bugs that hides in the system and kicks out posts and files to everyone in the e-mail address book.

The worm was scanning the files and attaching itself to any keyword that had to do with sex.''

Rex laughed. ''The Sensuous Collection files certainly qualified. But a company the size of the Luxurious Bedding Company shouldn't have had that problem. Their network should have been protected.''

Mooney smiled. This time a real smile that couldn't be mistaken for anything else. ''It was. But the network administrator had apparently known Blackstone was a porn puppy and had been tracking him online. She let the worm run loose to blackmail him into getting involved with her. From what Wilhemina said, he wouldn't give her the light of day otherwise.''

Rex had sensed something off between Jacqui and Charles, but he hadn't even come close to guessing the truth. ''I imagine they were both offered severance packages.''

''You got that right. This nonsense was about the last thing Wilhemina needed right now. She's been having a hard enough time trying to keep her people focused on business dealing with the launch. But you'd know more about that than I would.''

''The Sensuous Collection has had quite the effect on the staff,'' he agreed. ''But I'm sure Wilhemina intends to get her people back on track to get the launch off the ground.''

''And you'll help her?''

Rex leaned forward, and faced the man squarely. ''I will, but I want my assistant back.''

''April?''

Rex nodded.

''You might just stand a chance. She's currently out of work. If her business doesn't fly, she'll be job hunting.''

''Why did she quit?''

''''She has to learn to stand on her own two feet.' That's

a quote.'' Mooney gave another short laugh. ''You know, Holt, if Wilhemina had officially hired my company to investigate, I wouldn't have assigned April to the case. I didn't think she was up to establishing her cover and investigating. I was wrong.''

''Then I'm glad Wilhemina didn't hire you to investigate. For what it's worth, I don't think you were the only one who underestimated April. I think she might have surprised herself on this one.''

''You planning to point that out to her?''

Rex nodded.

''I've known her a lot of years. She's a live wire. You've got your work cut out for you.''

''I'm up to it.'' He didn't add that he planned to order the entire Sensuous Collection before he completed this job, just so he'd be stocked up on Fit to be Tied Restraints for the next couple of years.

John Patrick Mooney raised a grizzled brow. ''You made my favorite investigator go rogue then quit her job with my firm *and* you made her fall in love. But you still haven't told me what do you intend to do about it?''

''I intend to become your next son-in-law, sir.'' Rex stood and extended his hand in greeting. ''That is, if you'll tell me where April lives.''

ON NUMEROUS OCCASIONS through the years, April had been accused of hiding away in her apartment to pine. And though she hadn't realized it at the time, she supposed she had been pining. But this time was different. This time she was collecting her thoughts, deciding what she wanted out of her life and out of her future.

And gearing up the courage to face Rex with the truth, and then seeing if he was willing to take a chance on her.

Her apartment had always been her safe haven from the world, but today even the funky leather furniture and bright walls she loved seemed confining. There was no escaping the memories of nights spent asleep in his arms, her cheek pressed to his chest, his heart beating in time with hers.

She wanted to hop on a plane and fly straight to Phoenix to catch up with him, to visit the research foundation and learn all she could about Electro Hypersensitivity to see if it explained her unusual symptoms. She'd been researching both online and in the university library—*trying* to, anyway. Rex had been absolutely right in telling her there wasn't much credible information out there.

But she couldn't go to Phoenix. Not just yet. She had to wait for the green light that Wilhemina's investigation was officially over. Then she would e-mail Rex, explain the whole situation and give him a chance to decide how he felt and if he wanted to see her again to discuss things.

She wouldn't allow herself to dwell on what would come after if he didn't want to see her again, couldn't, not yet. So she worked on her post whenever doubts or worry set it, an exercise of sorts. She'd been writing, deleting, then rewriting to find exactly the right words to explain the situation and tell Rex how she felt.

She was writing now and she glanced at the computer screen, felt as if he wasn't quite so far away. It was the waiting that was killing her.

A knock sounded on the door.

The waiting, and the let's-keep-April-from-pining visits.

Lowering her head until her brow almost touched the keyboard she'd taped to the treadmill's instrument panel, she considered ignoring the door. Unfortunately Paula had been passing off April's apartment key to her daughters so they could all take turns popping up at odd times during the day.

As her car was parked downstairs the fact that she was home was no mystery, which meant there was no avoiding this visitor.

"Who is it?" she called out.

"John."

Her mood, which had been teetering on the edge, sank straight into the pit of her stomach. At first John had flat-out refused to accept her resignation. But he hadn't had much choice when she'd left his office and not returned.

She intended to stand on her own two feet if it killed her. She'd start small, take surveillance cases that she felt comfortable with before branching out. If her time working as Rex's assistant had proven anything to her it was that she needed fresh challenges, needed to find her work interesting, not something she could hide in.

Eventually she knew John would understand and accept that she'd done what was best, but at the moment...

More knocking.

April sighed. Stepping off her treadmill, she crossed the living room and swung the door wide. "Paula must have pulled out the big guns to get you to leave the office before six."

"She couldn't have blasted me out from behind my desk with a cannon. But *lover boy* here wanted to pay you a visit and I couldn't give your address to a stranger. You and Wilhemina might know this guy, but I don't know him from Adam."

Lover boy?

John stepped aside and April saw him.

That rich russet hair and that wicked grin. His star quality in place, looking as charming and as handsome and larger than life as he had on the day they'd met. His melting eyes caressed her, a look that didn't hide how much he'd missed her, a look that reminded her of all they'd shared.

Every drop of blood drained from April's face only to rush back again like an erupting volcano. Her cheeks prickled and burned. She had to be as red as a cherry.

A fact John corroborated by rolling his eyes. "All right, Holt. You win. She's got it bad." He scowled down at her, which only served to make her blush flare even hotter. "You going to invite us in or what?"

She had no clue what else to do, so she just stepped aside and let them enter.

They strode into her living room, two big men who seemed to suck up all the space with their broad shoulders and male intensity. John never took his gaze off her, but Rex looked around, summed up her place with that gaze that saw everything.

He smiled.

She didn't know what to say.

John stepped into the breach. "I'm not staying. I just need to know you'll be safe with this guy."

Safe was a relative term. Would Rex harm her? Never. But her heart was coming apart at the seams. If he was here then he already knew. She didn't need her letter because he knew. And she'd never realized what a wimp she was until then, when she faced him, not knowing what to think, what to say or how to act.

"You want me to hang around in case you need backup?" John asked and his wry tone snapped her out of her daze.

She reached up on tiptoe to kiss his cheek. "I'll be fine. Don't worry."

He slanted a sharp gaze between her and Rex, then snorted. "You call me the instant you work this out. I mean the second, April, or else Paula will have the girls there tonight to harangue me for details as soon as I walk in the door.'' He scowled. ''Better yet, *you* call her. That'll save me from being picked to the bone with questions. Got it?''

She nodded, going all soft and stupid inside, because he cared so much.

''All right. I'm out of here.'' He turned to Rex. ''You keep in mind what I said, Holt. Understood?''

''Understood, sir,'' he said, and April saw a smile twitching around his mouth.

John left and April closed the door behind him, needing some activity to occupy her, to let her avoid turning around to face Rex for just another few heartbeats....

''What did he say to you?'' she asked, barely able to hear her own voice above the alarm screaming in her head.

''I got the proverbial walk around the block.''

''Really?'' She clamped her hands behind her back and assumed the position before lifting her gaze to his.

Rex nodded. ''He made sure I'm clear that I'll be dealing with him if I hurt you.'' Without another word, he covered the distance between them and wrapped her in his arms.

The past week had felt like forever but the instant his arms came around her, she remembered with striking clarity exactly how she felt when he held her. The way her cheek fitted against his chest, the fabric of his jacket textured against her skin, her head nestled against his shoulder as though she'd been designed to fit. Her body molded against his instinctively, remembering every curve and hollow.

Then she tipped her head back, met his gaze...and erupted.

''Rex, I planned to contact you just as soon as the investigation was officially closed. I couldn't jeopardize everything and until I could tell you, I didn't see the point of contacting you. I needed to explain what happened and why I couldn't tell you and I never expected to sleep with you and then once we did I felt terrible because I couldn't tell you. Then I met your family and that only made things worse…''

April poured her heart out. Wrapped tightly in his arms, encouraged by his touch, she told him everything she'd written in her letter, everything she'd deleted, every doubt, every fear and every promise she'd made to herself.

She told him that she was tired of being a disaster and hiding from life. She was stepping out from behind her computer, stepping out from under John's wing and taking on the world one day and one step at a time. The good, and the bad right along with it.

And she let him off the hook, too. ''I understand if you don't want to be involved in a relationship with someone who's had to call 9-1-1 for every man she's ever slept with.''

''Except for me,'' he said huskily.

''Except for you.''

Darn if those weren't tears stinging her eyes.

''It looks like you arranged the furniture so you could pace right through the middle of your living room,'' he said, glancing around. ''Did you?''

April might have laughed had in not been for the huge knot of emotion rising in her throat trying to choke her. She did pace right through the middle of the room, so she could stare out the windows overlooking the park across the street.

She only nodded, touched that he'd recognize something so simple, yet so important about her.

''I'm sorry,'' she said.

''For what?''

''For deceiving you.''

Rex hooked a knuckle beneath her chin and tipped her face toward his. "I'd rather you were sorry for leaving."

"I made love to you with a lie between us. While you were being thoughtful and wonderful, I was reporting every phone call and fax you sent."

"I agree the circumstances weren't optimum, but you were doing your job. Why did you think I'd hold that against you?"

"I didn't. I just didn't want to hurt you."

He frowned. "I was surprised at having been a surveillance target, but all things considered, I appreciated Wilhemina's precaution. I was a legitimate variable and she made sure we were both protected."

"I compromised my surveillance by making love to you."

"You didn't think I was guilty, did you?"

"No, of course not."

His frown deepened, etching lines around his mouth, squaring off his strong chin. "I knew something was wrong, April, but I didn't know what. You wouldn't tell me, or at least tell me you'd explain when you could. I'd have accepted that. But you never gave me a chance to understand. That's what hurt."

Her heart was in pieces, and the stupid tears were prickling at the backs of her lids. "It wasn't that I didn't trust you, Rex, I didn't trust *me*."

She blinked, refusing to give in to the urge. But one rebel tear escaped. Rex thumbed it from her cheek, smiled softly. "I trusted you."

"I know." And that was all it took to pitch her over the edge. A week's worth of waiting, of learning how to stand on her own feet, and yes, a week's worth of uncertainty welled up inside. To April's complete mortification, she burst into tears, tears that had been building since she'd realized she would have to leave him, tears she'd refused to shed after she'd left.

She cried them all now, great huge dollops that made each breath a sob, rolled down her cheeks and smeared her mascara.

And through it all, Rex never said a word. He just scooped her into his arms and sat down with her on his lap, holding her close, an anchor to cling to while she toughed out the storm. He rocked her gently, stroked her back with a soothing touch, pressed soft kisses into her hair, as though he knew exactly how momentous this week had been.

He never said a word, until finally, *finally* she managed to catch her breath.

"All better?"

She nodded, swiping the tears from her eyes, collecting herself so that Rex could see that even if she faltered she could get right back up on her feet.

His smile told her that he already knew.

Then she found her voice, teary and trembly though it was, and asked, "How did you find out? Wilhemina can't say anything until the investigation is over."

Rex traced her mouth with his thumb, a light touch that managed to convey just how much he'd missed touching her. "I'm in research, remember? That means I have a curious streak and lots of resources at my disposal. Once I discovered you didn't work for the Luxurious Bedding Company, I did some investigating and got the basic idea of what had been going on. Wilhemina couldn't tell me anything, but she could confirm my suspicions and point me in John's direction."

"Good old Auntie Wil. I'm sure she's having a blast with all this."

Rex nodded.

"She's very fond of you, you know? She was willing to bet her career on your innocence. She's also bet her career that you can help her pull off this launch."

"I can, with some help." He eyed her pointedly and this crazy hope began to bloom inside her.

But Rex didn't give her a chance to savor the feeling or question him because he said, "Wilhemina was also very impressed with your work. So was your former boss."

"People are my downfall. I don't have a problem with computers."

"As long as you're standing three feet away." His gaze shot to her unusual computer setup. A corner desk sandwiched in between floor-to-ceiling windows with the monitor on top and a treadmill with a keyboard taped to the instrument panel.

The setup put distance between where she stood and the monitor, requiring her to have a nice-size twenty-one incher that looked like a movie screen and Rex was staring at the screen now. "Is that the letter you were going to send to me?"

She nodded.

"May I?" He didn't wait for an answer, just slid her off his lap and stepped onto the treadmill.

"I already told you everything that I wrote—"

"Not everything," his eyes were still fixed on the monitor. "You haven't told me you loved me. It's right here in your letter."

"I do."

He turned and his melting gaze caressed her, not hiding his pleasure at her admission or hiding what he felt inside.

"I love you, Rex."

He reached down and swept his hand across her cheek. "I love you, too."

The moment hung between them so unbearably tender, so rich and hopeful that April felt the darned tears again.

"And you didn't tell me what you wanted for the future. See, that's here, too."

"I want to be with you.

"I know."

A rogue tear escaped and he thumbed it away. "You'll trust me to tackle whatever comes up with you?"

She nodded, leaning into his touch. Then he reached for her hand, drawing her to her feet and onto the treadmill as he brushed his mouth against the inside of her wrist, right above the antistatic wristband. "You'll tackle whatever life tosses at me, too?"

She nodded.

"We're a pair, you know, April. I've been barreling right past life and you've been hiding from it." He laughed softly and met her gaze above their clasped hands. "I'm making a change. I'm making time to enjoy my life and I want you with me. You helped me see how much I've been missing."

"I'm making a change, too." She inhaled deeply, summoned the strength to voice her hopes and her dreams aloud, knew that no matter what happened that opening her heart was an accomplishment she could be proud of. "I've quit my job."

"John told me. He's sorry to lose you."

"And I'm sorry to go but it's time. There's something else I'd like to do with my life."

"And what's that?"

"Work for you."

Rex's smile told her that he wasn't surprised, most likely because she'd written that in her letter, too. But adrenaline was making her blood pump and her alarm start to head toward the red zone, so she said, "I've got this all worked out and it's perfect. You're a marketing researcher and I'm an investigative researcher. They fit together perfectly, don't you think? You like how I pinpoint potential liabilities and you've got to finish up the analysis on the Sensuous Collection. There's the Swiss Army Set and then the Faux Fur and the Incredible Edible. And those are just the gaming and adventure lines. You definitely need my help."

"I do." He wrapped an arm around her and pulled her close, the incline of the treadmill making her align against him at the perfect height for him to rest his chin on the top of her head.

She absorbed the feel of him against her, the warmth of his strong body pressed close.

"I'm guessing you couldn't have gotten too far starting up your own business in just a week."

"Didn't even get business cards printed." She barely got the words past the lump that was back in her throat.

"Good, because you've got the job. It'll always be interesting, I can promise."

April lost her battle with the tears again. They squeezed past her lashes as she stared into Rex's handsome face, saw the truth there. "That's it, Rex? No contract negotiations?"

He shook his head.

"You're sure? I don't switch jobs that often. I've only had one so far in my whole life."

"That kind of job history is a plus as far as I'm concerned." He turned with her in his arms and reached toward the keyboard taped to the instrument panel and typed out one-handed: *Marry me, April.*

She noticed he didn't use a question mark. That might have been because he couldn't manage the keystroke with one arm still wrapped tightly around her. But April thought it was more likely because he already knew her answer.

She brushed his hand out of the way and tapped out the letters to spell *Y-E-S*.

HARLEQUIN®
Temptation®

Legend has it that
the only thing that can bring down a Quinn
is a woman...

Now we get to see for ourselves!

The youngest Quinn brothers have grown up.
They're smart, they're sexy...and they're about to be
brought to their knees by their one true love.

Don't miss the last three books in
Kate Hoffmann's dynamic miniseries...

The Mighty Quinns

Watch for:

THE MIGHTY QUINNS: LIAM
(July 2003)

THE MIGHTY QUINNS: BRIAN
(August 2003)

THE MIGHTY QUINNS: SEAN
(September 2003)

Available wherever Harlequin books are sold.

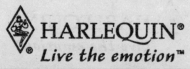

HARLEQUIN®
Live the emotion™

Visit us at www.eHarlequin.com

HTMQ

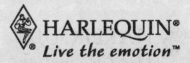

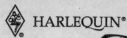

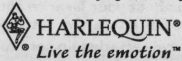

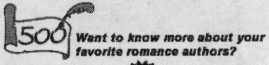

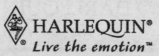

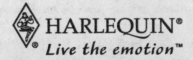

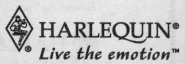

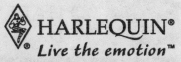